The Slave Harem

by

Wendy Rathbone

THE SLAVE HAREM

Copyright © 2019
A publication by:
Eye Scry Publications
www.eyescrypublications.com

Cover design: Wendy Rathbone

ISBN: **978-1-942415-27-5**

For Della, as always…

Kingdom of Slaves Background

*The **Kingdom of Slaves** series of standalone novels is set in a contemporary, fantasy version of Earth, present day, where the selling and owning of pleasure slaves is legal in most countries.*

Avilan is the largest and wealthiest country in the contemporary world and one of its top commodities is the selling of pleasure slaves both within its own borders, and to other countries. Avilan hosts three hundred slave training quarters called Slave Palaces.

While anyone may own a pleasure slave, only the truly wealthy can afford Palace trained slaves.

The Palaces thoroughly vet their buyers as well, and try to match the proper slave to the proper master.

But sometimes an offer comes that cannot be refused—the money is just that good—and a slave is sold to unknown realms...

Part One

Chapter One

The Training of Ren

Ren shivered. His vision blurred. He was rain-soaked through and through.

All day he had been walking. The pain in his muscles threatened to drop him. He concentrated on putting one foot in front of the other. Dark locks of hair stung his eyes. His chest ached and every breath he took tore at his throat.

His blue sweater—more gray now—hung from his starved frame in a hundred unraveled strings.

It had taken him two weeks to get to Lirangel. Walking. Hitchhiking. Begging bus fare. There were days he did not make any headway at all. Now, he had no more money. No more strength.

But just ahead, finally, there it was. He saw the Palace glinting silver and blue, reflecting the rainy day. The black iron gate soared twenty feet high.

The last mile had been all uphill to reach that gate. He had to push himself harder with every step.

The grass about him smelled of newly turned earth, the green of it lush as hope. Everything was hope or pain, beauty or chaos depending on how one looked at the world.

What kept Ren going was something one of his high school teachers had told him after his parents had died. After the horrible car wreck.

It's all interconnected. Nothing dies. There is only infinite change. Remember that. You choose how you want to walk through this world. How you want to experience it.

The Lirangel Slave Place was the best in the world. It was why he'd come here. He wanted the best to teach him how to be a slave. A *pleasure* slave. If they took him in, he could hide for the rest of his life. He would sign the consent forms and never again have to make a decision, or a choice. All would be out of his hands. The thought comforted him.

His teacher might be disappointed to see him now. To learn that his choice was to walk his life as an owned being, taking no responsibility for himself. But a part of him had died when his parents had died. It would never waken again.

What was left of him needed form and guidance. If it involved his body and sex, he didn't mind. Whatever was left of him, he wanted to open all the way to it, give himself over with all control to a master, *his* master.

It sounded strange even to his own mind. Hell, maybe he had lost his mind.

But now he was here. The black gate stood before him. Raindrops clung to the metal, making it look shiny, newly polished. The cross-bars dripped. They were icy against the palms of Ren's hands as he curled his fingers about them to steady himself. He was not sure how much longer he would be able to stay upright.

The uniformed guards beyond the double gate frowned at his rumpled, thin form.

Ren's voice cracked and broke as he let his wish be known to the intimidating strangers. "Please. Let me in. I want to be trained. I'm willing. Please."

One of the guards spoke softly into some invisible microphone. He had a wire coming up from his collar attached to an ear bud.

He stared at Ren without a word, unmoving. A few of the others wandered toward a kiosk to the left side of the gate.

The first guard kept staring.

"Please," Ren said. "I'm so tired. If I could just come in and rest for a moment. And if they don't want me, then I'll be off. I promise."

The guard's eyebrows narrowed. He did not move.

"Did you hear me?" Ren coughed and his whole body shook with the pain.

Finally, the guard spoke. "Hush. Someone is coming."

Ren tried to see past the front path that led upward. He saw the top part of the palace, its upper floor windows and two fancy towers, but not the front entrance. The hill of the pathway blocked it. Beyond the towers was a steep green hill covered with oak trees, and above that the darkening steel sky.

It seemed he waited forever. He'd not felt the cold all day. His fever and the walking kept him overly warm. But now he shivered as a chilled breeze rippled his damp clothes. It felt as if icy fingers had found their way to his bones and squeezed.

Finally, just as he had the thought that he might like to sit on the wet pathway, or collapse on the damp, freezing grass, a man all in black came down the path from the direction of the palace.

Ren watched him, how he walked with a kind of grace and purpose, head up, hands relaxed at his sides. He had neat, dark hair combed straight back, and a firm nose and jaw. As he got closer, Ren saw dark eyes hard around the edges, but he had a kind mouth. An assessing gaze and demeanor.

This was a master, no doubt about it.

Ren took a shallow breath, trying to hold back another coughing fit.

The master made a swiping hand motion to the guard, who came forward and punched in a code on a box by the gate. Suddenly, the hinges creaked and the gate opened inward by itself.

Ren let go of the crossbars and stood back.

The master came out past the border of the grounds and stood directly in front of Ren.

Ren blinked, trying to clear his mind and his vision. With the last of his strength, he looked the master in the eye.

"I'm here to train," he said.

The master put his hand on Ren's chin, looked him up and down and said, "Maybe."

Ren held his breath and waited. He was handsome. He knew it. But the trip had taken its toll. He had to look his worst right now. But there was nothing he could do about that.

"You are ill," the master said. "But I can see your beauty still. Are you running from the law?"

"No, sir."

Ren was surprised the man could see anything of his true looks behind his filth and rags and raging fever.

The master asked. "How old are you?"

"Seventeen."

"Ah, too young, then."

"I'll be eighteen in May," Ren insisted.

"Do you understand the nature of what it is you ask?"

"Yes."

"Why do you want to come through this gate?"

"I wish to be owned."

"Hmm. Have you any experience with being submissive? Do you even have a sexual orientation yet?"

For as long as he could remember, Ren had a sexual orientation. "Male, sir. No experience but my own thoughts concerning what I desire."

"You are still too young."

"Not for long."

The master allowed a soft smile to tease his kind mouth.

"Do you understand that your rights will be revoked? That you will be property?"

"I know."

"You will go through a thorough physical and psychological work up. If you do not pass, you will be sent away."

"I will allow it."

"If you pass the preliminary tests, you will be required to be physically trained in all the sexual arts. The training is hands on."

"Yes, I understand." Ren shuddered, but not from the idea of physical sex training. Simply, he needed this to be over. He needed to get himself inside, beyond the gates, locked away forever until he was sold to an owner who, hopefully, would keep him on a tight leash. Then maybe he could relax.

"You may enter," the master said. He swung his right arm wide.

Ren had to focus on each step he took, his legs growing heavy, his mind spinning.

In the post-storm gray mist, the shimmering gates closed behind them with a loud clang.

Finally!

Ren turned as the master came up alongside him. "Sir," he gasped, reaching out blindly.

He felt the master's hands suddenly clasp his upper arms, holding him up.

"Guard! A little help here!"

But it was too late. Ren collapsed into the master's embrace.

*

A long time later, Ren woke in the Slave Palace hospital to learn he had pneumonia.

He had been in bed for two weeks. Much of that time was lost to him in fever.

After the fever broke, he began to notice auras around people and things. In all his life, he'd never seen such color in the world before.

Faint light waved at him wherever he looked, as if the universe was communicating itself all around him in multi-colored glimmers, halos, and spirals of energy that came and went without sound or notice by other people.

Again, he thought of his teacher's words about interconnectedness, and decided it was a sign he'd come to the right place.

After another few days of learning to stand again, of short walks and full meals, a nurse brought Ren some clothing.

Wearing the simple blue coverall, Ren was allowed out of his room for the first time to meet with someone who, he was told, would see about his future here.

A young man in black slacks and a button-down shirt led him down one ornate corridor after another, all the walls on either side decorated with paintings. They depicted erotic scenes unlike any Ren had ever seen. Some showed forest gatherings where half-animal, half-human beings were depicted in detailed orgies. Others were of single beautiful nudes. Some showed couples in various states of sexual play, men with women, men with men, women with women.

Ren had looked at porn before, but this was nothing like that. These paintings were beautiful. They transcended the simple sexual act. They emitted a pink light that blossomed in Ren's vision over and over like a blooming flower in fast-motion.

As they came around another corner, Ren blinked the light away, only to nearly bump into another man in black.

"Ah, you are just in time," the man said. He had blue light coming out of his head in the vague shape of a tree blowing in the wind.

The man tilted his head at Ren. "Are you sure you are quite recovered?"

"Yes, sir." Ren nodded, ignoring the blue tree and looking straight into a familiar face. This was the master who'd met him at the gate. There had been no blue tree then. Ren had not seen lights emanating from people until only a few days ago.

"Do you remember me?" the man asked.

"Yes."

"Good." The master opened the door to a large room containing a round table and eight, office-style chairs. "Have a seat."

The attendant who'd accompanied Ren left, closing the door.

Ren sat and looked up. The master came forward and lowered himself into the chair closest to Ren. The master had an electric air about him. His aura was all golds and greens, apart from the blue tree above his head. Woodsy. Making the air singe with a hint of autumn bloom.

"Well," he began. "First, allow me to introduce myself. I am Eminent Master Locke."

"What does Eminent Master mean?" Ren asked.

"I, along with a board of other Eminent Masters, make final decisions around here on how this place is run, who is to be trained, who passes training and when they are allowed to be sold. This is like a school, but it is also run as a business. We are in charge of that business. I head the board. It is sort of like being the president of any other corporation."

Ren nodded his understanding. But he was also surprised. Why was the head of the board, an Eminent Master, in charge of his case? And why had he of all the masters in the Palace come to meet him at the gate two weeks ago?

"You have had quite an ordeal. You were a very sick boy, Ren."

"You know my name."

"Of course I do. The doctors and nurses asked you many questions while you were ill. They made their reports. I received them all. What you didn't tell us we found out through web searches, etc. Your file is quite full. So I know you've had a rough time of it this past year."

Ren looked down at his lap.

"It is important that we establish right now that your recent tragedy and runaway status cannot be factors in our decision to allow you to remain here. We do not take in strays. We are not a charity service. There are many services out there that can help you."

A knot began to twist in Ren's stomach. "You're not sending me away, are you?"

"Your case is interesting. There is a reason beyond your beauty as to why I opened the gates to you. Do you want to know what it is?"

"Yes."

"An intelligence and tenacity in your gaze. And something more I can't quite define. Quite compelling. When I found out how sick you actually were, I was even more compelled to have this meeting with you now, because truly you should have been unconscious by the time you reached us here at the Palace. Your fever had spiked at 105. Your electrolytes were so imbalanced I don't know how you kept standing. I am willing to give a chance to anyone showing that kind of strength."

"Thank you, sir. Uh, master." Ren folded his hands in his lap and squeezed tight.

"So you want to train when you become of age. Your birthday is in May," Master Locke said, glancing at an electronic pad and tapping it a few times with his forefinger.

"Yes."

"Why?" Master Locke looked up. "Please be truthful. There really are no wrong answers."

But there were wrong answers. If he said something the master did not like, he might not be accepted.

Ren watched fluorescent white light simmer about Locke's jaw. "I am most comfortable in the submissive role, sir. To have someone make the decisions for me, tell me what to do."

"In all of life? Or sexual situations?" The light at Locke's jaw turned almost purple.

"The world outside is a very uncomfortable place."

"Yes. It is for all. Especially teenagers on the brink of adulthood."

Ren thought he might be losing his way here. He tried to explain himself. "Yes, I am overwhelmed. Like anyone. But I seek more than just comfort. I don't want to be free. I want to be owned. It's as if I can't be whole out there. I know I'm young, and you probably think I'm just scared because of my parents being gone and having nothing left, but—"

"No. You have something left. It says here," and now Locke tapped the screen of his pad again, "that you inherited money from a trust and the sale of a house. It is in another trust for you when you turn eighteen. That is only a few months away. It could fund your college education, or the start of a business. This is why you interest me. That isn't enough to give you comfort?"

Slowly, Ren shook his head. He knew about the money. It was a lot. At least to his thinking. But even the thought of having money didn't change his mind. He had made his decision. He didn't want to be in the outside world.

"I—I think it's sexual, too." Ren stumbled over the next words. "Since I was twelve I've read about pleasure slavery. Some of my richer friends' parents had pleasure slaves. But I didn't read about them because I fantasized about owning one. I read the books because I wanted to *be* one."

"The crux of the matter, then. Now we get to it." Locke allowed a small smile to touch his kind mouth.

The knot in Ren's stomach loosened a bit. He watched as Locke touched the pad's screen, read something, then nodded. The pad itself gave off a white halo. Made of energy, but blank. No color. Not like the paintings. Not like people.

Finally, Locke sighed. "My dear, you are quite lovely. You must know this. I would be lying if your sweet beauty did not influence my decision somewhat. But you show me much more."

"Thank you, sir." Ren's cheeks heated.

"You will have a complete psych eval. You will be assigned to classes as befitting your age. These are not classes on sex training. Do you understand? I am making an exception for you because you are so close to your birthday. And I have seen your records. You scores, before you ran away, were consistently high. But your high school education is not quite complete. We will see that it is completed. Then you will come back to me for another evaluation."

"Where will I live?" Ren asked, throat tightening.

"Here, of course. We have a full compliment of classrooms and teachers. You will even have schoolmates. I will expect top grades from you, of course. I will expect you to have finished all your studies to complete your high school education by your birthday. Do you understand?"

"Yes, sir. Yes, master!"

"And when you turn eighteen, we will reassess."

"Thank you, sir."

Chapter Two

Several Months Later

The first time Ren knelt on a soft velvet pillow in front of a naked, erect man he noticed two things.

One: It aroused him very much to be allowed to do this.

Two: The cock itself was already erupting, but not with semen. Thin golden flares of light emitted from the tiny opening at the crown. Like miniature lightning bolts, they cascaded along the shaft, touching at pinpoints almost erratically.

Ren had studied fellatio from his training master by reading and watching videos, but this was his first hands on session since being collared. After he had graduated his high school studies with high honors, and been accepted for slave training by Master Locke, it had been three months of study, reading, videos, and watching live performances before he was allowed to touch another person.

Now they were in a private alcove of the main training room. Of course anyone could see in since there were no doors to the alcoves, but it was nice to have an area with a bed, pillows, and no distractions but the test subject and the training master who had been assigned to him.

"Are you ready, Ren?" Master Holden asked.

"Yes, sir."

"Remember the act is about more than just sucking."

Ren nodded. He was not embarrassed. Only eager. Happier than he'd ever been. Finally, he was allowed to touch another. Finally, the training would include real, actual sex.

He watched the golden lights play about the cock before him, mouth watering.

"Begin," the master instructed.

Using his tongue, Ren traced all the lines of the lightning, teasing and wetting the cock wherever those little lights touched.

His subject, a slave named Tony, began to gasp.

Master Holden said, "Tony, control yourself. He's not hurting you, is he?"

"No, sir. It's just already very good, master."

"You've been the recipient of many a student's first time. You act like no one's ever touched you before!"

"I'm sorry, Master!" Tony said.

Ren began again, following the golden light-paths, touching his tongue where they touched, licking where they lingered.

Tony gasped again.

"What is it?" Master Holden asked. "You can't be ready to come yet!"

"As I said, he's good sir. It's just that good."

The master shook his head, rolling his eyes. "He hasn't even started. Nor has he ever done this before. If you two are up to something, I'll hear about it."

"No, Master. I swear."

Ren sat back. "I don't really know Tony all that well, sir. We are not up to anything."

Master Holden made a motion with his hand. "Back to work, Ren. And Tony, I've never had a problem with you before. If you come too fast, the lesson will be thwarted. I'll have no choice but to send you back half a grade."

"Yes, Master." But Tony, always good-natured according to gossip, grinned. He had told Ren on the way to the training room that he loved being a test subject. He was patient. He had even said, "If you accidentally bite me, I'm cool. I won't tell. Just be careful."

Ren stared at the Tony's erect cock. It was a nice one. Not too big for first time fellatio. It stood out from his body and curved upward, sweet, not intimidating.

The little lightning bolts continued to sizzle around the shaft, and the light coming from the head now looked like puffs of bluish air filled with white sparks.

It made him hot to watch this.

"Ren!"

Ren looked up at Master Holden.

The master gave him a puzzled look. "You may start again. Any time now."

Ren followed the lights, laving the cock, leaving wet trails wherever the golden-white charges went. More light congregated, turning bronze on the places he'd been.

Tony tasted wonderful, and Ren licked all around the head, then kissed it lightly, inhaling to try to catch some of the light. But there was no sensation to his tongue or lips from the effect, not even a small burn. This was something intrinsic to Tony, his body, his cock.

Tony moaned loudly as Ren took the head between his lips and sucked it into his mouth.

Obviously, Tony liked it—loved it—which was wonderful. But more, despite Ren not feeling or tasting the electricity, other sensations washed over him. Arousal, yes, but more. Deep in his mind he heard a wind shushing by, and stars flickered in the corners of his vision. He felt as if he were sliding through barriers he could not see, as if reality were as fragile as a blown egg and he was peeking through to something beyond he could not name.

Good sex could be this way. Orgasms were a drug. Euphoria could cause people to have visions.

But Ren was not even near to coming.

Tony, however, was as Ren took more of him into his mouth and re-traced the lines he'd lingered on before with his tongue, his lips, sucking him into the back of his throat.

Time wavered in this moment. He did not hear anyone but Tony, not Master Holden or the other noises of the training room. He saw only light and more light of all colors sprouting from Tony's skin, floating in tangled beams upon the air around them.

Tony moaned some more, and the noises became garbled words.

"Wow."

"Fuck."

"That's the most amazing sensation ever!"

That last sentence was the least garbled. Encouraged, Ren's own energy increased. He felt a cascade of pleasure run through his limbs, his belly, his cock.

Something had changed in him since his fever. He knew that. He had accepted seeing the auras and haloes, but this? This was something so much more detailed than he'd ever seen during his months of schooling, and then the beginning of his training. It was as if his first hands-on experience opened more doors inside his mind. Now he could see more than emotion in the auras. He saw specific bodily desires. The lights led him to be able to touch exactly as a person craved.

All his focus centered on Tony, who was nearly yelling now. It went on and on like that until finally Tony screamed and Ren felt the burst, tasted the pleasure, drank the essence.

The cock throbbed for a long time before Ren let it go.

He could not say how long he'd been on his knees. All he knew as he leaned back, buttocks on the backs of his heels, and looked up into Master Holden's face, was it seemed the entire room had quieted.

Master Holden's eyebrows were so tightly knit together they made a single line of hair over his eyes.

Ren glanced over his shoulder to see a circle of aroused naked slaves and masters observing. This action was allowed. Ren had observed sexual acts himself in the training room, both inside and outside the alcoves.

Tony had not yet caught his breath. He rubbed gently at the base of his cock, almost absent-minded about it. His eyes were dark, his head still tossed back as if he was still reliving the experience.

Quietly, Master Holden spoke. "Ren. Excellent work. Tony. Report."

"It was like his touch, his mouth, his sucking reached inside me. More than touch. I can't explain."

"Compatible body chemistry," said Master Holden. "And his technique?"

"I—I can't find any fault," Tony said. His cheeks were pink. He breathed in long, letting the air out hard and fast.

Holden nodded.

Ren's own body ached with the still unspent pleasure of his own enjoyment in what he'd just done. His muscles were taut. His balls drawn tight. His cock jutting upward. When his gaze drifted from the group behind him and back toward his master, Ren could see the tent of Holden's own erection against the lap of his black slacks.

One of the masters outside the alcove stepped up beside Master Holden.

"That's quite an effect he had on everybody in this room," he said.

Holden started to shake his head. "That's how things are here in training."

"Not like this," the master said. He looked at Ren.

Ren bowed his head in respect, not looking him in the eye.

"You have a special one here," the master added.

Ren felt the praise like a tingle all over. He wanted to smile, but kept himself humble, head down.

Finally, Holden picked up the end of Ren's leash, and Tony's leash. He led them out of the alcove and the crowd had to move to let them pass.

"Come along," he said as if nothing interesting had happened.

Pleasure unspent, but definitely not unsatisfied, Ren followed, Tony right by his side.

Chapter Three

Training with the Master

The painting above Master Holden's head looked ancient. Surrounded by a weathered, gilt frame, it depicted a large columned room lined with fancy couches and a bathing pool at the center. The area edged off to a balcony showing a pink sky and yellow clouds.

All about the couches and over the edges of the pool beautiful men wearing nothing but white loincloths draped themselves. Some of the men were leaning or standing, showing off curved thigh muscles, or the grace of a firm bicep. This was a painting of a harem.

The painting looked old because the colors were muted, and the oils appeared cracked. But Ren couldn't be sure that wasn't done intentionally by the artist to make it look that way.

A silver light imbued the painting, flickering about the edges of the frame.

Master Holden reclined on the bed below the painting, shirt, belt and boots off. He had a lovely, firm chest, tanned and gleaming, covered with a dusting of dark fur. Today he had a lavender aura containing excited little spikes of darker purple.

Ren stood naked before him, holding a tray that contained a dozen bottles of fine oils of different scents and hues. Beside them sat anal plugs of varying sizes and girths, and a stack of neatly folded, soft white cleaning cloths.

Ren had prepared for this day. His special afternoon of first penetration. He'd had a long bath, and had attended to every part of his body with external and internal cleansing. A slave he knew and liked by the name of Mikal, had helped him with the permanent removal of his chest, underarms, anus and balls. He had agreed to the hair removal, liking the idea of it, the youthfulness of the trend. Mikal had left only a cropped triangle of hair, a perfectly shaped equilateral triangle with the point touching the base of Ren's cock. The stubble wasn't so short as to be sharp, but had a velvety feel when Ren ran his hand over it.

Ren's long, dark hair had been trimmed, then braided front to back on the sides and gathered in a single, shining braid that met the center of his back between his shoulder blades. Wisps of shorter hairs had come free at his forehead, and wafted over his face like a sweet, barely visible veil. Ren was not as dark as Holden, but his body gleamed, fit and with a more creamy tan than Holden's, skin stretched taut over slim muscles he'd refined over the months of training, spending two hours a day running and swimming and lifting low weights.

As Master Holden had earlier instructed, Ren brought the tray to the bed and set it down.

Master Holden stared at him. Rarely, did the master touch him. He had Ren perform acts upon other slaves for lessons in technique. So far, the lessons had been oral and hand pleasure. Nothing more. Always, Ren gave the pleasure. He did not receive. Holden was the teacher, the director. He did not touch his trainees unless they needed help or adjustment. He did not require them to touch him.

But now Ren had graduated to another level of training, and Holden told him he had requested to stay with Ren and not pass him off to another hands-on master. Holden would see Ren's training through to the week of finals when Ren would attempt to pass all his tests in front of the Eminent Masters over a five day period.

Ren was fine with Holden being his master for the rest of his time at the Slave Palace. He had not fallen for him, as some trainees did for their masters. Falling in love with a master was strictly discouraged, but it happened more often than not, especially with younger slaves. Human attachment and feelings of closeness during sexual lessons could not be curbed by a simple written rule

But Ren had no problem in that regard. He liked Holden, and trusted him. Holden was handsome and refined, extremely professional, soft-spoken and not scary at all. He was the perfect master to have so Ren could practice intercourse until he was skilled enough to take his final exams.

Today was a special day. His first time for penetration.

"Turn," Holden said from the bed. He was surrounded by plush, black pillows and a black spread. For this special time, he'd brought Ren to a private room.

Ren felt his lips press into a tiny smile and put his arms out about six inches from his sides. He turned his body slowly so Holden could see him from front to back.

Ren was already half erect and had been all day anticipating this lesson.

Holden sat up, careful to avoid the tray. "Come to me."

Ren approached the bed until his knees touched the sides.

"Turn again," Holden instructed.

Ren did.

"Stop."

Ren's backside faced Holden. He stood very still, waiting. He felt a gentle hand sweep the curve of his left buttock and glide downward until it rested against the back of his thigh.

Holden said, "Bend a little, please. Then reach back and spread yourself."

Ren did as the master commanded. He pulled his cheeks apart and felt the air touch his hairless bud with a slight tickle.

He heard Holden breathe out. "Excellent. Perfect. Good job. Your assistant Mikal will be commended in my report for leaving behind not one hair. Turn to face me, now."

Disappointed that Holden still did not touch him more intimately, but only looked, Ren obeyed.

Holden's lavender aura had spread outward in shapes of flower petals overlapping. The color had a calming affect on Ren. He wasn't afraid, but for his first time with a master alone, he was nervous. He didn't want to do anything wrong, which was stupid because this was a time of learning.

"Come up onto the bed," Holden ordered.

Ren obeyed, sitting with his knees folded under him, his cock bobbing against his thigh.

"Would you like me to undo your trousers?" Ren asked.

"I want you to lie beside me. On your back."

Ren moved to straighten his body until he was settled by his master's side.

Holden sat up. "Spread your legs."

Ren moved his legs apart, knees slightly bent.

Holden knelt between them. He took a bottle of pink oil from the tray and opened it. A faint scent of flowers brushed the air, not too overwhelming. It was as if a wind had blown into the room bringing with it the freshness of a garden.

Ren thought Holden would start right in, getting him ready for first penetration. Instead, he oiled his hands and ran them all up and down Ren's body, stroking, caressing. He circled his erect nipples again and again. He oiled his navel, lightly tickling. He spread his palms over Ren's hips and thighs, moving his way down the legs, then up again. He avoided Ren's cock and balls.

Finally Holden said, "You are beautiful."

Ren always enjoyed praise. This was no different. In fact, he needed it. He was so aroused, but his nerves made it difficult to relax.

"Lift your knees to your chest, please," Holden said.

"Yes, Master." Ren's hands slipped as he pulled his knees up. One leg slid down. Suddenly awkward, he shifted so his hands were behind his knees. He held himself open as Holden calmly watched.

Ren wanted this to go smoothly, to be perfect. His cheeks heated when he had trouble staying still and Holden did not help him. Finally settling, he waited.

"Very good," Holden said.

Ren bit the inside of his lower lip. He told himself over and over he was going to do everything right.

"I'm going to touch you now between your buttocks." He took up a blue jar of oil. "I will slowly get you used to my fingers. All right?"

"Yes, sir." His voice came out shakier than he'd intended.

The first touch was light, smooth. It felt startling but wonderful at the same time. For a minute, Holden simply caressed him there, over his entrance. Ren's cock yearned for touch as well, but got nothing. His balls ached.

"One finger now."

It went into him smoothly, but with a pressure and slight burn that Ren was not used to.

"Deep breaths and relax," Holden instructed.

Ren breathed in and held it.

"Don't hold your breath," Holden said.

Ren let the air out. The finger inside him pushed further in. Even with the oil it stung a bit, and the sense of invasion surprised him because he had never felt that way when he had imagined this act. And he'd already had another hole invaded time and time again. He'd loved it, loved sucking cocks all the way back into his throat.

Slowly, the finger inside him moved in and out.

Ren found no pleasure in it. But he forced a calm upon himself.

Holden looked down at him. "Are you all right?"

"Yes." The word came as a whisper.

He smiled. "Don't be impatient with yourself. You'll get used to it. That's why I'm here. That's why we're doing this."

Ren could only nod.

Holden poured more oil over his crack. Some of it got on Ren's balls and that felt good for a moment, nice and slick and cool. He felt them move with his arousal.

Holden said, "Ready for two fingers?"

Ren wasn't, but he nodded.

"First lesson." Holden withdrew. "Don't lie to your master. Second lesson. Patience. You are not wrong if you are not ready."

"But I want it," Ren said.

"Yes. And you will have this lesson again and again. And you will be fine. But if you aren't patient with yourself, or honest with me, then I will know you really aren't ready."

Trying to understand the words amidst his arousal and frustration, Ren wiggled. His cock smacked him in the stomach. He finally lay still.

Holden did not move or speak.

Ren closed his eyes and spoke. "One finger only, I think. For now. Slow."

"Good boy." Holden caressed his buttock, then slowly ran his finger around Ren's opening.

When the finger intruded again, Ren was ready. He relaxed against it, allowing it inside, focusing on the slippery way it moved, how it didn't really hurt. And how the idea of it eventually being a cock inside him thrilled him. He still wasn't sure how he could take a cock like that, but others did. He trusted he would, too.

Holden went deeper, finger moving, bending. Then it touched a spot inside him that had Ren seeing lights on the ceiling and thrusting up with his hips. The pleasure spiked. His cock jerked.

Ren gave a little yell.

All Holden said was, "Good."

"Can you… can you do that again?" Ren asked.

"Yes." And Holden did.

Ren writhed in pleasure. His hole seemed to open up. He wanted more.

"You can try two fingers now," Ren said.

Holden pushed another finger in.

There was pain in that stretch. Ren, jerked back a little.

Holden put a gentle hand on his hip and stilled his fingers. "Get used to it."

Blinking hard, Ren nodded. He wanted that pleasure again. He wanted to be open, but it was hard to accept the pain as well. He was not a masochist. He'd been tested for that.

Holden held him open, gentle fingers—two of them— shallow within but going no further.

Letting out a frustrated sigh, Ren tensed up.

"Easy," Holden said. Without warning, he leaned down and gave a warm lick all the way up the underside of Ren's cock. When he got to the head, he teased the slit, licking fast, then sucked in the swollen, pink head and gave a few wet, tight sucks.

The pleasure was so fast and intense, Ren arched up. He wanted more. Every part of him yearned, and he felt his hole squeeze, then open as he pushed himself against the two fingers, getting them to slide deeper.

Holden sucked his cock again and Ren began to fuck himself on those two fingers and all the pain seeped away until pleasure on top of pleasure encased him.

Holden let the cock drop from his mouth. "All right, then. Such a beautiful boy you are. A good boy. That's just beautiful."

The praise sent more tingles of pleasure up and down Ren's body. When he looked at Holden, he saw the lavender petals of his aura darken and lighten as if to the beat of his heart. Pink spiked within purple along Holden's naked chest.

But when Ren looked at himself, he saw only his body, his gleaming skin, his eager arousal. It was always like this, in the mirror or looking down on himself. Everything emitted light but Ren's own self.

He'd still never told anyone that he saw light around them, or that the light changed and grew more intense during sexual acts.

Now that Ren was comfortable again, and aroused to the point of almost coming, the two fingers moved in and out of him at a more rapid pace.

He took them in willingly, loving it. Holden held back from rubbing his prostate, touching the spot a few times only to keep Ren on edge.

Several times, Holden withdrew his fingers all the way and rubbed about his hole, oiling it more.

"It's open and I can get three fingers in now," Holden said.

"It doesn't hurt," Ren said.

"Excellent. You might be ready for a cock now."

"Yes, please." Ren pressed his lips together in a shy smile, seeing by the way his aura pulsed that Holden was also ready. Ready for him.

"Good boy." Holden smacked him lightly on the ass.

Ren held his knees up and apart as he watched Holden push his trousers down his thighs and throw them off the bed.

Holden's cock was larger than Ren expected. He was already erect. Ready. As Ren knew he'd be. The shaft jutted out hard, the skin taut, the head glistening and dark. Holden's hand came over his own cock and milked it from base to tip and Ren realized he had oil in that hand and had spread it all over.

Again, Holden knelt between Ren's legs. He used his fingers to play with Ren's hole again, stretching him open, and Ren felt a little burn that faded as the fingers played again, inside and out.

He was ready.

Holden said, "You're stretched well. So pretty and pink. I can't wait to be inside you."

More praise. That was part of the teaching. Masters were careful to tell trainees when they did well, and criticized in a style that encouraged. Never did they belittle or discourage a slave. Unless a slave really misbehaved, masters never raised their voices.

The head of Holden's erect cock bulged against Ren's crack. This was huge, not a finger. The cock slipped against him. That was nice. Sweet and intimate.

Ren felt the head push against his opening and go partway in. He was stretched enough that it didn't feel as if Holden had to push hard, but still it was like a giant finger, nothing like he'd felt before. This was a man. A man's cock. Breaching him.

"Oh!" He almost sat up in shock. Ashamed. Surprised. Unsure.

Holden pulled back immediately. "It's all right. You're fine." Holden then reached out and put one hand around Ren's cock, stroking him in comfort. "Just feel that. Relax. We'll try again. As many times as you need until you're comfortable."

Ren relaxed. His cock felt so good being stroked. He felt Holden push, the big cock head moving past the rim of muscle, stretching. And it hurt. But he wanted it.

He thrust into Holden's hand, forcing his concentration on the euphoric sensations Holden was wringing from his cock.

As pleasure mixed with pain, Ren's body opened little by little. His master's cock pushed deeper. Every time Ren thought Holden was all the way in, it went deeper. So many times that happened. A half inch at a time felt like six.

The oil made the way fairly smooth, but the muscles were not used to such an invasion. They would learn. Ren would learn.

All along, Holden kept up the praise. "You are the loveliest. Beautiful, Ren. So tight. The way you grip me. But we will go slow, slow. You need not fear I will lose control. I'm quite the expert at control which is why I teach." He chuckled and even that sound reached out to soothe Ren.

The time came when Holden went no deeper.

"Is it in?" Ren asked shyly.

"Yes. All the way."

"Oh." And wonder fluttered through him, a soft and profound joy.

"We can stay like this. Joined. Until you are used to it."

"Thank you," Ren said.

Holden reached between them with oiled fingers, circling the pads of his fingers around the stretched opening where his cock was buried. "Here, can you feel?"

Ren felt the touch on his tight skin. He nodded.

"You're so beautiful, so stretched, taking all of me."

He could only nod again, swallowing, wanting to move, afraid to move, loving it even if his body was still not used to it.

For a few minutes, Holden massaged his cock, his balls, and rubbed at his opened buttocks. He did not move. He stayed still. Ren admired his control.

"All right now," Holden said. "I'm going to pull out just a little. Slow."

"Okay."

Ren braced himself, but the slide was not the tug or pull he expected. His body had relaxed more than he realized and the cock moved within him easily, as if it fit just right.

"That's—that's nice," Ren breathed.

"Excellent. Beautiful. You feel quite wonderful."

Ren smile wide this time. "Yes. I like it."

"Do you want me to fuck you now?"

"Yes. I would like that."

Holden pulled out more, then gently thrust.

Testing his body, Ren drew in a quick breath, then let it out. Nothing hurt so far. "Again."

Holden did it again, pulling out what felt like almost all the way, then sliding back in with a well-oiled swish. When he slid in, the hard cock nudged his prostate.

Ren pushed up. "Yes!"

It took a few minutes and then they got a rhythm and Ren was being fucked thoroughly and well for his first time and loving it more than he could ever have imagined.

His cock leaked on his abdomen. His balls were drawn up tight and aching, longing to unload. But the fucking kept him at a peaked level that was downright criminal. He could not believe how good this was.

Holden himself was enjoying it, too, grunting and groaning, calling him "sweet" and "beauty" and telling him how hot and tight he was, how irresistible, adorable and a host of other descriptions that made Ren feel perfect, protected, and ultimately successful. This was why he'd come here. This was what he wanted. To feel protected and safe. Away from the outside world that held grief and car accidents and death.

He saw Holden's aura surge with a rainbow of colors as the master fucked him faster and faster.

Just when Ren thought he might be on the verge of coming, Holden pulled out.

"What?" Ren looked up at him in confusion.

"On your hands and knees. I want in deeper."

Ren obeyed, turning over.

Slow and careful, Holden penetrated him from behind, cock going into him well-oiled and deep.

At first it almost hurt. Ren started to tense, then it was the best feeling with Holden clutching his buttocks apart, cock plunging in and out.

Ren felt himself stretched to the perfect fit of the two of them together.

"Your ass is so pretty bent over for me," Holden said.

Ren liked that sort of dirty talk, and answered it all with excited yeses. He thrust his ass higher, pushing back to meet Holden's thrusts, fucking himself on that exquisite, rigid flesh. He thought: *If only this could last forever!*

He started to reach for his own cock but Holden, somehow keeping his wits, keeping all control, hissed. "Do not touch yourself!"

Ren let his hand down and braced himself as the fucking increased to fast in/out motions.

He heard echoes of yells. Himself. Unable to keep his cries silent, or soft. Holden, too, was moaning aloud. Finally, he reached around Ren's waist and grasped his cock, pumping it in his fist in time with his thrusts.

That was all it took. Ren was coming fast, his mind swirling into whiteness. The orgasm was so intense he shot and shot for what seemed like a dozen times.

Warmth flooded his insides. Holden was coming, pushing hard against him, grunting. And it was all animalistic and base but also magical and amazing. The two of them shooting, coming, crashing into ecstasy together.

When they were finished and Holden rolled off Ren, Ren collapsed onto his stomach, then rolled onto his side to be taken into his master's arms.

Holden kissed his forehead, his hair, his cheeks. Then, for the first time, Master Holden kissed Ren's mouth.

Ren opened, tongue thrusting out to meet his master's in a moment of enlightenment and a feeling of success. The kiss was enticing and intimate. But it was also a grade. He'd passed. He'd gotten an A.

When Holden pulled back so they could both breathe, Ren had only one thought before falling asleep.

I was made for this.

Chapter Four

One Year Later - Final Exams

During exam week, four Eminent Masters came to see Ren perform.

The masters were all wearing formal black jackets with tails, and all male since Ren would be offered only to male buyers.

Each master had a quality about him that basked in a sort of spiritual serenity, but each was different. One was tall and slim, another stockier, another very pale. They held their heads up, confident, and their gazes were peaceful, soothing.

They all had different auras, spike-shaped, or tangled spirals, or arcs that crossed over each other to form X's. Or petal-shaped like Master Holden's. Purple, blue, green, gold.

Master Locke's aura produced little firefly-like sparks that never stopped crashing and burning against each other. And he still had the blue tree-like shape of light throbbing from the top of his head. It was said that Master Locke was in love with an odd slave named Wulf he'd bought for himself on a dare. Ren did not know Wulf, for Master Locke kept him apart from all others and private to himself, but he'd seen the slave at a distance and what a beauty he was, with an aura bright as sunlight in spring that formed a mane about his head.

All the masters who'd seen Ren in the training room or about the Palace knew something was different about Ren. He'd heard them talking about his skill, his touch, and he could see in their eyes, and in the beautiful colors they emitted when they watched him in the training sessions that he caught their attention. They knew he felt different to those who had been his sexual partners, and that he performed seamlessly, knowing when, where and how to move, breathe, suck, squeeze. They all understood he was special, but none of them knew why.

Ren said nothing to anyone about how he saw the world now after his fever, or how he could see feeling and sometimes even taste sensation as if it were his very own. He didn't need to touch someone to know what they needed or desired. It was all communicated to him through the energy that made itself visible to him and only him everywhere but upon his own image.

Nervous, for this was the event he'd trained over a year for, first in quiet study, then hands on training. Now he now stood naked and ready before the small circle of four Eminent Masters and his own personal master, Holden. He knew he would pass all the tests, from the first which involved touching and intimate massage to the last that would incorporate his ability to submit and let his body be penetrated from all angles by a group of trainers, some of whom he'd never met. He was fine with it all. And after all this time, not shy about public sex. But still… these were Eminent Masters. The best of the best. They would scrutinize him. This was a turn in Ren's life on many different levels and deep inside his muscles trembled.

The masters all introduced themselves. Master Locke was the last to speak, and he smiled at Ren, saying, "You've come a very long way in the past year. You have grown into a beautiful and striking young man."

"Thank you, Master." Ren bowed his head. His voice came soft, showing his readiness but that he also had not allowed any pride to go to his head. His body language communicated to them that he could be confident but humble, perfectly trained in any act and yet still seductively bashful.

The masters sat in comfortable black chairs set in a semi-circle that surrounded a small area containing a backless couch—the stage—behind which flowed curtains of deep, red velvet.

The couch sat on a dais that could rotate so the masters could see the performance at all angles. They controlled whether the stage moved or not, and how fast it spun.

Master Holden had explained everything to Ren so there would be no surprises.

A young slave named Audi lay back on the couch, a red pillow under his lovely, blond head. Ren had only just met him that morning when he learned Audi would be participating in his first day of the final exam.

Ren took his position by the left side of the couch and faced the masters, head slightly bent, hands clasped in front of his groin.

Audi was to be given a full body massage and the masters would grade Ren on his effectiveness. It was about technique, of course, but extra points were given for creativity, style, and his ability to connect with his partner. How the recipient responded was fifty percent of the test points. Having just met Audi, Ren could not have practiced with him ahead of time, or coached him, thus the test was a fair assessment of Ren's talent to know and understand the needs of another based on instinct as well as training.

It seemed he waited forever, but only seconds passed before Master Locke said, "Ren. You may begin."

Ren lifted his head. His hair fell against his shoulders, cool and soft. He blinked, allowed himself a half-smile, and turned to his task.

Audi was a beauty, long-limbed and lean-muscled—though not quite as lean and hard as Ren—with lovely, soft gold skin. His blond hair glistened in tight curls. His lashes were so long and glittery-gold, they looked almost fake. His eyes were bright with arousal, and his sweet pink mouth smiled up at Ren. Already, Audi's long cock was lengthening, thickening, the pink tip pushing against the foreskin.

Ren took a deep breath, admiring him, then said in a soft voice just above a whisper, "My name is Ren. It will be my pleasure to take care of you. Do you have any special needs I should know about before we begin?"

He'd rehearsed the line for days, but changed it up here and there to make it seem natural, not rote.

"No, thank you for asking," Audi replied.

"You have a lovely body. I would like to start at your temples and then to the base of the neck and the spine. If you would please turn over for me and get comfortable, then we can begin."

Audi turned on the couch until he was face down, smiling now.

Audi had a light blue aura. In various places on his body an amber and pink light glowed. Ren already knew those would be the spots of greatest sensitivity.

He began the massage, working his way over Audi's head and shoulders, across his back and slowly down the spine. He paid more attention to the more colorful sections of light, and Audi groaned in pleasure at the deeper caresses and the expert manipulations of the muscles.

Audi's skin was like satin, and Ren grew aroused as his fingers and palms skimmed the surface, splaying over hard shoulder blades and the bony spine, curving about the gentle slopes and crevices of ribs, waist, and the dimples at the top edges of his buttocks.

Ren knew to not touch the buttocks until he'd done feet, calves and thighs. He forced himself not to rush.

The thighs were lovely, the skin thicker on the lean body, and he could dig deeper into them while taking care not to be too rough. The blue aura about the thighs and buttocks darkened and took on an amber back-glow.

Ren had learned that, though everyone was different, in general certain colors meant certain things. Blue for contentment, affection or love. Gold for arousal and desire. Often, colors combined. And some people's colors were bright, others dim.

Audi spread his legs in invitation as Ren's hands smoothed up the curves of his ass.

Ren doused him with more oils, the air growing fragrant with sandalwood scent.

He gave careful attention to the cheeks of Audi's bottom, running his hands just beneath as well, to manipulate the hip joints. But mostly, this was a pleasure massage. He was careful to watch how the colors of the aura shaded dark to light to dark again, and followed the little patches of amber and pink to make trails across the skin that would feel euphoric.

Ren heard Audi sigh again and again. He dared not take a peek at the masters to see what their reactions were. Instead, he focused.

It was as if Ren could see beyond the skin to where the blood flowed and warmed the body, to where the nerves connected in spider webs of sensation. His hands held no color, no light, but where they touched, he could sense the body give way and open to him.

Then his fingers slid down the crack, gentle and slippery and warm.

Though Audi had been instructed not to move, he lifted his hips just a bit as if he couldn't help it. Offering himself.

Ren used more oil and inserted a finger into him, massaging him slowly, and Audi moaned.

A few brushes against Audi's prostate had him nearly writhing, but that was all Ren allowed, for he was only half done.

"You are so lovely," Ren said low in his throat. "Now, if you please. Onto your back."

Audi turned. His cock was fully erect and wet at the tip. His eyes were half rolled up. He lay back and Ren began the front massage at his forehead, then to the jaw, the sides of the neck, the shoulders and arms.

Slowly, he worked Audi's upper body, aware that the erect cock was begging for attention with its flowering of nearly all pink light.

He lightly rubbed the pink nipples, eliciting more groans. Stomach, abdomen, hips. All were caressed and soothed while he ignored the straining cock leaking just below the belly button.

He then went to the foot of the couch and worked his way up the legs, shins, and the fronts of the thighs. Audi spread his legs again, unaware, arm thrown back above his head, mouth open, eyes closed so that the long lashes made golden shadows on his upper cheeks.

Seeing that the insides of the thighs were pink, which meant to Ren Audi was erotically sensitive there, Ren spent a lot of time rubbing them up and down. Sometimes he let the tips of his fingers touch the velvet balls that were drawn up tight against the center of Audi's body.

Finally, he moved his hands up and around the base of Audi's cock. The slave had shaved, so the skin was smooth. He pulled Audi's cock until it stood straight up, the pink head completely exposed now in his increased arousal.

Ren took one hand away and gathered more oil, then he put his hands together around Audi's cock and milked it slow, lovingly. He saw the pink aura at the tip go almost red and circled it with his thumb, causing Audi to cry out.

Audi's balls tightened further, and he felt the cock start to throb. He gripped it tighter, and ran his hands up the length over and over, going faster until Audi cried out.

The cock erupted like a mini-fountain, white semen rising up. Ren pulled the cock forward and up so that it could empty on Audi's stomach. It spurted seven times before the throb slowed and the liquid streamed slower over the head.

Ren rubbed it into the skin, gently soothing the underside of the cock as he did so, until Audi could breathe again. Until Audi was completely satisfied and his cock, though still hard, stopped its internal tremble.

When Ren took his hands away, he wasn't done. He moved to Audi's head, leaned over him and kissed his forehead right at where some people said lay the third eye, spiritually. It was lit up rosy there, like the cock had been. He just had to kiss it.

"Thank you for allowing me to touch your beautiful body," Ren said.

Audi said, "Ah, thank you!" His tone was breathless and filled with a still-aroused rumble.

Only after that, after the kiss and the final words, did Ren turn to the master, place his clasped hands in front of his ignored erection, and bow his head.

Looking up through his half-closed eyes, Ren studied their expressions and their auras.

Master Holden was smiling with pride for his student.

Master Locke's eyebrows were raised.

The others were looking from Ren to their tablets, tapping away on their notes.

"Audi, you may be excused," Master Locke said.

"Yes, Master." Audi grabbed a towel and got up. Ren heard the pad of his bare footsteps across the room, heard the big door open and close.

Ren stood still, waiting.

Master Locke said, "You did well. You have five more days of testing."

"I am ready, Master."

"I have no doubt." Locke spoke with almost sarcasm. But Ren knew he was impressed.

His body heated all over at the job well done.

"With the permission of your master, Holden, you may relax for the rest of the day."

"Permission granted to attend the exercise room, the indoor pool and your room," Holden said.

"Thank you."

Ren turned. Then he turned back to face all the masters.

"I want to thank you, all of you, for this opportunity."

The masters all looked up, mostly expressionless, but Ren could read their auras spiking blue and green and gold. They loved him.

"You may go now," Locke finally commanded.

Affirmed, Ren turned again and left the room.

Chapter Five

Sold to the Highest Bidder

For the next five days, Ren was tested not only on his sexual technique and skill, but in his manners. How he interacted with others from language to bodily expression was assessed. His own appearance depended not only on physical attractiveness, but through his demeanor. Of course, the care he took with his body through exercise, hygiene, hair and make up counted for a lot, too. Make up was not required for males or females, but they were taught the art of it in case their future masters requested it.

Ren had been taught to be versatile in sexual ability. He could top or bottom on command. He could receive or give blowjobs or hand jobs with equal abandon. He was able to handle two men at a time, one at each end.

And he truly enjoyed all of it.

For every test, the masters looked both proud and perplexed. He knew he excelled because of his ability to see through auras what others desired, where they wished to be touched, or where on their bodies to avoid. He had his random subjects, all strangers, moaning within minutes and begging for more of his perfect skills.

All of Ren's tests were filmed and put into a file where prospective bidders could view them before making their bids. He'd even posed for still shots, like a model, from every angle, for a portfolio. He'd written an essay on pleasure, quoting his favorite romance movies and poets.

He'd written another essay about himself. That was hardest. He'd had to do it three times over because Master Holden told him he sounded too vague.

In truth, Ren could perform all sorts of sexual deeds for a camera with no qualms, feeling no shyness whatsoever, but revealing his deepest thoughts in writing, including past griefs, or his desires to always be a pleasure slave, or how he'd almost died to reach the Slave Palace itself, made him balk and quiver. He did not like to think about the outside world and all the shadows it held for him. He did not like to talk about it.

Though Ren had had a complete psych evaluation from the Palace doctors and been given a clean bill of health, he still had problems expressing and understanding why he needed to be apart from the outside world. Why he had such a desire to be owned, to be taken away from the free world and have no responsibility for himself except obeying his master's commands.

For his final third try on the essay, he ended with some bold statements that Master Holden said were still vague, using language that separated Ren from the immediacy of who he was, but moving nevertheless.

In my heart, I am a pleasure slave.

I have known this from an early age when I watched videos of slaves for not only titillation purposes, and not because I wanted to own one, but because I wanted to be one.

I craved the feeling of being owned. Fully owned.

I have never felt whole. Perhaps no one ever does. This feeling sets most of us on quests or searches to find, in our adult lives, that which perhaps can give us some meaning. Some want families and children. Some want to be artists. Some meditate. Others look to even more spiritual answers.

To be whole, to completely celebrate the person within, nothing, no kink or peculiar habit or personality quirk or physical flaw should be erased, criticized, or ignored. Everyone is beautiful and has beauty to offer, and wants to receive beauty in kind.

I believe denial of this is like amputating the vulnerable and sensitive tendrils of what makes up our souls. It can scar us if we are dishonest and cruel. First we do it to ourselves, then to others.

The world is a place of cruelty, but also great beauty.

I wish to be a contributor to the beauty of the world in a way that pleases others. It is what I was made for. I believe it to the depths of my most secret thoughts.

But I do not wish to do so from an outside, free perspective. I want to be owned in order to feel safe and secure. I want to have my actions commanded and appraised by others. This is not because I look only for outside approval, but because the feeling of knowing that what I offer can please another makes me feel whole.

When I lost my parents, I was bereft. Some may have the opinion that I am merely looking for replacement authority figures, but I felt this way even when my parents were alive. From a very early age, I dreamed of a kind of abandon where I had no space or thoughts in my mind but that of pleasure, of pleasing a person who commanded me in all ways.

With these words, Ren passed the test of essay-writing on the subject most of his bidders would be interested to hear about.

It was not until a pleasure slave could pass all six tests with adequate vid-feed, and their essays and profiles were complete, that they were put up for sale.

By the end of the week, Ren's profile, called "extraordinary" by Master Locke himself, was made public.

All Ren needed to do now was wait.

*

Master Locke's office was clean, even austere like the master himself. It was straight-lined, containing a desk of chrome holding a computer and tablets and a phone—all black. All the Palace masters wore black, but many accented their outfits with colorful ties, belts or jewelry. Locke was more severe in his tastes.

Except for his slave.

When Ren was called to Master Locke's office, he expected to meet with him one on one. Alone.

But as the door opened and he delivered himself inside, he saw Locke sitting at his computer, fingers typing, as usual. But another man, naked and covered with paint, leaned against the white wall leaving smears of greens and golds, his glossy blond hair, slightly windblown, playing about his shoulders.

Locke looked up. "One moment, please, Ren."

Ren let the door close behind him and stood, hands behind his back, head slightly lowered. He could still see the entire room.

The man who leaned against the wall turned a cool eye on Ren, then looked away.

Ren had never met Wulf, Locke's personal slave. He had seen him about the Palace but always moving away, at a distance.

Up close, Wulf was stunning. His muscular body and golden skin drew the eye. Light played around him in hues of firelight.

This was the man rumored to be too dangerous to train. The man Locke had kept because, the gossips said, Wulf was a prisoner of war from an enemy country and if he could not cut it as a pleasure slave he would be taken back to prison and probably put to death.

Locke had saved Wulf's life by keeping him. But now that Ren could see Wulf up close, he realized it was no doubt more than altruism that made Locke keep him. Wulf was a prize. Too beautiful for words. Whatever problems Wulf might have, Locke was an Eminent Master. The best. He could handle himself with wild foreigners and errant criminals.

But Wulf didn't look that dangerous. And the beauty of his natural stature awed Ren.

These two men were meant to be together. Ren could tell by the colors of their projected auras which pulsed quite large and floated toward one another, mingling on the air in lavenders, golds and pinks. Ren associated these aura colors with sexual contentment and more—deep love. These two men were in love. And since the colors didn't lie, Ren knew Locke and Wulf were completely suited for one another.

Wulf let out a fast breath, projecting a veneer of boredom. But the man's aura said otherwise. It communicated to Ren that Wulf enjoyed being in Locke's presence at this very moment. The naked slave's impressive half-erect cock denoted impatience, perhaps, but not boredom.

The paint Wulf wore and which rubbed off on the white wall was the type used for the living statue gardens all about the Palace estate. In his days of training, that was one particular art-form Ren had not had time to participate in, but he had seen the statues often and admired them.

Finally, Locke looked up. "You are well, Ren?"

"Yes, Master."

"Excellent." Locke sat back in his chair, the light shifting over his dark, wavy hair.

Wulf watched Ren with his eyebrows narrowed.

"I would like you to please take a seat." Locke indicated a plush, black chair that stood before his desk complete with a clean towel placed squarely in the center. "That is not a request but an order."

Ren quickly complied, though the request seemed odd. Wulf's gaze never left Ren's form as if he was waiting for something. But what?

"I have news for you."

"Yes, Master."

"You have been sold."

Ren's heart rate quickened. "So quickly?"

Locke nodded once. "And for a very high sum."

It was good news. But Locke was not smiling.

"I am honored. Thank you, Master."

Locke took a breath, glanced away and then back at Ren. "This sale is red-marked. Do you know what that means?"

Ren shook his head. He had never heard that term "red-marked" before. He saw Wulf turn to Locke and tilt his head as well.

"The Palace as a corporate entity has many rules and regulations as you well know. Standards for slaves as well as buyers. A red-mark occurs when a buyer wins a bid but does not quite meet the standards himself."

"You mean the buyer is not qualified?" Ren asked.

"In this case, he is. In all the ways that matter to the corporation such as good credit, no criminal record, etc."

"Then he is qualified?"

"Yes. But he is shielded."

"What does that mean?" Ren asked.

"He has not been seen in public for twenty years. Little is known about him other than that he is wealthy. He is known to keep a harem of pleasure slaves on his compound. They, too, never venture outside and little is known about them. We suspect many have been purchased from the underground, the black markets and various other trades. Why? We don't know. Some masters who can afford it do collect pleasure slaves the way art lovers collect works of art."

A harem! Ren remembered the painting of the harem he had admired. It had overlooked him during his first time being penetrated by Master Holden. He'd not forgotten its beauty, and how enticing it was. Could this be a sign that this destination was the right one for him?

"So." Ren paused and took a breath. "He keeps a harem. I would not be his only slave."

"No. And I understand you were hoping for a master to purchase you and keep you one on one. Hoping for a relationship?"

Ren looked at his hands which were pressed to his naked thighs. "I—I confess I do have fantasies of being the center of my master's focus. But my training has taught me that is a gift, and extra benefit that may or may not occur. And I have also had a desire for a family. A harem seems almost like that."

"It could be. But you said it yourself. Your training has taught you not to expect the extras benefits of love and belonging. At least not at first."

Ren nodded. But his stomach flipped at the idea that he might never know the full attention of another. That he might be left alone too often and grow bored. In a harem he would have many more chances to find more opportunities to feel wanted, and valued.

"The buyer is red-marked not because he keeps a harem, but because he keeps them locked away. It is not a crime, for a slave is owned and a master can do as he wishes with his slave short of outright harm. But he is also red-marked because he does not allow photos, videos or anything personal about himself to be known. If he has any social presence, it is under a false name. This secrecy flags the Slave Palace system. The red-mark is a warning that he is an unknown entity who is also a first-time buyer from the Palace corporation. Through his solicitor, we know only of his credit reports, his official record with the law, and his country of origin."

Ren's realized his body had become tense. He tried to imagine who this buyer could be. Why the secrecy? Why the locked down compound? "What does all this mean?"

"It means you have a choice." Locke fiddled with his mouse and stroked a few letters on his keyboard.

"I do?"

"You have the freedom to decline this buy. In all other cases, you must adhere to our program where a purchase is final as long as the buyer is qualified. In this case, you get to make the decision to go with this buyer or not."

"Is anything else known about him at all?"

Locke started to shake his head. Then said, "All we have on him is that he is associated with the royal family of Pariny. But only as a distant cousin. He was known to have attended Cornell University for a time until he dropped out and was never heard or seen again. There had been rumors in the first years that he had even died. But of course he is quite alive. Nothing is known about his compound except it is located in the country of Pariny and is remote from major cities."

Across the sea. Ren would be traveling far if he decided not to decline.

"How can I make such a decision without more information?" Ren asked.

"That is the difficulty. But you should know that this particular buyer bid quite high for you. The highest I have ever seen in all my years here for one slave."

"For me?"

"Yes."

"Why?"

"Unknown." Locke let a smile press his lips. "You are exceptional, of course. Your tests, videos, essays—all exemplary."

"There are other exemplary slaves sold by the Palace every day."

Locked nodded. "There are. But this buyer chose you. He did not appear to care about other bids. He looked at our reserve and tripled it. And the offer is in cash."

Was that odd? Ren had no idea. But then he thought it probably was odd, especially if he went for as much as a house or something equally expensive.

"Would you like to know how much?" Locke asked.

"You're allowed to tell me?"

"In a red-mark case, I can reveal all of it to you so you are fully informed in making your decision."

Ren bit the inside of his lower lip. Nodded.

Locke leaned forward and put his elbows on his desk.

"Nine million."

For a moment, Ren thought he had not heard correctly. It could not be that figure. It was far too high.

Wulf, near his corner where the wall was streaked gold and green, grunted.

"I don't—think I heard you," Ren said.

"Nine million, Ren. Avilan dollars."

"But I'm not—I'm nobody."

"Certainly you are not! You are an amazing graduate from the Slave Palace. Smart. Talented. Beautiful. That was why we had a reserve of three million on you, and we expected to meet it." Locke rose from his chair and came around his desk, leaning his hip against the edge. "Never ever think you are not truly an amazing man and a perfect slave!"

"If not for you rescuing me," Ren began to say in a soft voice.

Locke held his hand up for silence. "You have wanted this. You embraced your dream for this with great enthusiasm. And now this is the reward. It is a lot of money. Someone wants you very badly. But we cannot know why. We only know that this man has purchased other slaves. There is no way for us to monitor their conditions, their health, or even if any are alive. This is a very important decision for you to make. The money is good. It means that should anything ever happen to your master and you end up back here, you will always be cared for. Of that nine million, a percentage is set aside in trust for you. For your life span. It means you will never not know wealth. But the decision for your well-being is more paramount. You do understand this, correct?"

"I do," Ren said. "I will be sent far away."

"Yes," Locke affirmed. "And you will have no contact with anyone, including me or any Palace representative."

"I'll be going into the unknown."

"That is essentially it."

Ren could feel his skin tingle all over in a variety of responses from anxiety to anticipation.

If he said yes, he would be part of a harem and probably never know what it would be like to be cherished by one, one on one, to be another man's one true love-slave. On the other hand, if he said no, gone would be the highest bid in Slave Palace history. A record-breaker. And he would never know who bid such a high price for him, or why.

A stranger wanted him that badly. It was the oddest feeling, both exciting and terrifying at the same time. But was curiosity on his part enough to risk his very life?

He did not want to be hurt again. Physically. Mentally. Other than the sexual games he'd been trained to perform which included

44

being restrained, taking the whip across his back, and allowing himself to be used by multiple partners, Ren did not invite more than that. What if this man was a true sadist? A torturer? A serial killer? Who could be sure if all that was known about him was that he was wealthy? If he and his harem never left the compound, no one would truly know what really went on behind closed walls, gates and doors.

Ren had already lost everything once in his life. He had almost died on the streets. But he'd made it.

The first and loudest voice in his mind spoke an immediate *no* to the situation. But deeper within, Ren had a strange desire rise up. He looked at Wulf.

He'd heard about that man's story. He had been captured, taken against his will, sold against his will, and labeled a one-night thrall to be taken and used and disposed of since he'd been labeled too dangerous to train. Wulf had not known what would happen to him day to day until he came to the Slave Palace. Even then, the story was told that Wulf fought his fate, and that only Master Locke with his great patience had been able to reach him. And they'd been together ever since. It was a lovely story.

Ren had the freedom to decline and wait for another bidder. But it was a gamble. That second bidder could be someone qualified but that did not preclude they wouldn't be cold, cruel, old, bitter. There were no guarantees at all for the slave when an auction was held. The winner of each auction could be anyone.

"How long do I have to decide?" Ren asked.

Locke met Ren's gaze. "Twelve hours."

Not long enough. And yet too long. If he had less time, his nervousness would end quicker. But he did not want to be hasty. He intended to take the entire twelve hours.

Ren bowed his head. "Thank you, Master."

"You have my leave to go. You may go back to your room or to the pools only. Order your food sent to your room. If you need to discuss this further, you may request the guidance of myself or Master Holden."

"Thank you, Master Locke." Ren stood and turned to leave.

Locke's voice stopped him. "Ren."

He turned. "Yes?"

"I am quite proud of your accomplishments here. You are one of the best. I want you to know I do not say this lightly. Your decision is yours to make and you will not be wrong either way. The Palace will stand by you, whatever you decide."

"Thank you, Master Locke."

As Ren opened the door and stepped into the busy hall, he heard Locke say, "Wulf, come here."

As Ren turned, he glanced back through the archway just before the door swung closed and saw Wulf, still glistening with paints, wrap his arms around Locke as Locke laid his head against his broad shoulder.

"What if he's not as lucky as I was?" Wulf murmured.

Locke reached up to touch Wulf's face.

The door shut.

Chapter Six

Bon Voyage

"You do not have to do this."

Locke stood by the wide window of Ren's private room, bathed in the deep ivory glow of morning light. His dark brown hair reflected golds and blues and his aura was a deep auburn fringed in pink. The blue light above him remained bright as always. He exuded success and fulfillment. He had a respected job. And a beautiful lover that was his own personal pleasure slave.

Ren longed to be even half as content.

"Nine million. The man wants me that much. I feel deep inside myself that I must go. I must honor this buyer's winning bid."

"You do not owe anyone."

But Ren did not quite agree with that. The Palace had taken him in when he'd been deathly ill. They had trained him well. This was the life he'd dreamed of. What he had always wanted. He owed the Palace everything. He lowered his head and remained silent.

"Come here to me." The words Locke spoke reflected those Ren had heard him speak to Wulf before he'd left his office the previous evening.

Ren moved toward the window, blinking at the brightness, the view a green field swept by willows, oaks, and eucalyptus.

As Ren faced Eminent Master Locke, Locke's aura lightened and the pink outline sparked with tiny flames.

"You are one of the most incredible slaves to graduate the Palace. You have other bidders who are wealthy and will take you. Possibly even love you."

"But not at nine million." He could not help but be awed—and proud—of that figure.

"True." Locke reached up and pushed a tendril of hair back from Ren's face. Ren felt himself flush all over. To be revered by Locke—and touched. This master simply did not do that. Not since Wulf had come to stay with him. Rumor was Locke no longer consummated physical sexual acts with those under his authority. Once, he used to be the best. So gossip said. He interacted on all levels with trainees. But now he oversaw the Palace itself. When he took on trainees, he had hands-on masters who worked for him to train them. Locke remained in authority, but did not touch.

Ren liked to think it wasn't because Locke was jaded, but because he was in love. And completely devoted to Wulf. Completely monogamous.

It wasn't that unusual, actually. From what Ren had learned during his time at the Palace, many masters did like to play with many different partners, not just slaves in training, and in groups, and they remained polyamorous for years and years, but others ended up retiring to long-term relationships with one partner. As in any work place, everyone was different.

But now Locke touched Ren. And his dark eyes softened, gold around the edges. His aura pinked even more.

"It may be obvious that I have taken an interest in you."

Ren's lips twitched, wanting to break out in a grin.

"There will be no outside contact after you are gone. I will never know what happens to you. So this is of great concern to me."

All masters cared about their trainees, but relationships were not only discouraged, they were forbidden. Not that this was a relationship, but there was something more. Locke had taken a personal interest. He had shown altruism to Ren by taking him in when he was half-starved and feverish. All trainees were shown good treatment by their masters. They trained them well so they could take care of themselves out in the world, after they were sold and left the Palace.

This made the parting easy and smooth. Already, Ren felt fine about leaving Master Holden. He had no feelings for him beyond teacher/student.

But Locke— that was different. Ren had always felt an affection for him. Perhaps it stemmed from that rainy day he'd collapsed in Locke's arms.

Anyway, he was ready for this. Ren was ready to face the world now. As a pleasure slave. He had been well-trained. If he shied away from this secret bidder, he'd always wonder for the rest of his life what he had passed up.

"I want to go." Ren swallowed and his throat was dry.

Locke nodded. "Then I will put the final stamp of approval on your bidder. And you will leave in two days."

Ren nodded. But his eyes welled.

Locke's eyebrows almost met. "You must be sure."

"I'm sure. I just—I do have emotion about it. That's all. I'm happy, Master. I truly am."

Locke took a deep breath. "Ren. You make the Palace proud."

"I am proud to have learned all that I have. This is what I want."

Locke nodded. "Not everyone has this conviction deep inside in the beginning or even after they graduate. This sureness you have in your identity—I believe it will help you. I will never forget you."

"Thank you, Master." Ren flushed again, wondering at his heat. Had the air in the room been turned off? But no, that wasn't it. It was the approval. The sense that he had done well beyond expectations. To be told by Master Locke he was the best made his heart light.

For a moment, Ren thought Locke was about to embrace him. Instead, Locke dropped his hand from where it had touched Ren's hair and turned away.

The room fizzed with pink light for a long while after he left.

*

Tradition dictated he walk the Rose Path before passing the Slave Palace gates to the outside world.

Ren's mostly hairless body had been freshly oiled for the occasion.

Cascades of red, pink and yellow rose petals fell over Ren's naked form. Silver spring sunlight streamed into his eyes. Tears slid down his cheeks.

The glare, he told himself. *It's just the glare.*

But the celebration moved him beyond definition. The crowd of masters and trainees exuded light of emerald, pearl, ruby, all denoting excitement, happiness, and maybe even a little jealousy from the trainees. So bright.

They were all proud of him. Even the ones he did not know. But they knew who he was. Ren was the boy who sold for the highest bid ever known to any Palace. The boy who would cross the sea and enter a mystery of a life with no outside contact. He would never be able to tell anyone about it.

Deep inside Ren's chest a tremor threatened to produce more tears, and a singular excitement enfolded him the likes of which he'd never known.

He'd come such a long way.

He was a little afraid. Not for his life, for who would part with nine million dollars only to murder his acquisition? But his apprehension for the unknown coursed through his veins.

Ren smiled as more flowers and petals cascaded through the air and into his hair, thrown by his peers. They slipped down his shoulders, some sticking to his shining skin. His hair was loose, cascading down his back.

At the end of the path stood the Eminent Masters in a rainbow fog of colors. In the center of the group, Locke smiled at him and held out a single black rose. He gave the black rose only to graduates who passed with the highest of ranking.

Ren took the rose, bowing, then kneeling before the masters.

Out the corner of his eye, he saw Wulf nearby at the front of the crowd. He stood apart, aloof, naked and goldenly glorious, and not without interest in the proceedings.

Wulf would never walk this path. For a moment, Ren was almost jealous.

He looked up through his shining hair as the masters bid him to rise.

Now they would feast.

Then Ren would sleep one more night in his own bed, awake at dawn and board a helicopter which would take him to a private plane on a private runway a hundred miles from Lirangel.

*

Eminent Master Locke, Master Holden and Wulf met Ren at the helipad.

Ren was surprised to see anyone there. As a graduate, he had the freedom to come and go unleashed, though he would always wear the collar. He was expected to get himself to the helipad on time.

50

The sky was green on the eastern horizon. The sun had still not poked itself above the low mountain range beyond the city. From their vantage on the high hill, Ren could see the city lights below still twinkling in the pre-dawn shadows.

A breeze blew cool through the deep, thick leaves of the oaks.

For the first time in two years, Ren wore clothes. White shirt, black silk trousers. He had on black slippers and his hair was tied back with a neat black string. Some of the shorter hairs brushed his cheeks and eyelashes.

The calmness of the scene left dark blue auras surrounding the four of them.

But though Ren did not have regrets, he was far from calm. He could not eat and had drunk only half a glass of orange juice before leaving, for the final time, his luxurious Palace room.

Master Holden stepped forward. "To my finest student, I bid you farewell." He kissed Ren on the forehead.

Master Locke stepped forward. "I hope with all my heart you find happiness."

Ren blinked back the sting of tears.

Master Locke then stepped forward and brought Ren into a tight hug. He had never seen Master Locke hug a student before. He stood in the midst of that hug and took all the warmth and strength of it into his heart. He put his own arms around Master Locke and pressed tight.

He was breathless when the hug ended. "Thank you, Master."

"A rare jewel. That is what I told your new owner in a letter to him. Of course, I received no response, but I can only hope my words and recommendations for your character found their way to him."

Master Holden nodded in agreement with Locke's words.

Wulf stood to the side, silent as always. Unmoving. But in his eyes there was a hard resolve. He did not look away from Ren. His aura, spiked with green bolts this morning, told Ren Wulf was astounded, but also admired him.

Ren boarded the helicopter. The pilot had already started it up, the propeller spinning faster and faster.

As they lifted, Ren looked down on the entire estate on the hill. The Palace itself glowed in the pre-dawn light, the golden turrets like a vision from a fairy tale. From on high, it all looked like a child's toy set in a miniature garden, and the masters and one slave looking upward to send him on were but tiny dolls receding into the past, the way of all childhood things. Blurred. Lost on the edges of pearlescent, faded memory.

But Ren knew he would never forget them. And maybe, if he was lucky—who knew?—he might see them again. One day.

Part Two

Chapter Seven

Arrival

After eight hours of flight—most of it over ocean waters—Ren saw a city with tall buildings that gleamed dark gold in the sun's glare. It looked as if it had just come up for air from sea, glittering like a lot of broken pieces of a child's toys scattered about. Beyond the spill of that city, a range of mountains swept like a wave on the land. Dark green contrasting with the white edges of the dark sea. He could already smell the forests of those mountains, spiced and sharp, and with the fresh clean scent of shade.

This was the entrance to a country called Pariny.

He was headed for somewhere in that vast range. A secret compound. An isolated retreat.

He had dreamed of it twice before leaving the Slave Palace. In one dream it was full of light and flowers, as if flooded with life. In another, he heard a darkness full of moans and sighs. He could not decide which was to be his fate. If either.

Ren shivered though he was not cold.

The plane landed and as he descended the stairs, two men with dark hair and dark suits immediately came up to him, separating him from the line of other passengers.

"We have a car waiting," said one. He had an accent that was thick but pleasant.

Ren kept his head bowed, as he was trained to do even in the outside world. He was a slave. Not a free man.

The other man also had dark brown hair. He looked older than the first, and had a scar on his chin. He did not speak.

Both men were trim and tall. Bodyguards. Or something very like that.

He could not read their auras. When he was too nervous, the lights of other people faded from his vision. Right now he was too keyed up to see much in that regard yet.

He did not ask questions. He had been instructed not to.

The car was a sleek, black limo that smelled of new leather. To Ren, that meant he was to be presented in style at the very least.

The seats in the limo ran parallel to the car's length. The two men sat on one bench facing Ren. Ren sat alone on the other.

He had no luggage. Nothing. Not even toiletries. He'd been instructed to bring nothing as all would be provided for him. His i.d. was an embedded chip in his wrist, and had been scanned for him before the already paid-for flight. He had no rights. No money, nothing to his name but his collar, and his status as a pleasure slave.

But he'd been well taken care of already so far. He'd been served brunch and early dinner on the plane, which had been large but a private charter with only a few other passengers who seemed very dignified and important. He had not been chained or treated disrespectfully by the staff who served the meals. He had been allowed to get up and use the lavatory when necessary. No one spoke to him except to ask his preference in drinks.

The windows of the limo gave Ren a view beyond the men sitting in front of him. First buildings and cars and sidewalks crowded with people passed by the windows. The city did not look much different from other cities Ren had been to, including Lirangel. They entered a freeway which led to the city outskirts and dusty rows of modest houses.

The limo took an off-ramp that quickly led to a two-lane highway lined with maples and pines. The road became hilly, more desolate. A half an hour passed.

Ren stayed still and quiet. Neither of his escorts spoke a word. One had a phone in his hand and was tapping on it. The other stared straight ahead, the muscles of his face stiff as if he were angry, perhaps mulling over a past event.

Ren had been trained well. In his life as a pleasure slave, he was expected to remain submissive in every situation he found himself in, unless otherwise instructed by his master. Though he had not yet met his new master, he belonged to him now. His expected decorum would be one of utmost obedience and deference.

He kept his head slightly bowed. He did not meet his escorts' eyes. But he could see their auras now, the stiff-faced one's a reddish brown, the other's a more sedate yellow. Both colors revealed that their attentions were less on him and more on other matters.

It made sense. They would not be worried he would run. He was Palace trained. Willing. And he'd been bought and paid for, all legal with his own signature tying the bond.

The limo slowed, and Ren braced himself against the motion of the abrupt turn. He looked through the front part of the vehicle and saw a break in the trees and a dirt outcropping. Beyond that was an iron barred gate, much like that at the Slave Palace. Through the bars he saw an asphalt paved drive that wound through the trees out of sight.

The gate opened for the limo and they glided over dirt and rocks and onto the smoother blacktop.

Soon, the trees cleared and Ren could see more of the grounds they had entered, an estate to rival even that of Lirangel's Slave Palace.

Looming out of the ground cover like a fantasy world come to life, giant marble sculptures reared. Unicorns. Griffons. Dragons. They looked down upon the narrow lane as if to guard it from invaders. On both sides of the road the sculptures loomed. Ren counted six, then a dozen. White lions, an onyx Pegasus, a tourmaline dragon with transparent wings as if carved from green ice.

Around another bend, the compound came into view. Huge. Imposing. A black mansion surrounded by large, white, flat-roofed outbuildings. Neatly trimmed lawns sloped between the buildings and the main house, lush and emerald. The four-story house itself sported a "V" roof. Poised at the top, balancing on two back legs, was a black unicorn, reared up, hooves pawing at the air, head back as if it wanted to conquer the sky.

The limo pulled along one of the outbuildings to a concrete porch that led to a door.

Ren's escorts exited first, and motioned Ren out.

Ren stood by a curb where the neatly trimmed grass looked so full and green and shiny he thought for a moment it was fake. But all around him was lush, real. Amazingly serene.

He had arrived.

Chapter Eight

Preparation

His escorts pushed a button that rang a bell at the outbuilding's door. Soon it opened, and an older man, about forty-ish, in a white shirt, black trousers and bowtie stood at the threshold. He had wavy light brown hair styled neatly back from his face.

"I will take him from here," the man said, gesturing almost violently for Ren to come up the two steps to the little porch.

Ren obeyed, not looking back.

The man said, "Ren is your name, correct?" For nine million, Ren expected his name to have already been confirmed. But he answered in his trained, polite tone. "Yes."

"I am Niko. You will address me as such. Follow me. And shut the door behind you."

"You are not the master?"

Niko laughed. "You are not ready to meet the master yet."

Ren looked up, forgetting his lessons in submissiveness for a moment. "I am quite well-trained and quite ready."

Niko's eyebrows rose. "Well, all right then. But I say not." He shook his head as if already disappointed by Ren, and that was when Ren saw his aura, blue and green with soft fuzz at the edges. Ren interpreted that to mean this guy was content in his job. Even loved it. "This is the preparation house. You will bathe. You will be given a new collar, among other things, and you will be instructed as to the rules. You will pay attention at all times. If your mind wanders, I have permission to use whatever methods I deem necessary to get your attention. Do you understand?"

"Yes, sir. Uh, yes, Niko."

Niko led Ren through a front room that looked like any sitting room or living room of a typical medium income household with sofa, two recliners, a flat-screen TV, and a coffee table.

One area of the room led to an open doorway. A kitchen perhaps? The other led to a hall and that was where Niko took Ren.

At the end of the hall was a brightness and as they walked, Ren saw the hall open to a large bathroom, as big as the living room, maybe bigger. There were two toilet stalls at one end, and a huge open shower at the other with multiple water spigots in the center wall.

Two men in white shorts and nothing else stood by the shower.

"Let's have a look," Niko said. "You will disrobe now."

It all felt rather strange, but Ren was not shy. Not anymore. He began to undo his shirt.

Niko stood before him, arms crossed, and watched.

Once Ren had his shirt off, he folded it and looked around for somewhere to put it.

Niko said, "You won't be needing those clothes anymore. You may dispose of them here." He indicated a hamper by the wall outside the shower.

Ren put his shirt in the hamper, then proceeded to take off his shoes and slacks.

Fully naked, he hesitated to place the shoes in hamper as well. He didn't know why.

"All of it," Niko instructed.

Ren nodded.

"Come here and stand in front of me."

Ren obeyed.

Niko looked him up and down, then took a small tablet from his pocket and tapped on it. "Turn," he said.

Ren turned slowly, letting Niko see his whole body.

Niko looked bored, again tapping at the tablet screen.

Once, Niko took a step forward and peered closer at his cock. Then he motioned to the grooms who stood by the shower. One came over.

"Take his collar."

Ren must have given some indication of surprise, because Niko added, "Don't worry. You'll get a new one. The master likes them fancy."

Niko made more notations as he circled Ren's body, glancing at it now and again.

Ren held his breath. He had had assessments like this at the Slave Palace, but he'd always felt secure. Here, he had no idea what to expect. Niko had spoken of rules. Ren longed to hear them. Rules made him feel safe. Rules let him know what to expect, what to do, how to be.

Niko took a step back. "Now, before we go any further, you will let these men bathe you. You will be getting the full treatment inside and out. Including an enema. Do you have a problem with that?"

Ren was almost offended. He was Palace trained which meant he was prepared—the best. But if they wanted to do it all again, he would obey. "No, sir."

"Good. They will groom you while I watch. If I see anything out of line, you will be punished. Know this. You will never be sent back from where you came. Once you crossed the border of these grounds, you became property of its owner for your lifespan. But you can still be rejected. And believe me, you do not want to be rejected for any reason. Then you will live a lonely life, isolated and un-revered. I am sure your purpose in becoming what you are is not to end up like that."

"No, it is not, sir, Niko."

"Good."

One of the men by the shower turned on the spigots, then motioned to Ren.

The other stood by a cabinet, opening it. Within, Ren could see bottles of shampoo, soaps, enema tubes and other necessities for preparing pleasure slaves.

He was too nervous to see the auras of these men, these grooms, but he didn't really care about them. He cared about presenting himself in the best light possible.

He cared about how he might be welcomed by their employer, his owner.

The grooms were thorough but the shower was quick. They knew their job and Ren was used to being handled, and used to being clean inside and out. Usually, however, he did the job himself.

When he was dry, Niko came forward with something that looked like a combination of a collar and a necklace in his hand. The main part was embedded with blue and green gemstones. The part that looked like a necklace was made of an elaborate weave of chains, all silver, spilling across Niko's hand like captured rain.

"Bend forward," Niko ordered.

Ren bent his head. Niko put the collar on him and the chains tickled the skin of his chest and they made a sound like tiny bells clinking together. Chimes.

"This way," Niko ordered, abruptly turning.

Ren followed Niko out of the large bathing room and into another area that contained a couple of straight-backed chairs and a long, white table scattered with tablets, and what looked like gaming equipment, but wasn't. Ren tried to see, but Niko stood in front of him and motioned to the nearest chair. "Sit."

Ren obeyed, the cushion of the chair hard and cold against his backside. His hair, still wet, streamed little cool drops of water down the center of his back. He suppressed a shiver but sat with his back straight. Yet even with his training, this was all new and unknown and his muscles remained taut, his pulse thrumming in his veins.

The air in this small room smelled faintly of old dust, though it appeared quite clean.

Niko, in his clean white shirt and bowtie fiddled with something on the table. Something hummed, then dinged. When Niko turned, he had a sort of wand in his hand. He leaned toward Ren and said, "Remain still."

"What is it?" Ren began to ask, but before he could finish, the wand touched him on the right side above his pec and it felt like a thousand flaming needles invaded his skin.

He could not hold back his cries and his mind went black at the edges and spun. A sharp, metallic taste coated his tongue. He jerked forward but Niko took the wand away and it was already done.

Through streaming eyes, the tears falling so fast he could not control them, Ren looked at his chest. It was already red and swelling, the ash salt scent of burnt skin invading his lungs. The skin blistered where it formed a design of a generic flower with open petals and a solid center. He had been branded.

The pain of it continued to slice through his body, making his stomach clench, making him want to be sick.

He looked up at Niko, who set the wand down and came at him with another tube.

Ren flinched, but it was only salve. When Niko rubbed the ointment onto his skin, Ren groaned in pain, feeling stabbed and hurt all over again.

"Master's orders," Niko said unapologetically.

Ren was still catching his breath as a simple square bandage was placed over the brand.

"It will heal in a week or so. If the redness doesn't subside by then, you need to report it."

Report it? To whom? He clenched his teeth and tried to swallow away the bitter metals that had been released in his mouth at the sudden pain. His training told him endorphins would soon kick in, but in the meantime he was dizzy from the assault and could not think what to say in response. His body began to sweat all over. He shivered.

"There now," Niko said, handing him a small towel. "Wipe your tears and chin up. Everyone gets the brand here." He pointed to his own chest, which was covered, crisp shirt buttoned to the edge of his bowtie. "Even me."

That did not make Ren feel better. The pain of a burn did not subside quickly. He was still resisting the urge to double over. He used the towel to wipe his face, and the sweat from his shoulders and the unassaulted portions of his chest and stomach.

When his thoughts settled, he thought of Master Holden and Master Locke. What would they say? There were those who liked pain, who were trained to take it. He was not one of them, and that box was not checked on his auction bio.

Master Holden would say in his cool, unaffected manner: *Be brave and always obey.*

Master Locke, in a warmer tone, would no doubt remind him: *There will be an adjustment period, and you must endure, take time to settle in.*

Ren envisioned Locke's dark brown eyes narrowed, and tried to focus on remembering the flickering warmth he noticed in them, and in Ren's mind the man's pretty blue-green aura spiked with pure blue love. Love for his partner. His private pleasure slave Wulf.

He took a deep, shuddering breath. His voice came out thick? "Even you?" he asked Niko.

Niko nodded.

"Are you a part of the harem?"

"No. But I am owned just the same. The master has younger tastes. But I perform a function. I see to the initiation of all new slaves. I oversee their well-being through the grooms. I am the master of the grooms."

Ren nodded. He did not feel well at all. Not after what Niko had done. But he had to muster all his courage, for Niko had told him—with no reason to lie—that the branding was done to all of them here in compound. All of them were bought and owned, perhaps even the bodyguards who'd brought him here from the airport.

Niko crossed his arms over his chest. "Can you stand now?"

Ren slid off the chair, his skin sticking to it from leftover sweat. His legs wobbled for a moment. The pain had been that shattering.

"Yes," he finally answered.

"Good." Niko motioned toward the hall they'd come through. The shadows became golden as they passed the huge bathing room and approached the front room again.

The grooms exited the hall to the bathing room, and Ren was left alone to follow Niko. To obey.

Chapter Nine

Master

When they stepped out of the little, square white house a slow breeze washed over Ren's still-hot skin. Between the outbuildings that surrounded the giant mansion, the grass glowed, and little white flowers lined their path. Bees thrummed about them. The air had a sweet quality to it, fresh and unfettered by city smog. The sky beyond the hill and the trees drew into itself a moonstone blue radiance that soothed both mind and eye. A trail of small white clouds wrote themselves upon the air.

Ahead of them, the mansion was like a shadow of itself, shiny and surreal as if carved from black onyx. The windows sparkled like many open eyes, square and staring. On the lower level, blots of pink and lavender marred some of the windows. As they moved closer to the big house, Ren saw they were curtains. One window was open and the breeze had stolen the lightweight, pink chiffon and pulled it over the sill to play with it along the bushes that grew there.

That color—pale against such a dark, stark visage of architecture—seemed almost out of place. Like an escaped bit of hope, an energy of a fulfilling dream Ren hoped for in his most secret heart.

Now they walked up raw, unpolished marble flagstones—all gray and black—that led to a shaded porch supported by large, dark columns. Ren's collar chains chimed as they climbed the even, black steps.

His naked skin had cooled a little in the fresh air. His hair was drying fast, unbraided and long, like a little jacket against his back. The pain on his chest had receded a little, but not much. It made him feel more alert.

Coming up the porch, Ren saw tall, double doors, and they opened inward at their approach. He squinted to see inside, blinking. When his eyes adjusted, he saw no one. Just a room richly carpeted with rugs of Asian design in maroon, ivory, and black. The walls were red, and lined with masks of all shapes, colors and sizes. Some looked carved of wood, others made of metal. Some had feathers. Some had hair.

Ren's skin prickled, not from pain now, but the strangeness of it all. His feet brushed against the soft rugs. Niko, one step ahead of him, stopped in the middle of the room where an arrangement of pillows lined the floor. The doors closed behind Ren, obviously operated by sensors. Or perhaps by someone unseen pushing buttons in a nearby room or office.

Niko made quick motion with his hand, and whispered, "You will kneel." The well-dressed, older man dropped to his knees on one of the pillows.

Ren quickly stepped up beside him and did the same on the other pillow. He saw Niko had his hands clasped behind his back. Ren copied him, looking up at the vast collection of masks, so many faces, so many eyes watching.

Ren watched as Niko, facing forward, eyes unblinking, said coolly, "I present your newest acquisition. Ren. From the Slave Palace of Lirangel in the country of Avilan."

A strange, almost metallic-sounding voice seemed to emanate all around them. "He wears nothing but my collar and the brand, I see."

"This one's beauty has not yet hardened. As far as I can see, he required no make up or mask to create his features to your preference. But I bow to your judgment on the matter."

"I agree with your assessment."

The voice almost seemed to echo. Perhaps various hidden speakers throughout the room created the affect. Ren wondered. The air seemed to vibrate with the intensity of it.

Ren glanced about the room all while trying to remain still and not turn his head. Glittering faces, round open mouths, cheeks like buttocks, chins like dildos. Some of the masks might have been called obscene by some, but with his training Ren thought many were imaginative if not downright beautiful.

"Very good, slave Niko. You may go now."

Without a word or even a nod, Niko stood, his clothing rustling, and turned. Ren listened as his footfalls whispered across the rugs and felt the breeze as the door opened behind him.

Ren stayed very still, kneeling on his pillow. Alone in the mask-room now. Waiting for a voice. Minutes passed.

Ren studied more of the masks. They did not unnerve him, but interested him. He'd never seen such a vast array of them. So unique. Colorful. Each one different from the last. He wondered about his new master now that he knew he was a collector. Why Ren? Why nine million dollars? He knew he was good at his training, handsome even. But was he that special?

The amplified voice interrupted his thoughts. He had no idea how long he'd been kneeling, silent and alone. But now the voice had returned, offering some company.

"Ren, welcome to my abode."

Ren's hands squeezed together behind his back. "Thank you, Master."

"Will you please stand?"

Ren obeyed quickly, letting his hands fall to his sides. He arched his back, lifted his chin.

"Turn, please."

Ren began to turn his body.

"Slowly, please."

Well, at least the master was a polite one. He'd used the word *please* twice now.

When Ren had turned all the way around and again faced forward to a long wall of masks, the master said, "Excellent form. Not overly muscular, which is preferred for your purpose. Long and lean limbs. A face that could be a poem. You are even more exquisite than your videos and personal file from the Slave Palace portray you."

Ren let out a puff of air from his nose. "Thank you, Master."

"I am a collector. I acquire rare and beautiful things that appeal to me, that sharpen my appetite for the unusual, the exotic. Art. Sculpture. Jewels." He paused. "Masks." Another pause. "People."

The voice surrounded Ren. Its sharp tonal quality, male but pitched in such a way as to hit a tenor pitch, still felt unreal. As if it operated through some system, like a machine. But behind it, he could hear the man. Faint but there. Not soft. But not cruel. It commanded him.

"Usually slaves come to me in a more formal manner."

Ren flushed to hear that maybe he'd already done something wrong. But that would all fall on Niko, wouldn't it?

"Hair done up, make up to enhance, widen, lengthen, brighten. But you are the way you are naturally, and one reason to be chosen, I should think. But something else as well. Care to reveal that to me?"

"Something else?" Ren almost forgot his manners. "Master."

"More than physical beauty, you have a talent. It has been recognized through a thorough study of you. You read people. I could see it as you found their pleasure without any tentative hesitation on your part, without exploration of their bodies, or verbal questioning as to their needs or desires. You pleasured those you had not even met as if you had known them before, or had been with them before. How?"

Ren swallowed. He'd never told a soul, not even Master Locke, about his ability to see so much light around and on people, to see the trails of longing on their bodies, of desire, of arousal, and simply follow them with hand, lips, tongue, cock. He'd never revealed that sometimes, rarer times, he even received images in his head out of context of beautiful venues, smiling faces, happy people while pleasuring another.

What had this man seen? Was this why he'd been purchased? Master Holden and Master Locke had never mentioned they noticed Ren was able to *read* people. They only knew he was expert in technique, quick to figure out where another wished to be touched, and how.

"I am not sure I understand what you mean, Master."

"A lie on our first meeting. Hmm. This is not an amenable start."

"I do not lie, Master. I am sorry if you think so."

"Withholding information I ask for is the same as a lie." The statement seemed to bounce from wall to wall, not yelling, but echoing, louder than before.

"You will tell me what I ask, or I shall call slave Niko back and have him take you back to the branding room. You will receive another permanent brand that marks you as hostile, untouchable. Then you will be whipped and placed in isolation."

Ren's mouth fell open. "Master, I want to be honest. But I am not sure how to speak. How to begin. I am afraid you will not believe me. But, please. I will answer your question."

"Very well. I am waiting."

Ren focused on one mask, a simple gold eye covering; it gleamed with an outline of white diamonds. "I s—see. Colors. I see colors."

"Continue."

"On people. Like light. Clouds of it. Or ribbons. Like lightning almost. Playing upon the skin. The lights are like storms and they tell me to go ahead, or stay away. They tell me how a person will respond. And auras around people. I see those often. They communicate emotions to me. I can almost taste the colors."

"Are you aware there is a term for tasting color? Or smelling color?"

"No, Master." Ren waited.

"It is called synesthesia. Can you taste or smell the colors?"

"No, Master. Unless I put my mouth upon the skin of the person projecting a color on that part of their body, I cannot taste it. And even then, sometimes all I taste is skin."

"And when you do taste the colors, what is it like?"

"There are different tastes, Master. Bitter. Sweet. Salt. Tart."

"Did you see Niko's aura?"

"No, Master. I was too nervous. Sometimes I do not see another's aura right away. Sometimes I do not try to see, and then when I try, it is there."

"Perhaps some people are closed off to you."

"I do not think so, Master. It is this way only when I am closed. When I am too anxious."

"Perhaps there are ways to test this."

Ren swallowed. The continuing throb of his burn made his whole body tense, and even as he forced himself to relax, his training kicking in, there remained an inner tremble to his muscles. He also began to be afraid he might disappoint this master.

He'd never trained with his gift for seeing auras and colors on and around people at full disclosure. No one had ever asked him about it and he had only ever followed his instincts concerning the ability during sexual contact. And, of course, he'd read the true love in the blues and coppers that darted about Wulf's aura, and the pure blue of Master Locke's aura and the tall sapphire crown at his head.

He wanted to explain all of this to the nameless voice. Instead, he merely said, "Yes, Master."

"I shall make the proper arrangements soon. You will be called upon then."

Silence.

Ren filled the space with a final response. "Yes, Master."

Chapter Ten

The Harem

Suddenly a door opened amid the largest wall of masks. The voice, somewhat faded now, said, "Move forward through to the next room. You will abide there. You will be shown where you will sleep and eat. You will be informed of the rules."

A loud snick filled the room, as if a machine that had been on was turned off. Sounds of voices came from the room beyond the open door, and a not-so-quiet murmur like rain.

Ren stepped over the threshold and realized he faced the side of a tall waterfall. Water poured over a rocky edge and into a huge swimming pool. The waterfall was taller than Ren and about seven feet wide.

He felt the coolness of the spray on his face, arms and chest as he stepped around the fall and the entire room came into focus.

An enormous atrium met his eyes. It probably took up the entire first floor of the mansion. This was the room of the pink flowing curtains. This was the room where, it was now apparent, his master, the great collector, kept his people collection. His rare and beautiful humans. His pleasure slaves. He immediately spotted about a dozen naked men in various areas.

This was the room of the harem.

He couldn't help his first thought. What made each one of these men so special that they, like Ren, had been collected?

Ren did not know where to look first. Surrounding the swimming pool were several couches and chairs and tables. Beyond the pool and up two steps was what looked like a combination living room and playroom, with more couches and chairs, a giant flat screen TV on a half-wall, and just beyond that a sort of bar with a counter, sink and refrigerator.

Beyond the other end of the pool were alcoves that contained beds with lamps, pillows and plush rugs. These were small bedrooms, open-ended, but divided by half walls. He saw at least a dozen, and in the middle a hall that he surmised led to a bathing/restroom area.

Light flowed in the main area from dozens of recessed lamps in the ceiling. Plants decorated the room near each window, half a dozen to the right, same on the left, lending a bit of natural green color to the slick, luxurious interior. In one corner, beyond the TV area, were sets of weights, three treadmills and two stationary bikes to form a large exercise room.

This place was meant to be a cage, yes, but a very gilded one at that. Ren tried to count the naked men. Two were swimming laps in the pool. Three watched TV. Two reclined on different couches by the pool. Another two, who looked like identical twin brothers, sat at a table playing some sort of board game Ren did not recognize. One sat on a bed in one of the alcoves reading on a tablet. Two more were standing by the waterfall near Ren. One approached him, tablet in hand, as Ren came into the room. He was followed by another man who moved with jerking motions. He was like a stuttering shadow to the first greeter, but extremely pretty, Ren could see.

"Been expecting you." The first man was about six foot, Ren's height. He spoke with an accent, like the bodyguard at the airport, which reminded Ren that the machine voice of their master did not have any detectable accent. For a moment, he wondered why, then forgot about it.

"I'm Ren," Ren said.

"Yes. I know. I'm Cam. This is Zanti." He motioned to the man behind him, who ducked his head and moved even further behind Cam, as though shy.

Cam had blond hair cut above his shoulders and long in the bangs. They swept his handsome face. His blue eyes were rimmed with black eyeliner. His eyebrows were golden and trimmed.

Zanti had coloring more like Ren, dark hair pushed straight back, not as long as Ren's, the edges curling under his earlobes. He was a couple inches shorter than Cam. Exactly Ren's size and type.

Both men had amazing bodies, lean with firm muscles, perfectly curved asses, and thick cocks resting against hairless balls. One dark, one light, their skin gleamed healthy and would probably be like silk to the touch.

"Here's the thing. I do this rarely, only four times since I arrived here, so it's not routine."

"What?" Ren asked, confused. The swimmers in the pool splashed a bit as they went by doing laps.

"Greet the green ones. The freshers. The newbies."

"Oh."

Zanti's lips curved upward and he peeked out from behind Cam, staring hard at Ren. His gaze was hard, almost angry. It was unnerving. Ren kept his attention on Cam.

"Rules are important." Cam pressed his lips tight. Zanti smirked, then let out a strange snort as if he were about to laugh.

Ren blinked and nodded.

"Remember them well," Cam said.

"I promise," Ren replied.

"Okay. Rules." Another pause. "There aren't any!" He let out a big laugh. Zanti giggled silently as if he was ten years old, his breaths coming out in hisses.

Ren gave them a small smile but did not laugh.

"Seriously, the biggest rule here from on high is we all have to get along. Fighting is punished, of course. Physical, I mean. You can yell all you want. If Master gets tired of it, he'll have Niko bring you in to set you straight. Only if you hurt someone are you hurt in return. Space is respected. If someone says to get away, or not touch, you respect that. Otherwise, we can do as we please. Play, fuck, drink, even trash the place. Anything but leave. If we make a mess, there is a cleaning crew that comes in early mornings before most of us are awake. Got it?"

"Yes," said Ren. "Do we have chores?"

Cam let out a sputter of air. "No. Just look pretty. Do as Master tells you. If he wants you to wear your hair a certain way, then do it. It's as Master's commands, nothing else. He isn't strict about how we behave within this room, but you always do what he says."

"Yes, I know. I am well-trained to obey my master," said Ren.

"I'm sure you are or you wouldn't be here."

"Do we see the Master at certain times?"

"See?" Cam laughed. "No. Only if he calls you upstairs. Which you will learn isn't always what you think it might be."

Zanti, who had not said a word, nodded and raised his eyebrows up and down as if to mock Ren. Ren decided he would stay away from that guy, pretty as he was. Maybe if Zanti had been sweeter, Ren would have melted a little on the inside to look at his beauty, but Zanti was already being a dick in more ways than one. He was too nervous to see Zanti's aura and read him, but thought the guy might be jealous. He had already figured he'd have a lot of work to do to settle into his place among all the men here.

Ren nodded, wanting to know more, but keeping his mouth shut.

"You can find new toiletries, toothbrush, toothpaste, hair brush, etc., in the bathrooms behind the beds. Do you need a shaving kit or is that permanent?" Cam indicated Ren's hairless body.

"Permanent."

"All right." He waved his arm toward the alcoves. "You can pick an unused drawer in the bathroom—there are plenty—and stash your stuff there. You're to be clean inside and out every morning, no exceptions. You know what that means."

Ren nodded. An enema if needed every day. He was trained for that.

"The alcove on the far left has been newly made up for you. You're number thirteen. Lucky, huh?"

Ren nodded. "Does the master have a name?"

"His name is Master. He's not *the master*. He's Master."

"Got it." Ren blinked. His burn ached and he realized he'd lifted his hand to rub around the outside of the square bandage.

He glanced from both Zanti and Cam. Cam had the flower brand above his right pec. It looked long ago healed. The scaring formed the flower's edges and inner pattern perfectly, the skin darker and slightly raised where it had been burned.

But Zanti's chest was unmarred. How could that be? Niko had said all the men had brands. Even Niko had one.

Ren frowned. "He doesn't have a brand."

Zanti flipped him off and turned away, walking a few steps, his back to both Cam and Ren. Apparently, the guy did not talk.

"Yes," Cam answered. "We have all questioned it. But if you're thinking Zanti is the master hidden within the confines of this harem, think again. Zanti is as much one of us as anyone here. But he has problems. He doesn't speak. He is different. There are more reasons, but I am not at liberty right now to discuss them. We've all come to the conclusion that the brand would just make his condition worse. The pain of it is an ordeal."

"What condition? Why doesn't he speak?"

"That's Zanti's story, and Zanti's not talking so accept it is none of our business. Leave it at that, ok?"

Ren nodded. Not a problem.

Cam tapped something on his tablet, then pointed at Ren's chest. "You'll find pain pills in the kitchen area in the middle cupboard under the bar. Use them. They aren't much stronger than aspirin, but they help."

"Thank you."

"Any more questions?"

"How often do you see the master? I mean, *Master*."

Cam's smooth eyebrows narrowed. "Are you asking about me or all of us? And this may seem confusing at first, but we do not *see* Master."

"What?"

"We do not see Master. He sees us. He asks for one or two or more of us. We go upstairs and do whatever we're told. You'll find out soon enough."

They didn't see Master? Ren was unsure if Cam meant that literally, and was also disappointed. He had expected a strange set up, maybe even an unsafe environment, but he did not foresee an invisible master.

"You're quite pretty," Cam commented, looking Ren up and down. "Maybe the prettiest of all so far aside from Zanti. So far I see no orders incoming for your make up or hair style. You're to be allowed to go rogue, as we say here in our little world. Wild."

"I usually braid my hair," Ren said.

"You can do that. But if Master commands otherwise, you must obey."

Ren glanced about the vast room, taking everything in. It seemed so big, and the waterfall gave off an outdoorsy scent and feel, but he suspected it all would grow smaller to the mind week after week when this was to be the extent of his world from now on. A prison with fine things and pretty men and room to move about, but still a prison. Well, he had chosen this.

"Oh!" Cam waved his tablet under Ren's face. "I forgot. We all have tablets if we want them. I can set yours up for you in a blink.

You can access most things on them about the outside, but it's one way. There is no contact with others allowed. You cannot receive or send information to people, organizations or anything of that sort, no emails, texts, comments, messages. It won't work. You can only view. You can see movies. You can play games. You can keep a diary. But you will be unable to submit any of what you do or see here to the outside."

"That was clear to me from the beginning when I was sold," Ren said.

"Good. Then you understand." Cam and Zanti exchanged looks, as Zanti sidled up alongside Cam again. "You have only us. It can be hard sometimes. Confining."

Zanti stared hard at Ren, then frowned again.

"I understand," said Ren, looking away from Zanti as his heart skipped a beat from his nerves. He was still too nervous to see any auras.

"Come along, then, let's give you the tour."

Cam led Ren all about. Zanti followed several feet behind them, wordless, almost darkly withdrawn except for his almost hostile interest in the newbie. In Ren.

As Ren was shown every section and every space, the other men lounging about or swimming or playing games all quit what they were doing and came over, surrounding them. They all looked Ren over, some with friendly gazes and grins, some with cold stares and noses held high. They represented all skin tones and hair color, but their sizes and shapes were relatively the same. Lean, wiry. All somewhere between five ten and six two. The age range appeared to be twenty to thirty years of age.

In the living space beside the couch with the TV on mute, Ren stood very still and let the crowd of men have their look at him. It did not seem odd they were curious. If Cam was telling the truth, they did not see new men enter their ranks all that often. Maybe they were jaded and tired of each other. Maybe Ren represented something new and interesting to fill the long hours of the day waiting for Master to call. Or, maybe because he was new and untried, they resented him. He hoped not. He wanted friends. And he wanted to do everything right by his new master.

All the naked bodies came close and surrounded him. He was used to men, used to nudity and that included the friendliness of other pleasure slaves. The swimmers smelled fresh and damp, and faintly of chlorine. The others also smelled good, sweet, their colognes mingling.

Cam stood back, and Zanti went with him, grasping Cam's free hand in a possessive way, pulling slightly.

Cam whispered something in his ear.

Zanti lowered his head and shut his eyes, shaking his head hard. His dark hair reflected the lights in pale blues and gold and suddenly, from one minute to the next, Ren could see his aura. It was dark, almost solid black, but there were little lightning strikes of brilliant blue within and blooms of phosphor green. It was unlike any aura he'd ever seen. He did not understand it. Black might mean angry… but then again something else. He had never seen a black aura.

Zanti stomped his foot, spun and sauntered off alone. Ren did not see where he went for the others were demanding attention.

He glanced at Cam and the men around him as a multitude of colors assaulted his senses all at once. A rainbow of essences. So much instant emotion. Excitement. The others were all suddenly easy to read.

To Ren, this meant connections were being made. For better or worse, these men would be his brothers for the rest of his life, or until he was tossed from the harem for being too old. He wondered if that had already happened to slaves before him. If so, where did they go? Were the other outbuilding complexes for men retired from Master's central harem?

He supposed one day he might find out, but for now he did not allow himself to worry about it.

Now the men began to introduce themselves. Ren had no chance to remember all their names, but later he would learn them. For now, he heard low voices, a strum of introductions. "Finn." "Michael." "Li Po." "Tomo." "Aiden." And so many more.

Cam came forward after a few minutes. "All right, all right," he said, shooing them away. "Ren, are you tired after your long trip here?"

Ren nodded. In truth, he was exhausted.

"Are you hungry? Dinner is delivered in an hour. The food here never disappoints."

"Thank you. I might like a nap."

"Of course."

Most of the men wandered away, bored now that he said he wanted to sleep, but still eyeing him. Some of the men sported half or full erections as well, which had not been the case moments before. Did they want to test Ren out? To fuck him?

Ren could not think about that right now. He was still in pain from the brand, and his energy definitely drooped.

Cam showed him his private alcove which wasn't very private since the entire inside of it could be seen from most angles of the atrium.

Cam said, "I'll bring you the pain pills and some water."

Ren sat on the edge of his assigned bed on a silken spread of blended lavenders and golds. Cam's aura was pale green, bobbing about his head and shoulders, open, friendly as he left the alcove.

Ren pushed the bedspread out of the way of his feet and lay down just as Cam returned with a glass and some medicine.

"Here." Cam held out his hands.

Ren sat up and drank down the pills and set the water on a bedside table. "Thank you."

"No problem."

Ren felt instantly vulnerable in this strange place, and pulled the spread past his hips as he turned onto his side.

In seconds, he fell into a dark encompassing shadow, soon deeply asleep.

Chapter Eleven

Acceptance to the Harem

Li Po's aura fluttered like a garden in bloom. He was the most colorful of them all. And the first real friend Ren made in the harem.

All the men in the harem had cat-like muscles, long and firm and lean. A type, it seemed, Master preferred. Despite what Master had said about collecting rarities -- people like Ren -- Ren still had not yet ascertained what each man's gift actually was beyond their good looks. He did know now some had actual super-weird gifts like Ren's, but more mundane.

Cam had told him he himself was a whiz at organization. Finn could do complex math in his head. Torrance and Seth, the twins, had black belts in kung fu. Aaron had a beautiful voice and sang the weirdest, old-fashioned ballads *a capella*. He said he could play six instruments but didn't elaborate. But lots of people in the world had talents. Ren had been expecting them to be perhaps more strange, like seeing ghosts or making people's heads explode with a thought. In fairness, he had watched a lot of science fiction as a kid. His imagination might have gotten away from him a little.

As it was, Li Po informed him that Master liked performances and the men were exceptionally talented in that manner. He wanted men who could perform. "And not just sexually," Li Po laughed. "Acting. Singing. Dance."

"Like putting on plays?" Ren asked.

"We do that, too."

Zanti remained a peculiar, darkly shining thing, his aura like a shadow, always dark gray or black with bits of exploding stars breaking through now and again.

Ren learned that Zanti was deliberately mute. It wasn't that he couldn't speak, but according to Cam had chosen not to. He made only a few small sounds like grunts and squeaks, and that very rarely.

"You said his story is his to tell, but do you know his history?"

"He's been hurt. That's all I can say."

"What is his talent?"

Cam smiled. "Looking beautiful."

"Really?"

Cam shrugged.

Ren slept through his first night, exhausted beyond what even he had realized. He missed dinner and woke only once to use the facilities. Other than that, he was out cold.

The next morning, after he'd obediently followed the strict cleansing regimen of the harem, at breakfast, Cam invited Ren to sit by him and Zanti.

"So, you are Slave Palace trained?" Cam said.

"Yes."

"So is Michael, but he didn't pass the tests, so he wasn't sold as a Palace slave. He went to another distributor and that's how Master found him. The rest of us are not Palace trained at all. We come from all over. You can tell by some of our accents."

Ren nodded, realizing some of these men could have been from back alley deals, maybe not even consenting.

"What's Michael's talent?"

"He's a great actor. He can sing, too. Not like Aaron, but he's very good."

Ren nodded.

"Slave Palaces are famous, known for producing the best. Are you the best, Ren?" Cam asked with a smile.

Awkward, Ren could only think to say, "I do my best, yes."

Cam chuckled. "Can't wait to see."

Whatever that meant, Ren did not feel like asking just yet. He was still getting his bearings.

Breakfast was wonderful, complete with a vast selection of foods. Ren chose eggs and bacon, the standard fare, and when he was still hungry after downing his orange juice, he filled up on the best honeyed oatmeal he'd ever tasted.

He was not surprised when several men paired off afterward. He watched as a dark-haired man named Jaxon and a fairer one named Calder entered the shallow end of the pool, sat on a low step and began to make out. He saw their erections grow, flushed and strong, and their auras bounce pink to red, the colors for arousal.

Seth and Torrance, the twins, went to the weights, but they seemed to be helping each other with more than just exercise, their touches on each other's bodies as they worked out far from platonic. After awhile, they started to do some sort of *kata* or dance. With every move, their cocks lengthened. They moved as one, eyes on each other only, the rest of the world locked out.

Cam and Zanti went to watch TV. Or rather, Cam did. Zanti just seemed to follow, mostly uninterested in anything. But he kept stealing glances at Ren, and Ren kept a curious eye on him.

Others wandered about. Ren stared at his empty plates.

Li Po came up behind him and said, "Don't worry. The servers will return to clean this all up."

Ren looked away from Seth and Torrance but Li Po was staring at them now. "They're something. Beautiful together. Master has a kink for them." Li Po winked.

"They're twins." Ren did not know what else to say.

"Yeah. Cute, eh?"

Of course they were. Ren was not shocked at all. He looked up at Li Po. "They are. You all are. I was not sure what to expect, but I am surrounded by loveliness everywhere I look."

"As lovely as at the Slave Palace? I have heard stories…"

"Yes. As lovely." Ren smiled. He sighed.

Li Po said, "Are you still nervous? Are you all right? I know a great way to help you relax." He winked.

Li Po had a hard, wiry body, thin-skinned, almond dark, and narrow at the waist. He was friendly without being too forward. He had a lovely, dark cock, thin but long. His straight, fine hair was like curtains of pale brown silk falling about his cheekbones, and his angular eyes were soft and gentle, exotically gorgeous. It might be lovely to push that hair back from that beautiful face, and feel it slide through his fingers.

But Ren was still tense. He had not been ordered to do anything. He still felt he needed to settle in. Watching other men have sex and lounge about was enough for now.

"Maybe later," Ren said. He raised his eyebrows in the hope that his words were not seen as rejection to a man who seemed to be trying to form a friendship with him.

Li Po took a deep breath. His aura remained a friendly gold-green. "Sure. That's fine."

Ren stood. "Will you sit with me, then? Talk? I have more questions. I want to learn. Everything."

Li Po had the sweetest, low laugh, a mix of a rumble and hum. It went right through Ren's chest. Li Po's aura came better into focus now. So many colors flitted about the edges. So many designs. One of the prettiest Ren had ever seen.

They found a plush, unoccupied couch facing the pool and made themselves comfortable.

Ren wanted to know about the other men, but more, he wanted to know about Master. There was an urgency in his chest about this subject, which was still an unknown. All he had to go on about his new owner was an echo-voice that sounded faintly mechanical, and what Cam had said. *We do not see Master. He sees us.*

Either Cam was teasing, or this was quite the riddle.

"I want to know about our Ma—um, about Master."

Li Po sat forward, his legs bent, feet up, resting one arm across his knees. "Everyone does, of course."

"That's not an answer."

"I know. Here's the thing. Master is very private. Shy, perhaps? He is what some might call a voyeur."

"He doesn't like to participate, you mean?" Ren asked.

"Something like that."

"Wait. So none of you have ever actually been with him?"

"No."

"Why didn't Cam just say so? Okay, but some of you must have seen him at some point, then?"

Li Po held up an elegant hand. "I know what Cam says to everyone who is new. And it's true. We don't see him. None of us have. Tomo was the first, before there was a harem. He came to be Master's slave and lived in luxury alone until called upstairs, sometimes once a week, sometimes once a night. Master ordered him to do things. He was alone for a year before Master bought more slaves."

"But you said Tomo saw him, or…?"

"No. I didn't say that." Li Po glanced about the room until he saw Tomo. Ren followed his gaze. Tomo stood by an open window, the long pink drapes moving about his legs and hips from the outdoor breeze. He was very dark-skinned, with a regal face, close-cropped black hair, and gleaming, long muscles. Tomo had his hip cocked, head back, but he was watching the twins. As he watched them dance together, he pleasured himself with his hand.

"Look at him. Like a king," Li Po said.

Ren saw it was true. Tomo held himself like a man of power, as if he'd been born to it. His cock was long and thick, pink as a rose at the tip. Breathtaking.

"His ass is like nothing you've ever experienced." Li Po scrunched his face as if he'd said something funny. "Seriously. I'm not trying to be crude. Look at him."

Ren looked at how Tomo's ass curved outward from his lower back, plump but hard, and the way it met the backs of his thighs—so much flesh to touch, to stroke, to grab hold of. It was in prime condition. They all were, but Tomo's buttocks were somehow richer, fuller. Pillows to sink into.

"He's very handsome."

"Master is a voyeur, like I said," Li Po went on. "But he could not resist Tomo's ass. Tomo said Master fucked him. But only once. And no, they did not meet. There was a wall between them."

"He used a glory hole," Ren supplied.

"Yes. Fucked him from behind. Tomo never saw him. Or his cock. Maybe it wasn't even Master. He said he tried to see into the hole in the wall, but every time Tomo turned around to look, only darkness from the hole in the wall was there. Not even a bit of light. He didn't even see the cock because it withdrew whenever he tried to see. Tomo is special. He's the only one of us Master has ever actually touched with any part of his body. If it was Master touching him at all. It might have been a guard, or a servant. Master is an enigma. So it is possible he used surrogates."

Ren's heart sank. He could not help but be disappointed. He knew he was being a bit spoiled, but he'd hoped for a master to take him, tell him what to do all the time, order him to be whatever he wanted. But in the master's bed. Not apart from him. Yes, Ren could perform and was taught well, and he did not mind playing in groups with other pleasure slaves, but a master's pleasure was what he'd trained for. What he'd dreamed of having for the rest of his life. He'd hoped for a sort of real love, hands on, not games of love.

But Master Locke had warned him. It might never happen. And in a harem any master's attention would be divided.

Ren could understand voyeurism well. He'd enjoyed looking at men from an early age. But he had wanted to be someone to be looked at as well, controlled. The men he looked at were men he wanted to be, not have. He had always wanted to give pleasure, to be wanted, desired, coveted.

He glanced away from Tomo, and from the twins with a pang. It was almost jealousy, but not quite. More a feeling of anxiety as to whether he might match up to these men in areas of talent, beauty and prowess. He was Palace trained. Of course he was the best. But deep inside him a wavering insecurity still lived, as if he were a child still yearning to escape, still trying to deal with the deaths of his parents.

He had rarely felt insecurity at the Palace because he was with others like himself, trainees focused on revelatory acts of sex day in and day out. But here he was not a trainee. He was one of thirteen collected men, all of whom were unknown to him. With Master being the biggest mystery. He would be judged. It would be anyone's nature to judge their newest acquisition, their newest cellmate. If he had rules, tests to pass, that would have been fine. In this black mansion, the harem had few rules. And Master kept a cold distance.

This threw Ren off his game, making him feel lost.

Li Po continued to talk softly, filling the silence that seemed to encompass Ren. Ren listened with half-attention, dazed, confused that he didn't fit in right away, that these men who had their own pairings, their routine unions, had gotten along fine without him and had no reason to open to him. Li Po was being friendly, and Ren welcomed it, but there was an underlying feeling here of less camaraderie and more competition.

As Li Po talked, Ren learned he'd been in the harem five years. He liked Cam and Tomo just fine. Zanti remained a stranger to him. He said with a laugh, "Aaron argues everything. He takes everything personal. He's blunt with his opinions. But his voice…"

"Have people been dismissed from the harem?"

"Twice that I know of." Li Po leaned forward, voice low. "One got really sick. Weak and thin. He needed professional medical help. Master does not deny us quality care. So he was taken away.

We all thought he'd get the help he needed and return. But he never did. The other I knew was violent. Some of us are more moody than others, and it's to be expected, but Brandon was always picking fights. He'd yell a lot, and go into rages where he'd bulldog his way into anyone nearby, knocking them around, shouting nonsense. He lasted two weeks before he was taken away."

"Where do you think he went?"

"Master keeps other compounds I've never seen. They house staff. You know, anyone who works at this place from cleaning crews to groundskeepers. There's even a medical ward. I went there once for a twisted ankle. We have everything here. Why not compounds for those who don't fit into the harem? It beats considering the alternative."

"Master wouldn't kill an unfit slave, would he?"

Li Po shrugged. "Honestly?"

Ren nodded.

"I truly don't think so."

"But why all the secrecy? Why can't we ever contact the outside world?"

"It's about control. He owns us. We are his property and his alone. He's very territorial, I guess. An eccentric rich dude."

"But why won't he let anyone see him?"

Another shrug. "Maybe he's shy. Or maybe hideous. No one knows."

"How old is he?" Ren asked.

"No clue. But Tomo says he was the first of the harem and that was ten years ago. Tomo loves living here. He's one of the oldest and the happiest. If Master started this harem young, he might only be in his thirties. But if he was older, well, who knows? He could be thirty or sixty."

"So no clue about how old this estate is? Its history?"

Li Po shook his hair from his face. "None. When I came here, I had no clue where I was going. I'd never heard of this place. I had some training. I love sex but I didn't want to whore myself to different people. I wanted one master, and not just for play. The real thing."

Ren could relate completely to this penchant. It was a desire he could not ignore, one that was as much a part of him as the skin on his body.

"I belonged to a master who traded slaves right and left," Li Po said. "He got bored fast. Didn't appreciate I was educated. He sold me online to a mystery man. I actually thought I was being carted off to some underworld hell. But I ended up here. Master bought me based on my profile."

"What in your profile do you think attracted him? Other than that you're good looking, I mean. Because you are."

Li Po smiled wide. "Thank you. So are you. But I speak six languages fluently, and a smattering of five more. My parents moved all over the world as I grew up. Master likes to hear me read and recite lewd erotica in different languages. Says I have a nice speaking voice, too. It's weird but fine with me. No one ever appreciated my languages before like Master does. And also, he apparently gets off on great voices. He calls Aaron upstairs sometimes just to sing to him for an hour or two. Doesn't even make him touch himself, according to Aaron's stories. Oh, and I also dance, sing and act."

"Where upstairs do we go when we're called?" Ren asked.

"It's a room. Well, there are several rooms. You'll see." Li Po smiled.

Chapter Twelve

First Afternoon

Ren found a chair by a window and for most of the morning sat in it looking out through parted, pink chiffon. It wasn't that he wanted out. He knew he'd be in a harem when he was sold, of course and reminded himself he liked the idea of feeling part of a larger family some day.

It was simply that everything was different, strange, and he needed to see it all to process his new reality. To figure out where he fit.

Li Po let him be for now. But Ren could feel eyes on him. Eyes from every corner. And Master watched as well. No one told him there were hidden cameras in the atrium, but he could sense it.

Ren needed some time, that was all. Time to acclimate. He would get to know these guys, of course. But everything was too much too fast and he wanted to go slower. Even the public sexcapades did not rouse him. At the Slave Palace, everything roused him. But he'd felt safe there. He'd loved that place. Loved learning all he could from it, and from Masters Holden and Locke.

His eyes stung as he thought of them. Over a year he'd lived there. It had become a home to him. Inside his chest, his heart trembled. As if pieces of it had split off. First his parents. Now having left his training nest forever. His body fidgeted in distress. He was too old for coddling, but there were broken things inside that let their sharp edges be known.

The waterfall poured into the pool making a lovely sound of rain that Ren liked. It soothed him. It filled the air with a dew-scent that made everything seem new and clean.

He drew his legs up into the chair and watched the view from the window he'd chosen, a landscape of emerald dotted with patches of white flowers. There was a huge, many-branched oak, gnarled and ancient, that shaded a white compound about a hundred yards away. The windows of that building were white and shuttered. He sensed no life within it. Maybe it was for storage. He tried to imagine what was in there. Food supplies, perhaps. Or yard equipment. Or maybe it was a garage filled with more collectibles, old cars, or sculptures, or boxes and boxes of more masks from all over the world.

By lunch, Ren was still not feeling quite content.

He ate chicken soup and a salad, wanting to go light. Feeling small.

Li Po sat beside him looking pretty and made idle talk. Ren nodded in the appropriate places. Throughout lunch, Zanti stared at him, brows narrowed. Ren ignored it. The guy was just too weird.

Later, ignoring the continued public randiness of the men which almost seemed to evolve from boredom more than love or lust, he took a nap.

Adjustment periods are normal. Ren remember both Master Holden and Master Locke saying this to him at various times. First, in the context of settling into the Palace routine, the phrase was like a lesson. The other times, it was about the future. Eventually, when he would be sold, he needed to know that even in the best instances, people needed time to adapt and face any life changes, pleasure slaves most of all because they were the most vulnerable in their position of no rights. They needed their training to help them, to speak for them when they had no voice. They needed to be strong of mind and body, both, to contend with the unknowns they might face every day, every year.

Ren needed to be patient with himself.

He sat on his bed among soft pillows and watched the cleaning crew come for the lunch dishes. Two men in white slacks and shirts gathered everything up on a wheeled cart. They cleaned the kitchen area even though it was still sparkling from the morning wipe down. They took all of the trash generated by thirteen men in half a day. Which was minimal, mostly bottles and cans of drinks.

The soft rattle of their work calmed Ren, gave a normalcy to things.

Cam sauntered over and stood in the entryway to Ren's room. "I have your tablet. It can play games, movies, collect books. Anything that needs to be paid for is on auto. You can't order physical items to be delivered, of course, but anything digital can be transferred. Physical items desired go through me."

"I know how it works," Ren said. "Thank you."

A raised sleek golden eyebrow. Taut naked chest expanding with his breath. Cam looked both mystified and disappointed at Ren's low energy.

"No worries. It'll get better. You'll get used to things around here," Cam said.

"I know. It's just the trip wore me out and all," Ren lied. "And why is Zanti staring at me all the time?"

"Is he?"

Cam turned as Zanti came from another alcove. Cam raised his eyebrows at Ren, shrugging, mouth shut. Zanti looked as if he were almost about to laugh.

Ren shook his head.

Zanti offered half a shrug. As Cam turned and moved back to the center of the harem, Zanti sauntered along behind him, sashaying his ass as if he knew Ren was looking. And, yes, Ren was looking, but all of Zanti's gestures felt more like mocking than a tease. It was a really nice ass, though.

Ren fiddled with the tablet for about fifteen minutes before growing bored. He didn't want to read or watch movies. He didn't want to do anything right now. Good thing he had all the time in the universe to do nothing.

The light from the windows lent a pink veil over the atrium. The falls splashed, the perfect peaceful white noise. Two men were fucking in the alcove next to his. He could hear the grunting and groans, the smacks of flesh on flesh.

Fucking. His favorite subject. Favorite pastime. At the Slave Palace he never had trouble watching, getting aroused by it, learning the best moves. But right now nothing twitched. Not one single part of his body. Surrounded by luxury and beautiful men, and he wasn't interested?

How could this happen?

He'd pondered his lessons. His youthful enthusiasm for men. His love for sex as he remembered the splash of auras caress all the bodies he'd ever touched and brought pleasure to. All still alive and well in his mind. So what was wrong? Was he sick? Homesick? That was ridiculous! He'd strived hard to make no attachments at the Palace.

Nine million dollars had bought him. Paid for him. He was proud of that. It should be enough and everything else would fall into place. He would obey Master. He would live to serve him no matter the conditions and whether he was called to serve once a day, a week or a year. The honor of that could not be disputed. He had agreed to devote himself without even knowing a thing about the man. He had made that decision. He had no right to mope now.

Forcing himself up, Ren went to the pool and sat on the edge. Three men swam and played in the water. Two tossed a ball back and forth. Laughing. One was Li Po, who looked at him through damp bangs, smiled and waved.

Ren smiled and waved back. The cool water lapped against his shins. He swirled his feet, making more tiny waves. The falls created a mist in his hair.

Ren noticed some of the other men about the atrium watching him. Curious. That was how he read their mildly faded auras of green and gray.

After about five minutes, two men came to the edge of the pool from the other side of the room and sat down, their feet plunging into the sparkling water. If Ren was remembering correctly, one was named Calder, and he was very fair. The other was Aaron, the one Cam said had an incredible singing voice but wasn't overly talented in bed. He couldn't believe that if he was here in the harem. Maybe Cam, like Li Po, simply did not prefer him.

"Hi," said Aaron.

"Hi." Ren gripped the pool's edge tighter and pumped his legs a little in the water.

"So what's the special thing about you?" The tilt of Aaron's head and his side glance belied the boldness of the question.

"I—I—um." How to say it? He'd never talked about it with anyone until his conversation with Master in the mask room.

"Don't want to say, huh? We'll find out eventually. Is it only that you're Palace trained? So is Michael. He's not better than any one of us for it, though."

"I would not assume that." Again he stopped, swallowed hard.

Aaron's grin was quick. There was a gray fog above his head as if he were confused or unsure. Across the pool, Zanti sat on the couch with his tablet. He was watching them intently, poised like a tense rabbit.

Zanti's attention seemed to be on him quite often. He should have been flattered. Instead, he was annoyed at the little imp.

"So if you're so great, why don't you prove it?" Aaron lifted his leg and turned, thighs spread, toward Ren. His lovely cock, pink as dawn, rested semi-tumescent against heavy balls, pressing the side of one thigh. He was handsome but that didn't matter. Ren could have shown anyone a good time, handsome or not. But if not ordered to do so, why should he?

"Not friendly?" Aaron asked.

Li Po swam over. "Aaron, god! You're such a bulldog. It's why I warned Ren about you."

"You did? I'm so hurt. Is it because I say what I want?"

"Because you have no tact."

"Tact? Here? Ren's no prude, either. Li, you just want to be his first, now am I being honest and forward enough without any tact?"

Li Po splashed water all over him. Some of it got on Ren and Calder, but neither flinched. It felt good to Ren.

"You want some of this?" Aaron dove into the pool right at him, and Li Po swam off, Aaron playfully chasing after him. Li Po apparently took no offense and laughed as he swam under the waterfall and came up on the other side. The screen of water veiled him, his dark body a glittered silhouette. Aaron came up from underwater alongside him. The two men embraced, Aaron slightly taller, lighter hued.

Maybe Aaron had been confused or unsure around Ren, but his aura changed when he was with Li Po to friendly green and lusty pink. Ren chided himself for being somewhat surly. He would not get off to a great start as the newest of the harem if he remained too aloof. But he wasn't ready to be open and playful. Not yet. Not with his heart hammering in his chest like a stuttering engine afraid to start.

He glanced over the pool again and saw Zanti's brows narrowed, lower lip caught between his teeth. When Zanti raised an eyebrow at him, Ren's heart fluttered. What was it about that boy? This continued hands-off silent enticement gave Ren a start as he felt the first, warm spark of arousal since his arrival.

Calder, a few feet away, kicking at the water and wiping droplets from his eyes, drew Ren's attention. "Aaron's pretty sweet.

Really. Everyone likes to say he bugs them. He's just got a big bold mouth. He can seem rude. But he's good. He's really good."

Ren said, "It's okay. It's all fine."

And it was. It had to be. Of course he wasn't shy at all, either, and he watched Li Po and Aaron make out standing up in thigh-high water behind the waterfall. It was fine. All of it. Beautiful. Sex was beautiful. But he needed something else. An impetus he wasn't getting. Something to make him respond, because he hadn't gotten hard in two days since leaving the Palace. Simply, that was not like him. Even after a day of training, he was ready for more. And every morning at the Palace he woke with an erection. He was young and insatiable and he loved that feeling.

But now? Nothing. No such feelings. For two days.

He glanced at Zanti who had gone back to reading, then back at Aaron and Li Po behind the waterfall caressing, kissing. Aaron knelt for the smaller man, taking him into his mouth.

"They are good together and they know it," Calder supplied, voice barely above a whisper.

As Ren idly watched, he thought about Master's voice. About their brief meeting and how all the masks had watched as he turned proud and naked for Master, as he answered his questions. An edge of heat swept through him at the memory, on top of what he'd just experienced when he'd looked at Zanti, a too brief encounter with no visuals, no touch, no scent or burnt-sweet taste of excitement on the air. Only a mechanical voice. Echoing. Yet he wanted more. And that mystery fueled something deep inside him.

Li Po had apparently finished for now, and pushed Aaron back on a rocky outcropping, lifting his long, golden legs up, bent at the knee. Li Po's dark head bent between Aaron's legs and Aaron groaned.

Calder had dark blond curls thick about his face, giving him a cherub look. But he was neither plump nor an angel. His lean body, sporting a proud erection, slipped into the pool and he slowly swam over to the falls and walked right through them. Ren watched Li Po reach out to him and pull him into an embrace, and just like that they'd created a threesome.

Ren heard Master's voice again, distant and cool. *I acquire rare and beautiful things that appeal to me.*

Ren needed to remember that. He was one of them. This was a good thing. And his body fluttered very slightly again at the thought.

Chapter Thirteen

First Summons

Ren woke to thicker light denoting late afternoon. No one had bothered him when he'd decided to head back to his bed for another nap. Though he had not done much at all, he was tired and wrung out.

Seeing he was awake, Cam approached and stood at the open alcove entrance, perfect body glimmering with a pink-blue aura. "Do you need an aspirin or something more? I can put in a note on my tablet for Niko to take you to medical if you're not feeling well."

"No." Ren sat up.

"All right. Dinner is in ten."

"Thank you."

There was a common oval table made of brown oak, the edges carved with ivy, where most of the men sat for their meals. But some took their plates and lounged, feet up, on various couches and chairs, maybe needing to be alone for a while, or simply enjoying the more luxurious cushioning for their primed and toned buttocks.

They had dumpling soup, plates of roasted chicken dripping with juices, warm tortillas with melted butter, tossed salads, plates piled with cheeses and fruits, golden hot rolls, beans, rice, steaks, broccoli. It was a buffet of choices, and you could dish up whatever you wanted.

Ren had more appetite after his second nap and ate both steak and chicken. He piled up on the fruit and salad, too. For dessert they all had more choices: fresh baked cookies and cakes, slices of lemon meringue pie, strawberries dipped in chocolate.

If they ate this well every night, including the rest of the days' meals, Ren wondered that they all wouldn't become obese in a matter of years. But of course they were young. They swam. They worked out. They fucked. These restless men were burning the calories, no question.

As they were finishing up, something happened that seemed to make the entire room rattle, from waterfall and sleep alcoves, to the kitchen area, TV and exercise abodes.

The table gave a faint tremor.

Then came the voice. Master. All the men stopped what they were doing and looked up, though there was nothing to see but recessed lights and a tall, white ceiling which was the bottom of the floor of the mansion's second level.

Ren looked up as well, as if the tilt of his head might increase his hearing.

"These names only." The tone echoed throughout the room. "Zanti. Jaxon. Aiden. Finn." A pause. "And Ren."

There was a stirring on the air as the men shifted, waiting, silent. Finally the voice, returned. "Cam, you have instructions on your tablet. By eight at the door. Thank you."

Ren had been called.

Aiden, Finn and Jaxon all surrounded Cam.

"What does it say?" asked Finn.

"We have not been given time to prepare for anything! That's one half hour from now!" said Aiden.

Cam shushed them all, looking down at his tablet, tapping every few seconds. He finally said, "There is little to prep. Make up for some, of course. And you should all shower."

"But who--?" Jaxon began.

Cam interrupted him, turning to Ren. Now all their eyes were on him. "Ren gets braids, so we all must help. He is to wear the mask and the cock cage."

Ren frowned. "What?"

"You do as you're told," Cam said. Walking over to him, he raised his hand and patted Ren's cheek. "It's the position of honor, my new friend."

Ren thought of the mask room. So many. Which one would be for him?

Already, the others were hurrying about, those chosen, and those who were helping.

"I'll do your make up," Ren heard one say to another.

Cam looked up, raising his voice. "We all have to help Ren. He has a lot of hair. And Zanti, too."

*

Ren had no time to think. The men pushed him and the four other chosen ones into the showers, spraying them down quickly with soap, washing them all over. Zanti was furthest away from Ren, but his presence was the one he was most aware of. Zanti, the one with no voice. And no brand. Zanti. The guy who kept staring at him.

By the time Ren emerged only a couple minutes later, the twins were there, one with a towel and the other a blow dryer, and they were friendly as they helped Ren prepare.

Out the corner of his eye, he saw Zanti sitting and Cam before him applying dark eye shadow that made his already large eyes look bright and glimmering.

Ren did not get to sit. Someone came up behind him and as Ren looked down, hair blowing every which way, arms came around his waist and fastened a thick gold chain. Hanging low from the chain was a cage. For his cock.

The man came around then, and knelt at Ren's feet. Aaron. Grinning up at him. Being nice now. "I'll try to be gentle."

Ren had seen all sorts of cock cages, but in all his training somehow he'd never been required to wear one. Other slaves did, but he had figured it was upon request, because Master Holden had never bothered him with one.

This cage was gold mesh and slightly curved. It had an opening in back and his limp cock slid right into it with ease. Aaron fastened the other part of it to the waist chain so it held his cock aloft. There was a little extra room for him to grow inside the cage, but not much. It might be painful because Ren's cock nearly doubled in size when aroused. A fact he was proud of.

There was another chain below the cage that Aaron pulled tight underneath Ren's balls. It was a bit uncomfortable at first, but Ren didn't care. This was for Master and he would obey. In fact, his excitement, now that it finally sank into him that he'd been called and placed in a place of honor, was the first surge of real energy he'd felt since his arrival.

"There," Aaron said. "Okay?"

"Yes."

"I didn't hurt you?"

"No."

"Pity that." Aaron gave him a wide, fake-bored grin.

One of the twins pushed him into a chair that someone had brought to the center of the wash room. Ren fell back into it, the cock cage tugging at his genitals.

Suddenly, he was surrounded. Uncounted hands began separating his hair into tiny bunches and the braiding began, none too gentle. They pulled and tugged. It was obvious they'd done this before. Prepared the guests of honor.

Zanti stood to one side, his make up already done, and it made him look wild, his gaze voracious, completely an antithesis it seemed to a man who couldn't or wouldn't talk. What a pretty man he was with dark skin, slim hips, and veils of black-brown hair. Finn, Aiden and Jaxon were still being groomed, but each only had one helper applying lip gloss, eyeliner, hair spray, and glitter.

Hands tugged and twisted Ren's hair. His collar jingled. All their collars did whenever they moved. All were of a similar style, but different. Zanti's collar had emeralds. Cam's flashed moonstone. There were sapphires, diamonds, rubies of pink and pale green, and of course Ren's own flashing white with emeralds, more like Zanti's than anyone else's.

Colors. Everything was colors, excited auras mixing like a rainbow above them all as they worked.

In no time, Ren had a head full of braids and he smelled like fresh rain, not too sweet, not cloying, but a perfect scent to project cleanliness. Willingness.

He had no idea what would be expected. Sex, of course. He could handle that. If he knew Master was watching, wanting him to perform, he would do so with great ease and pleasure.

This was what he'd been waiting for.

When they were all finished crowding the big wash room, Cam herded the five chosen to the center of the atrium. Ren thought they'd be going through the door he'd arrived through behind the waterfall, and into the mask room, but instead they went to the opposite part of the room to a blank wall past the TV area. A green tapestry of a tree hung there. Pretty, but not something Ren had given a second glance.

Cam pulled the tapestry aside and draped it on a hook protruding from the wall. A flat door was revealed, already swinging open.

Two grooms in white button up shirts and white shorts, both with black hair, waited inside the door on either side.

Cam leaned toward Ren and whispered in his ear. "This is as far as I go, and the rest of us as well. You follow the others and do what the grooms say. You'll be fine. You were trained for this."

Sexual performance? Yes. Ren was not worried. "Thank you, Cam. For everything." He meant it.

Cam nodded. Zanti had already gone ahead, the first to enter the hallway.

Li Po came up, patting him gently on the shoulder. "Have fun, friend. You're a star."

His new braids tugged as he walked forward, the last in line. The ends, fastened with thin silver rings, batted at his upper back and shoulders. He had never thought to glance in the mirror to see his altered appearance.

As Ren crossed over the threshold, he saw a white staircase leading upward. One of the grooms touched his arm, motioning him to stop.

Ren looked at him, eyebrows narrowed.

"Mask first," said the groom without emotion. From a table behind him, he brought up a sleek mask wrought of thin gold with slanted blank eye-holes. It was not a full face-mask. It would cover Ren's eyes, and part of it dipped down on one side, and would cover his right cheek.

While the others waited at the foot of the stairs, the groom fastened the mask onto Ren's head with an elaborate system of ribbons, which fit almost like a net over the top of his head. The mask would not come loose that way, or even go askew from abrupt motions. It wasn't heavy or uncomfortable. Just strange. It shut out all his peripheral vision. And he could not see the full picture of what was ahead of him. Thus, it blinded his ability to see auras for the moment.

Now that he was ready, the group moved, one groom leading, one groom trailing. Following Ren. They went up the staircase in single file.

Chapter Fourteen

Room of Moons and Suns and Sins

Music played with a strange, seductive cadence. Instrumental only. The drums in the background created a heartbeat.

They had entered the first room that faced the landing of the staircase on the second level of the mansion. The two grooms in white, silent, their faces hardened with determination, focused on their job, and quickly ushered the five harem men into the center of the room.

One wall had a sunset mural painted in a sparse style of colorful slashes, still leaving most of the wall white. The orange sun dipped below curving lines of blue-black which could be interpreted as a sea, or mountains.

The next wall contained a moon and stars on dusky blue, a pastel tableau of night as if the moon shed almost as much light as the sun.

The third wall depicted a purple night, golden stars, and black lines overlapping it all as if one was looking through a jungle of tall grass.

The fourth, the one marred by the door they'd just come through, held large black and white sketches of men in various erotic poses, very simple, elegant. All the colors of the walls were muted, the light in the room giving off a bronze haze. It confused Ren's senses. At the moment, he could not see any live auras.

In the center of the black carpeted room were lounging sofas, plush chairs and a large king-sized bed with a blue spread. Wordlessly, the grooms directed the men to sit in various places. Zanti lay back on the blue bed. Aaron sat on the edge of it. Aiden and Finn each took chairs which faced the bed as if they were going to watch the scene.

This left Ren alone, standing on the carpet and facing the bed. The grooms stood aloof and did not look at him. Behind his mask, Ren's cheeks sweated. He had to turn his head back and forth the see the entire set up, and try to follow what was happening.

The others appeared excited. Aaron sitting on the bed was already half-aroused. No one moved. No one did anything. Ren stood very still in the center of the room. His cock cage was tight. His mask felt strange. But it was all right. He would willingly play Master's games.

From one second to the next, the pressure in the room changed. A static energy seemed to charge the air.

The voice split the air. Not quite as mechanical. More melodious tonight. Low-toned. Beautiful.

Master.

Ren turned his head from side to side to see if Master had actually entered the room but he already knew the sound came from all around, again as if multiple speakers were hidden in every wall, as well as cameras.

"Once upon a time there was a beautiful boy named Zanti."

Zanti raised his face, chin up, stream-lined chest puffed out. Ren looked at him with a sense of both hope and annoyance, the beautiful, voiceless guy still not aroused but lying seductively on the blue spread like a fairy prince.

Master's voice continued. As if he were reading them all a bedtime story.

"Zanti came from a poor family. His mother and father were old by the time they had him, and older still as he grew into an adult. When they both became ill, Zanti sold his beauty and his obedience to the highest bidders in the darkest back rooms of the city to pay for their care. Zanti had a rare beauty, lips like rose wine and long-lashed eyes so big they gave him a look of innocence, though he was not. It was said he was feisty in bed, tense, almost angry, but eager, a player among men like no other.

"Why was he like no other, you may ask. The men told stories around the bars and in the smoke-filled, drug-glazed back rooms. Zanti fucked like a fiend, made men come from just stroke, or a lick. Allowed them their pleasures in any way they wanted. But he himself never produced an orgasm in return. He did not come from any stimulation. The best had tried. No one could move Zanti beyond obedience, and when they were done with him Zanti would collect his payment and leave, only to show up the next night and the next."

Master cleared his throat. That made him human, at least, Ren thought.

"One day, Zanti came to the attention of a rich count who offered to pay for not only one night with him, but a hundred. At triple Zanti's usual price. His parents' medical bills would be paid. They would be taken care of on that salary for at least a year.

"And that was how Zanti found himself in the count's bed in on a remote island in the middle of a stormy sea. Far from home. Awaiting the caresses of a stranger who, perhaps, hoped to win Zanti's love. To milk from him the essence Zanti had refused every man he'd ever been with."

Master paused as a groom motioned to Zanti. Zanti lay back, his beautiful body in repose, sleek against the blue spread, his legs splayed, his cock on display where it lay still soft against his thigh.

"Count Aaron had prepared himself to win Zanti's heart."

A groom motioned Aaron to stand and face the bed.

"Count Aaron came into the room where he lit all the candles."

As this was spoken, the other groom lit some candles on nearby tables.

Aaron's cock was hard as he faced the bed. Zanti eyed him up and down, then turned his head away as if too shy to see more.

It was an act. It was all acting. That was what Cam had meant when he said they put on performances for Master.

All right. Ren could get into this. If he didn't have to be himself, if he didn't have to think, all the better. But where did he fit? He hoped to soon find out.

The story, though a narrative, was not entirely bad. It was fun. It was a fantasy, and Ren wondered of Master had written it himself and used the harem to see his creation come to life.

Master continued to recite. Aaron and Zanti did everything the words described.

"Determined to win Zanti's passion, to control it, Count Aaron choose to make love to Zanti rather than control him right away. He began with his feet."

Aaron climbed onto the bed and took Zanti's right foot in his hand and began to massage the arch. As Master read on, Aaron took each of Zanti's toes into his mouth and sucked. The other foot received the same treatment.

"He made love to Zanti's legs with hands and mouth."

Aaron began to work his way up Zanti's body. In his bent position, his ass faced the audience of Ren, Finn and Aiden, and it was lovely to look at, hard and round, the hips strong, the curve of his back and shoulders showing muscle lines and ribs. Zanti was astonishing in his relaxed position, head back, lashes fluttering, legs bent and lifted as Aaron left kisses all along his calves and then paid special attention to the insides of his knees.

"The count placed his lips at the bend of Zanti's knee, and the warm mouth left his skin tingling. The count kissed gently, the way a flower kisses the sunlight, and Zanti lay against the rich bedclothes and ornate pillows, a sculpture of beauty, still like stone. The only evidence that Zanti might feel something was a slight pinking of his cock."

This was true, as Zanti's cock was not fully erect, not even close as Aaron reached the divots of his hips.

As Master narrated, Aaron made love to Zanti's entire body. Zanti obeyed Master's story beautifully without becoming aroused. "He lay in a self-imposed languor, naked and exposed, but as if time itself had stopped and the count's gestures could not be felt."

As Master read about how the count licked and stroked Zanti's cheeks, his erect nipples, his underarms, his neck, Aaron obeyed. He did everything right.

Zanti squirmed and whimpered a few times, which was not in the script, but it was a great performance and fascinating all the same.

Ren could see their auras now through his eye-holes, Aaron's so pink with arousal and reddish with desire. Like a perfect magical fog winding and intertwining around them, and filled with lightnings of white and gold. But Zanti's aura did not have color. The usual blackness lightened only a little to a silvery, haunting gray.

Aaron kissed Zanti's cheeks and forehead, ran his hands through his hair. He caressed his lips with his fingers, then with his tongue, forcing Zanti's mouth open. But Zanti did not kiss back.

"The count left delicate kisses along Zanti's arms. When he got to the fingers, he sucked each one in turn."

There were many pauses as Master waited for the words to play out on the stage he'd set up.

"Only after he finished with Zanti's hands did he turn to his cock, which was sweetly reposing against his plump balls, but still not hard."

Still true. Zanti was perhaps not as soft as he had been, but he was not hard, and the rosy tip of his cock remained dry.

"Zanti lay very still, legs spread in obedience, as the count took his cock in hand. No expression crossed his features. The count placed a feathery kiss at the tip of the neglected cock. Then licked delicately all around the head, making it glisten."

Zanti squirmed as Aaron obeyed.

Ren loved to see it, how well they obeyed, how gentle Aaron forced himself to be, how patient. Pleasure slaves obeying, not in control, aroused Ren. The question now became, could Zanti hold on to his indifference. And for how long? And was it all an act? Had he been trained to control to that extent? Or was he jaded?

"The count stopped when he got no response from Zanti and turned him onto his stomach."

Aaron flipped Zanti.

The lovemaking began again, only from the back this time. All up and down the legs, arms, and waist until finally spreading the plump and pretty buttocks so that flower kisses could be placed between the crack and on the cute puckered hole of the beautiful boy who'd sold himself so he could pay his parents' bills.

Zanti pushed himself up on his hands and knees, and Aaron kept his cheeks pulled apart, displaying Zanti to the onlookers: Ren, Aiden, Finn and the grooms. And to the cameras in the room. Aaron licked him up and down, from balls to hole, wetting the skin there. Then finally thrusting his tongue in and out of the little hole which had now turned pink and flexed against the onslaught of pleasure.

Zanti squirmed.

Master continued the story. "Zanti presented himself to Count Aaron for anything the count might like, but he still did not show any prelude to orgasm. He was stone. A man waiting for some unknown miracle no one, perhaps not even Zanti himself, had any clue of."

Parts of the story had wildly poetic phrases like the fact that Zanti's skin gave off a sweet fragrance like a summer wind. And that to touch him was like touching silk stretched across hard marble. The youthfulness of Zanti, and the suppleness of him, was described over and over. His nipples, his thighs, his sweet buttocks all soft and hard in just the right places, and completely shaved, no hair down there, nothing to get in the way of naked, arousing, exposed flesh.

Ren thought the count would mount Zanti, who offered himself and his hole with lots of squirms and wiggles, but Master's story wanted Aaron's lips on Zanti's cock again, so Aaron had to turn him over and obey.

Aaron laved that lovely cock without sucking for a long time, edging Zanti, clearly challenging his control. Zanti did not get hard.

Ren's cock cage was tight as it forced his own arousal down. His balls began a faint ache. He told himself it was the story that aroused him, not Zanti. But it was a lie. Zanti and his behavior was more physically appealing than anyone Ren had ever seen.

When the story finally got around to Aaron sucking Zanti off, he did not hold back. He suckled and stroked with his lips and tongue with great enthusiasm, taking Zanti deep into his throat and swallowing. After all this, it should be enough to get any man off, Ren thought, but Zanti managed to hold off. Maybe over-stimulation kept him on the edge, or maybe Zanti was that well-trained. Again, he could not know. But he did note that Zanti's cock was pinker now, and bigger. Who could resist such a good sucking?

Ren knew nothing about him, or any of the men in the harem for that matter, except Li Po who'd told him some of his back story. If they were used to performing, then holding back until Master ordered them to come would be ideal. They would be good at it, or they wouldn't be here.

Ren suddenly worried he would not be as good.

Master's beautiful, but somewhat mechanical voice hummed along with the words. "Count Aaron sucked Zanti's thick, pink cock for hours, it seemed, and nothing happened. Maybe he thought he felt a twitch, or sensed a pulse, and the cock became longer by some measure, but never quite fully hard, never erect to the edge of orgasm."

Zanti's cock swayed in Aaron's grip, thick and long, the tip swollen and flushed and wet with saliva.

"Finally the count grew impatient, flipped Zanti over, and oiled his hole. With his finger he found the internal mound of nerves that sent men over the edge of pleasure and into whole new worlds of delight. He milked him there, and with his hand on Zanti's cock, then replaced his fingers with his own cock.

"The count, aroused from his hours of ministrations to Zanti, was ready to fuck, but still he took it slow, trying to bring any response from Zanti through their joining. But Zanti was cold as the northern sea. Frustrated, the count fucked Zanti harder, with force, smacking his hips hard against Zanti's backside."

Aaron obeyed. His hard cock withdrew, then re-entered Zanti's spread and welcoming hole with more force. Zanti was gorgeous splayed like that, hips thrust up, teasing. Ren could barely breathe to look at him. Aaron grasped Zanti's hips to hold him in place and began powerful thrusts that knocked Zanti back and forth.

Zanti opened his mouth and let out wordless grunts of air. His hair fell forward and over his face. He lost his balance a few times and slammed his face and chest into the mattress as Aaron pushed in and out of him, eyes closed, face flushed. Sweat rolled in crystal beads down Aaron's face.

Cam had indeed lied. Aaron had great talent in bed. He was fantastic at following orders.

As Master spoke the words, "The count came hard inside Zanti," Aaron cried out, pounding harder, then pulled his still twitching cock from Zanti's ass to prove to the audience and cameras he was coming. To give a show.

White liquid shot from the tip of his cock and all over Zanti's back as Aaron stroked himself to completion, head thrown back, mouth open, eyes shut tight.

Aaron, just then, was the essence of youthful beauty, his sculptured body perfect, his cock stiff and jutting out from his body, producing the essence of ecstasy. His buttocks clenched, the muscles rippling under his skin, the dimples above them deepening.

Ren gasped. It might not be literature they were enacting, or any sort of classic, but it was beautiful just the same.

"The count fell breathless across Zanti's body."

Aaron fell against Zanti's back, embracing him tightly. Ren could not see if Zanti had come, but he thought not. Aaron's aura had brightened, the pink fluorescent bright, with zigzags of white and red flashing. But Zanti's was still silver-gray with only flickers of pale white at the edges.

"Next, the count's assistant came into the room to offer water."

A groom pointed to Finn, who got up and, taking direction like a pro, brought a pitcher of water and cups to the bedside table.

"The count, exhausted but still wanting to see his newly acquired treasure, bought and paid for, owned by him, show some sort of response—any would do—then ordered his lovely assistant named Finn to spread Zanti's legs and give his cock a good, inspired suck. Finn was known far and wide for his expertise in deep throating, for taking cocks of any size and milking them with his talented mouth until they spilled all their essence into him. He hungered for men's essences. He thirsted for the white milk and would suck cocks daily to get his craving filled."

Finn bent before Zanti and teased his cock. Zanti was barely half-erect, so Ren knew that, incredibly, he had not yet come. His control should be rewarded.

After a while, the story moved along. Zanti still did not come and the count decided Finn should fuck Zanti.

And so it went until Finn came in long, hard spurts on Zanti's back, after fucking his loosened hole, and Aiden took his place, trying his best to make a frigid man come.

Ren watched and waited. Would his turn come? What would be expected of him?

Zanti did not seem to suffer, nor did he tire. Nor did he come. He seemed to love all of the attention, bucking at times, panting as if in pleasure.

Finally, the story took a turn and mentioned Ren's name.

"The last servant, a lad from a hidden room in the attic, kept from the world, was beckoned. The lad wore a mask and cage on his cock, for his virginity was being protected, saved for a special moment, Ren was ripe and ready. The count collected virgins for himself, so it was odd that he used this virgin not for himself, but through utter frustration and desperation, to try to get a rise out of his handsome, newly bought boy.

"Little did any of the men in the room know, though the count had observed Ren and suspected, that Ren was special. Not only was Ren a virgin, but he could see colors on people, colors of pleasure that left trails on the skin that led him to know exactly where to touch, and at which precise moment, to give the ultimate experience of ecstasy in sexual gratification. Ren didn't even know it himself until he came into the room and saw Zanti, and touched him, and that was when he understood. That was when he knew he could bring this boy an orgasm the likes of which he'd never known."

Ren startled at the revelation of his true gift to the others. But they didn't react as if it were strange. They all thought it was still a fiction. All but Zanti whose brows rose. His head tilted and his mouth opened in surprise. Ren noticed, though no one else seemed to, Zanti move back a little on the bed.

"The count slowly and tenderly removed the cock cage from Ren's aching cock."

Zanti took a deep breath and held it, glowering now.

Ren took it all in stride. He told himself Zanti was acting. It made the story more interesting if he continued to withhold his pleasure.

Ren was hard now, after watching all the others follow Master's orders and make love to Zanti. This was for Master. This was ordered. Even if Zanti hated him, Ren would make Zanti feel good. He would be gentle and kind. And he was getting into the story. Role play was fine with him, he simply had never imagined it would be with anyone other than his new master. He had only ever thought as far as that. How could he have been so naïve?

Zanti sat up and continued to watch Ren, dark eyes bright and languid at the same time.

Through his limited vision, the eye-holes of the mask obscuring all but what was straight in front of him, Ren tilted his head down to look at Aaron. Aaron was also frowning, his mouth half-curved into what was more grimace than smile.

Finn and Aiden were standing by the side of the bed, both sated, their cocks at rest, but they were staring straight at Ren with no smiles, and gazes steady enough to be almost unnerving.

Ren stepped forward. They were emotionless because he was new. That was all. They had never seen him perform. They were perhaps proprietary toward each other after living in close confines for years.

He tilted his head back, trying to see their auras. Darkened around the edges, all of them. Anger? But that could not be it for he had done nothing wrong, and nothing at all to them. He felt quite suddenly like little more than prey.

Master's voice commanded him through the narration of the story.

"Ren, the virgin, came into the room ready to give himself for his first time to a man who could not be moved. The count ordered Ren to approach the bed.

"Ren wore a mask and this, along with the cock cage he had worn for so long, had inspired gossip all around the estate that night by everyone who worked for the count and had seen Ren emerge from the locked space upstairs. People suspected Ren had been bought as a toy. But he had never seen any action. No one knew why, nor the reason their master hid him from view and kept his chastity intact, never touching the boy himself.

"But now, uncaged, he stood before the bed, looking through his mask at Zanti. Ren was naked and untouched, unsure what to do, unsure what the count expected of him.

"The count said, 'You will offer yourself to this boy. You will climb through his invisible barriers and re-start his heart. Do you understand?'"

Zanti scowled. Ren tensed.

Master continued. "Ren shook his head. He did not understand at all. He lived in an attic. He was a virgin. But the count ordered him to climb onto the bed and begin to caress Zanti's face, then his arms and chest."

Obedient, Ren moved onto the mattress on his knees, and bent to his ordered task. At first he felt awkward. The mask was in the way of his view. But Zanti, still sitting up, remained still, body taut.

Ren could not see the usual lights on the skin of his partner. But to the touch, Zanti's skin was smooth as new leaves, baby soft, the muscles of his arms and chest gently curved in all the right places. A pretty boy with a delicate beauty like lace, like clouds. He looked fragile, but he was anything but. He was wiry and wound tight. Lace did not give way easily, and clouds brought storms. Ren could see it on his skin the mask eye-holes revealed to him as slowly, almost too slowly, the colors of passion he was used to seeing finally began to simmer on the surfaces of Zanti's body.

Zanti had already been played with by three men, fucked and sucked until he was almost bored, yet still half-aroused. Like the story, Zanti need more. The over-stimulation, the edging, the strict admonition not to come as Master's story unfolded, had actually made the man withdrawn. This was Ren's test. He could tell. Zanti would play his role and not make it easy. The character of Zanti in the story was closed to emotion. In real life, Ren guessed Zanti might be jaded about the harem after so many years. All the men might be jaded.

Was that why Ren saw dark streaks of color across Zanti's body, instead of flickering, more colorful light like he'd seen in the wash room when they were all getting ready for Master? Was that why he seemed to glare at Ren? Was he just tired of it all?

Ren would show him, then. He could do this.

He tried to convince himself of this as he ran his hands up and down the smooth arms, showing his skill at touch. But he hesitated. Zanti had welcomed the other men: Aaron, Finn and Aiden. Encouraged them.

Was it the story that had him holding back now? Or Ren?

Master's voice trembled the air. "Ren had an ability to see Zanti's deepest desires through his skin. Through the energy that made beautiful lights seen only by Ren's eyes."

Ren followed the patterns with his fingertips, though dark and hard to see, especially with his mask, searching for any brighter reds and pinks in Zanti's aura.

He found them. At the junctures of his body. Underarm. Inside of the elbow. Just below the hip. At the wrists and knees. At the base of his cock and on the softest of skin that made a pouch for his balls.

As instructed by the story, Ren used his hands and mouth on all these places.

Zanti had long since fallen back on the bed. He looked bored, or maybe confused. But Ren didn't pay much attention to his facial features and focused on the lights on Zanti's skin.

Thankfully—or maybe just obedient to the story—Zanti's cock stiffened and began to leak tiny pools of clear fluid as Ren worked. His aura brightened to paler silver. But glancing now and again at Zanti's face, Ren noted he did not look pleased. It was the character in the story, Ren told himself. He was not used to resistance like this. But it was role-playing, that was all. And Ren had been trained for that.

He pressed his lips to Zanti's hips, to his belly button, and left breathless kisses on the elbows and in between his fingers. He turned Zanti, as the story instructed, and kissed the line between thigh and buttock, licking until it was wet and gleaming.

Zanti shifted and hissed. His aura trembled. This was a good sign Ren hoped.

Master's story unfolded in intricate detail, almost but not always matching the places where Ren saw the pleasure zones on Zanti, and tortured him there with lusty licks and caresses.

His mask got in the way sometimes. He ignored the barrier, doing his best to obey.

The count's story unfolded. Aaron, the count, became part of the play again. Instructed to touch Zanti where Ren had just touched. Following Ren's lead. He did not seem happy. Aaron or the count?

Master's story took a turn.

"Then Ren did something none of the others had ever done. He offered himself for pleasure. He straddled Zanti and stroked him upward until the wet tip of Zanti's cock probed his hole. Slowly, Ren lowered himself on Zanti's stiff cock, taking him into him, letting the boy feel how tight he was, how virgin, how saved he was for this special night when the count decided two boys must use each other to waken themselves to true manhood.

"Zanti had never fucked a man before. Ren had never been fucked. It was time to see them locked together in new passion, time to rouse their sleeping souls."

Zanti was lean but big when aroused. So were they all. Ren knew Master had collected them with care. Maybe they had talents, but they were all of a size, lean, hard, big-cocked, young and energetic. Maybe they had not been Palace trained, but Ren was no snob. Young men could fuck with sustained energy many times a day. Some slaves at the Palace were able to maintain themselves through ten sessions a day, with only short breaks for food and rest. They craved sex. The more insatiable ones always sold first, Master Holden had told him.

"This was a new sensation for Zanti. So new it took him by surprise and broke his control, as the count was hoping," Master recited. "Zanti's eyes went wide. His hips bucked up. And the sweet virgin ass he plunged into was hot and tight and irresistible."

Suddenly, Ren was no longer in charge, no longer required to do anything but be a hole.

Almost as if too eager to obey, Zanti grabbed Ren about the waist and pulled him down until he was fully seated on Zanti's cock. Ren had been made ready before ever coming upstairs, so he was well-oiled, and moved his hips in a way he knew men liked, but Zanti's fingernails dug into his waist, like a warning.

"Zanti took full control," Master said, voice a bit more breathy than it had been all evening.

Zanti bucked up again, hard, and Ren felt slight pain. He'd been trained for that as well. Ren moved to adjust his position, forcing his muscles to relax. But Zanti did not seem to notice, or care, that Ren was re-settling for more comfort and better sex. He seemed not to notice at all. His hips began to move up and down, and his cock dragged out hard, then in again, over and over as his hips moved in a more rapid rhythm.

Zanti pushed against Ren's chest, not to embrace him, but to show some sort of, what, force? Ren listened to the words Master read.

"Zanti became lost in pleasure so great it took all his senses away. He knew nothing but that he wanted more of this sensation, this hot grip on his cock, this fucking he had never before experienced."

Okay, so Zanti wanted more. But the words did not paint a picture of carelessness. That was all Zanti. And it was downright rude. It was all right, though. Ren knew the abandon with which men could fuck, the losing of control, the moments they lost perspective or any focus on other than their own satisfaction.

Now Zanti piston-fucked him so fast and hard it took Ren's breath. Ren looked down and saw a sideways grin slashing Zanti's face, a first smile that was not a smile but more a feral look that took over his dark eyes, as if he was a beast, as if he were raised by wolves.

Ren bounced, his own cock smacking him in the stomach hard enough to sting. Then Zanti sat up and pushed him hard, his grin showing teeth, not humor, and definitely not friendliness. He bounced Ren up so hard, withdrawing fast enough to burn, and came up over him like a creature toying with prey. He shoved Ren hard again, and Ren fell back, legs going up, and Zanti attacked his ass before Ren could even settle, pumping into him with Ren sliding back and almost falling off the bed.

Aaron was there and caught him, holding him down as Zanti pounded him, as Zanti pinched his thighs so hard they would most certainly bruise.

"In and out, Zanti pumped into the virgin boy," Master crooned.

Ren let it happen. He didn't mind rough. He wasn't a BDSM boy, though, and not sold as one. But this was a performance, nothing more. A final conclusion to the Zanti character's frigid pact with a world gone mad that forced him to sell himself to pay for his elderly parents' care.

Yes, that was it, Ren told himself. That was all. He closed his eyes behind his mask and let that fiction claim him even as Aaron held him too tight, as the beautiful boy who was Zanti in the story pummeled him as if he wanted to tear him apart.

When it was done, when Master read the description in the story where Zanti's whole body exploded in such a fierce orgasm his cock wouldn't stop pulsing, Ren lay very still, letting the liquid fill him, feeling it run down his stinging crack, his mouth open, the dry air of the room coating his throat, making him want to cough. Tears burned his eyes but he would not allow them to fall. He would not!

Aaron's grip on his shoulders had come close to Ren's neck. Close but not quite. Was this how Master had re-trained them? To be harsh? To be cruel to the newbie? Or did they truly hate. Hate this. Hate the harem. Hate Ren. It hadn't seemed that way only hours ago.

"In conclusion," Master read, "the boy Zanti's sex drive had been awakened so violently, and so quick and with such passion, that he could not hold back from wanting to rape all the men he saw in the count's possession. The count lost control of him. The count kept him only for entertainment, so he could watch Zanti fuck and come over and over now that he owned him. He bought more virgins for Zanti to plunder, bodies for Zanti's uncontrollable passion to wreck. And watched it all with hooded eyes, his blood steaming, boiling, for he had not known how good it could be to see a sweet boy who loved his parents be turned into this monster with a sexual drive that could not be sated. The count and Zanti lived for conquering. They became one and the same.

"Zanti never returned to his parents, but he kept them in good care, his money to them never stopping. His urges for the depraved and underground dungeons of the sex world grew. He broke many a soul. His appetite for doing so never ceased.

"And as for Ren, the broken boy from the attic was never the same. He wore his mask to hide his shame. And his own disgust for all things human. He moved through a world a ghost. The count dropped him in an alley of a shadowed city with a bag of money.

"Where Ren is now, none can say. What he did with his life and his money and his ghosthood is another story for another day.

"The End."

Well, that was rather awful. And the ending for Ren. It was humiliating. He almost forgot it was a play.

He looked up through a daze and the limited vision of his mask. The others had strange looks on their faces. Aaron said, "That's never happened before."

Finn said, "Some game."

Ren wondered what they meant. What had never happened before? But he had not time to ask.

The grooms began to move, gesturing the men up, ushering them to line up by the door that led out of the room and back to the stairwell.

Ren's legs would not cooperate and for a second he thought his hips had frozen in place. His thighs had been forced so wide. He'd been given no respite, and his muscles shuddered, threatening to cramp. He felt a trickle down the insides of his thighs and looked down through his mask but had trouble seeing.

A groom shoved him forward. As he took a step, he saw pale pink trails on his skin. Blood. His ass was one big burn, but he could take that. The blood on the other hand unnerved him a bit. It wasn't much, but still… He assessed himself for more damage but could not be sure. The pain radiated everywhere. And the still-bandaged burn on his chest felt like sharp stabs.

He blinked. His face was hot, wet. He wanted the mask off. His skin couldn't breathe with all that gold metal pressed up against it.

Just as Ren had that thought, one of the grooms came up behind him and said, "I'll take this now." He lifted the mask off

Ren's head. It was weird to hear a regular voice after hearing only Master for so long in that room.

The air hitting his damp cheeks was cool, soothing.

The groom set the mask on a table by the door. As they all walked into the stairwell, Ren the last one out, the groom touched his arm and led him down the shadowy hall while the rest of the men began to descend the stairs.

Ren was motioned through another door. He entered an all white room with a counter and sink, cupboards, a chair and an exam table. Another man who also looked like a groom, dressed all in white, motioned him to the table. "Let's have a look," he said.

Ren obeyed, blinking fast, trying not to tense. Trying not to feel singled out, picked on, afraid. Everything was fine. The groom seemed nice. At least they'd noticed he was bleeding.

Ren scooted up onto the table, wincing.

"Turn on your side."

Ren obeyed. The groom's gloved hands gently prodded him. Ren felt something slick go inside him.

The doctor took off his gloves with a snap. "You can sit up."

Ren rolled up and into a sitting position, crossing his arms in front of him.

"Minor abrasions," said the doctor. At least Ren *thought* he was a doctor. The groom had technically not introduced himself as such. "You'll be a little sore but you'll be fine. Use this ointment twice a day for two days." He handed Ren a tube of antibiotic cream.

Ren took it. The groom turned to the sink and began to wash his hands. The water churning into the metal sink with a drumming sound. He said, "Master wishes for you to abstain from sex for two days. The others have been informed."

"Informed?" Ren's face heated. But of course everyone in the harem would know everyone else's business. His veins stung with a weird anger and he pushed it down and away. That anger would not do. Not here.

The groom turned from the sink, a small smile on his face. "There are very few secrets in the harem."

"I don't know any of their secrets." He refrained from adding he didn't want sex with any of them anyway. If Master called him, so be it, but the others? Aside from Cam and Li Po, none of them had been too welcoming to him. Their indifference was probably normal, but at the moment Ren didn't care. And Master? Ren began to think something was very very wrong with their master. Why else wouldn't he show himself? The voyeur thing was all right, but never to allow his harem to see him? That was unusually weird.

"You will come to know them all. Give it time," the groom said.

Ren shrugged.

The groom continued. "If you experience further pain, inform Cam. He'll make a record of it and I'll see you up here again. Otherwise, we're done."

Ren slid off the exam table. The white paper fastened around the table stuck to his ass. He was still sweaty. Unclean. He pushed himself away from the paper and stood. It tore a little at the end.

Ren strode to the door where the groom who'd escorted him waited.

The groom-doctor said, "I suggest a shower, then use the ointment and rest."

Nodding, Ren followed his escort out the door. He half-turned, Palace manners instilled in him from day one. "Thank you."

Did he mean his words of thanks? Of course. But his annoyance would not abate. He felt as if he'd been betrayed. Which was odd because how could he be? He had no rights. He was owned. Nothing had changed. But in his heart he felt Zanti, beautiful Zanti whom he had actually felt something for despite his silence and his oddness, had taken some liberty, and Master had not stopped it. The others had shown no empathy.

He could not help but think they all hated him.

Chapter Fifteen

Pariah

The groom brought him back to the atrium through the door behind the tapestry. Half the men were loitering there, waiting to see him return, staring.

Ren inhaled a deep breath, then walked through their circle as if he didn't see them.

Cam hurried along by his side. "You wore the mask and the cage. That always makes it tougher. It's the hardest role. Now you know. But you're okay."

Ren turned to look at him, his braids flying, almost hitting Cam's face. He opened his mouth to say he was fine, wasn't it obvious with semen and blood dried on his thighs?... then closed it when he saw Zanti a foot behind Cam and to the side. Zanti frowned and parted his lips a fraction, turned his head about half an inch. His eyes were glistening with unshed tears. But Ren wasn't in the mood to process that.

Ren glared back with all his might until Zanti lowered his gaze. Zanti's aura was like a pin cushion of white on black. So many new tiny spots of light—had Ren put those there?—but still so dark. At the moment, he was too exhausted to care.

Ren glanced at Cam. "I'm fine."

He heard a laugh and turned. Aaron, the one they all said had such a beautiful voice, who himself was as gorgeous as a cologne model ad—they all were—raised his eyebrows as if in challenge. Aaron who had never been trained, or so Cam said.

Ren let out a forced breath and shook his head. Were they hazing him or something? Fine. Ren walked right up to Aaron, who stood his ground. He gripped the tube of antibiotic cream in his left hand so hard he thought it might break. He was still greasy, still dirty, his thighs a mess, and bruises were aching on his shoulders near his neck. Aaron's fingerprints.

Voice low, Ren said, "Thank you for keeping me from falling. It's very nice when the new guy gets treated so well, since it takes time to acclimate, you know, to get used to different styles, a different life."

Aaron took a step back, head down, and began to mumble. "Hey, I wasn't laughing at you…"

Ren turned to Zanti, ignoring Aaron. "And thank you, Zanti, for your prowess at fucking that knows no limits. You were impressive. You all make me feel quite at home especially when I was feeling out of place and alone."

Aaron's mouth turned down. Zanti looked completely lost, then shuffled behind Cam who, eyebrows raised at Ren's words, clueless, said, "All right then." Cam's face brightened. He clapped his hands together. "We're all good, then, right?"

"All good," Ren said coldly, and sauntered off to the showers.

*

Ren emerged from the shower still thinking about the evening. Trying to distract himself with other thoughts. Happier thoughts. Palace thoughts. How Master Holden would have reassured him he did his job correctly. How Master Locke would have come to visit him after something like this to make sure he was well, see to it that he was cared for and pain free. He would have brought him aspirin or something stronger. He would have stayed and talked with him in that soothing voice of his, and explained any questions he had until Ren understood the lesson.

This wasn't a lesson, though. This was Ren's life now. A life in a harem where the men were reluctant to accept him. Where they all seemed so easily two-faced, so moody.

What had he expected? That high school behavior ended with high school?

It was stupid but it still hurt. His vision blurred. His breath stuttered.

He quickly brushed his tears away. Only awhile ago, they'd all been prepping right here in the showers and wash room for Master's summons. They had all worked together, helped each other, and no animosity existed. Or if it did, none of it had been projected in Ren's direction.

After, they had behaved like children. Every one of them.

A shadow motion caught Ren's attention. He stood up from drying his legs, towel in hand, and saw Li Po standing at the entrance, lean and golden, constantly sweeping the pale brown hair from his eyes. Lovely.

"It's because they found out what you can do."

"What?" Ren asked.

"Aaron's a big bulldog, a blab-mouth. He's not a bad guy and I enjoy him immensely, but he has trouble with talking too much." Li Po looked up at the white ceiling as if searching for words there, lost words stuck, hidden, trembling. Like how Ren felt.

Li Po continued. "As soon as he came back, he announced it. To the room. That you see auras. It wasn't just a story you all were acting out at the end. He said the colors tell you about passion, make you the best of lovers because you can predict where someone longs to be caressed. He said you made Zanti come."

"So?"

"No one ever makes Zanti come. Not even if it's in the story."

"Zanti made himself come. He was rough and wild, almost as if it was rape to him."

"That's in the story. We've done it all before. But he still never comes. Not until tonight."

"Never?"

Li Po shook his head.

Ren had never lived with this quirk of his—this talent—being publicly known. He had kept it secret for this very reason. He did not want to be seen as different or weird. And yet, Master had said he collected rare things. These men were odd, too. But Ren's talent was different still. Psychic. Maybe even a little scary to those who didn't understand what he saw or how he saw them. It figured he would be the different one.

Now they would all act uncomfortable around him. Unnatural. Suspicious. As if he could read their sins or their fears or their deepest, most secret and shameful dreams.

"In the harem we're all brothers," Li Po said. "And lovers. And we tease and we comfort and there's even love. But when it comes to Master, sometimes the balances of power affect us. It becomes a fucking competition. Get it?"

Ren nodded. He did get it. Everyone wanted to feel important. Chosen. And they all were. Except they weren't special if there were thirteen of them. It diluted the pool. Made no one person stand out unless he was different.

"Are you sure you understand?" Li Po pressed.

"I am. I do get it."

"So don't let it—them--touch you here." Li Po pressed his hand to his naked chest. "It's not worth it. It's not personal, okay?"

Ren was glad to hear these words. Li Po was right, too. This new situation he was in was about a lot of things such as power, obedience, slavery, sex. A lot of issues came attached to those words, especially if they were all in one place. The need for approval, to be told you're good, to feel worthy. They were like children. Competing. Vying for Daddy's attention. An absent Daddy. A Daddy who never showed himself but took care of their needs, then commanded they do things for him. Things that exposed the self. And brought about a sort of dark eroticism that made everyone hungry, jumpy, and wanting it and not wanting it, competing for who could be the best.

Oh, Master had them all exactly where he wanted them. He probably got off on the dramas he created. He'd made them into some reality show of his own. All under his control as was his right.

Li Po nodded. "All right. Good night, then."

Ren finished drying himself, his necklace jingling. Then he went into a private bathroom stall and applied the cream he'd been given. After that, he replaced the bandage on his burn. He had another special cream for that which would be healing for a week, or so Niko had said.

When he was finished, he went to his alcove. He had to pass several to get to his on one side of the line of small open rooms. Some were unoccupied. In a couple of them, men were lounging together, not fucking, but talking. Cam slept alone. So did Zanti, who lay curled and unmoving, his aura all black again, vying for supremacy over the alcove's shadows. In another, the twins. Yet another, Calder and Jaxon, necking.

Ren entered his own alcove and immediately lay down in his bed, pulling up the covers. His tablet sat by his head on the nightstand, but he ignored it. He was too tired to read or watch anything.

For the first time in hours, alone at last, he could relax. Here in his own bed he felt contained, whole to himself. Unless there were cameras in the thin dividers between the alcoves, he wasn't watched here. He wasn't judged. He drew up the covers, their crisp coolness against his skin offering a strangely clean and safe comfort. He curled around his extra pillows and escaped into sleep.

*

Ren pulled out the dining table chair and saw its cushion was missing. His ass ached.

All right, then. He'd grab his food and go sit on a couch away from prying stares. He didn't want to be that guy who remained aloof, or acted too good to eat with the rest, but surely they'd understand. That chair was polished wood. And hard.

Aaron came up behind him, an extra pillow in his hand. He placed it in the chair, then looked up. "Sorry, dude, all right?"

"Yeah." Ren had to sit now. Or he'd look like an ungrateful bastard douche. He sat.

Elbow on the table, Ren leaned his head in to his upturned palm. He was not ready to forgive Aaron just yet, but he didn't want to push the issue. Honestly, he didn't really think Aaron was sorry. Just showing off for the others.

The eggs were fresh, the toast hot and buttered, the orange juice thick and sweet. His stomach rumbled. He had two helpings of everything, including pancakes. He had to have burned a lot of calories last evening.

After breakfast, Ren went to the side of the pool with his tablet and dangled his feet in the water. He wanted to swim but dared not. Not with his ass on fire and brand still healing on his chest.

He tried not to pay much attention to the others. He did not see Zanti, but Cam was at the breakfast table, which meant Zanti was probably not far behind.

Ren was still annoyed, so he didn't care if he ever saw that feral-looking fiend again.

He must have been giving off some real "don't touch" vibes because everyone left him alone. Even Li Po. They had to know he was recovering. Fuming and healing. Wrestling with issues each of them had probably wrestled with in their beginnings here in the harem: pride, importance, pain, homesickness, a pissed off mood and lamenting that maybe sex might never be fun for him again.

Ren didn't believe that; he loved sex. Lived for it. Planned his life around it. Wanted to be a pleasure slave. Of course he'd romanticized it a bit, even in training at the Palace, even with his masters' warnings about expectations, hopes, errant dreams of love. But his body told him what it wanted. His libido craved to be the pleasure source for whoever might want him. If he found love, that would be better. But sex itself—he'd wanted that. And he'd gotten it at the Palace. Now he was here with twelve other men. He'd agreed to a harem situation. He'd willingly walked into an unknown situation with an anonymous master. So be it.

This was his decision. He needed to be adult about that. He would find his place here, he told himself. There was Li Po. And Cam. And he could ask for things and they'd be delivered to him. He had every movie and book at his disposal. Porn. TV shows. Magazines. News. Music. If he wanted, for example, to paint, he was sure brushes and canvas would be brought. Or video online classes in digital art. Musical instruments might be brought in for them. Or the digital equivalents.

He had not been here long enough to see everything that these men did. What they wished for. What they received. But Cam had assured him they did get wishes granted.

It was a cage. He knew that coming here. It was gilded. It was a tiny world made of light, water, chiffon curtains, huffy beautiful men, and pleasure. He certainly could have done worse.

Lunch was a buffet of sandwich makings. All ingredients fresh and jumping with flavor.

After lunch, Ren had another shower, then applied more antibiotic cream to his brand and his ass. He sat in a soft chair by an open window and gazed out at the fresh lawn and sky. He glanced about, now and again, for Zanti, but never saw him. If the boy was hiding, then good. He should hide. Maybe not show his face for a time.

After a while, Li Po came to him and asked him to play some video games.

Ren followed him to the big screen. No one was around so they commandeered it.

Ren began to relax more. Li Po didn't try to talk to him. He was just there. As if he knew Ren wanted him to think he was okay. Which Ren was, actually, even if he was annoyed, in pain and struggling a bit.

A noise interrupted their game. They froze and turned at the same time, watching as the door behind the waterfall opened.

Was there another newcomer?

But then Ren saw several white-clad grooms pushing something large on wheels. It was black and huge... took five guys to maneuver.

Li Po met Ren's questioning gaze with a sideways grin. "Aaron ordered a piano."

"He did?"

"Six months ago." He shrugged. "I truly believe he'd given up on it."

"Wow."

"Master has one in the music room upstairs where he brings those of us who can sing or play to perform. He has all kinds of musical instruments. But we've never thought about having one so big as a piano down here until Aaron ordered it. Well, Master must have said yes."

This wasn't any old piano, either, Ren could see. It was a grand piano. A big, sleek monster of large proportions. One groom followed the moving crew, carrying a bench still wrapped in brown packing paper.

Aaron met the movers, bowing his head as they rolled the thing in, walking alongside it, examining it from all sides.

"Do you play?" Li Po asked.

"No. Do you?"

He shook his head.

Ren watched Aaron get his reward. And after last night, it stung. He still kind of hated the guy but couldn't deny the piano was an elegant piece of work.

Li Po said, "We can ask for things at any time. No question. Master delivers on our requests most of the time, unless you ask for something completely outrageous. One time Calder asked for a dog, specifically a weenie dog, and that never came, though."

"We could get a ping pong table. Or air hockey. Or a bowling lane," Ren suggested.

Li Po chuckled. "We had the first two. After a couple months, they sat dormant. They were removed. We can ask for them back at any time. They're probably in storage somewhere on the property."

"Hmm. Master doesn't like clutter."

"No. If we don't use it, after a while we lose it. It's that simple."

"But what if we want to be like Master and collect stuff?"

"Like what?" Li Po asked.

Ren shrugged. "Rocks. Or ceramic dragons. Or comic books."

Li Po glanced about them. "Nowhere to put it all. You could have one of those things you mentioned. One rock. One dragon. The comic book he'd deliver to you digitally, though. But the other stuff, you could keep one by your bed in your alcove. But Master doesn't allow us to accumulate what he calls junk."

Ren watched the men place the piano in a ray of light by one of the windows. They turned it and turned it, looking for the best position.

"Master's a collector. He wouldn't call what he collects junk," Ren said.

Li Po leaned back, scratching his chest. "Yeeeeah. The world isn't fair, is it?"

"True." Elbows on his knees, Ren maintained an eye on Aaron who kept circling the piano, and who seemed impatient that the groom unwrapping the bench was moving too slowly.

The lid over the keys was lifted. The bigger lid went up exposing the strings. When everything was in place, Aaron finally sat at the bench. For a minute, he just stared at the keys as if they were the most beautiful creatures he'd ever seen. The sunlight from the window streamed onto his face and fair hair, and his aura was a transparent gold. Aaron was tall, broad-shouldered, but the piano nearly dwarfed him. He looked like a little prince, all golden and pure, ready to play his first recital… albeit naked.

The first chord struck. It seemed to fill the room with the resonance of a storm. The next chord brought the wind. The next brought rain. And then Aaron played the keys with a furious, quick pace as if the world was ending, everything breaking, everything needing to find a new place, a new path.

Ren felt his breath stall in his lungs. Then his chest heaved. Li Po nodded at him, eyebrows raised. "He's good."

Ren swallowed hard, the notes swirling about him, getting into his head. He offered a reluctant, "Yeah." Then touched the bruises on his shoulder as he continued to watch Aaron conquer the new instrument. Tears came to his eyes. They weren't from pain. More like awe.

And he knew he'd barely begun to know any of these men here in Master's harem.

Chapter Sixteen

Rain

It had been raining for three days and Aaron played the storm, reflecting all its tones, plinks and crashes, the wind in the eaves, the rattling of panes.

Master had not called on any of them since Ren's night wearing the mask and the cock cage.

He was completely healed from that night. The brand on his chest was better, too, reduced to ugly scabs and flaking skin. It no longer pained him.

Zanti had made himself scarce. Barely seen. He came for food now and again, taking it away and eating it in his alcove.

Ren stood by an open window letting gales of air and water batter him, inhaling the tart scent of rain water, and wondered why they did not have a yard to play in. Even the worst of prisons had outdoor areas. Ren would have liked to feel the wind in his hair from more than an open window. Maybe he could request a yard. With a garden. And a gazebo with twinkle lights. And lawn chairs and a fire pit and sticks for hot dogs and the makings for s'mores.

Maybe he would see Cam about all of that. Put in an order. A list of requests. See what turned up in a year or two. He wondered if others had ever asked about a yard.

One day ago, Ren decided to start a routine for himself. The treadmill for half an hour. Light weights. Then a swim. His was healed enough now so his brand could take more than water from a quick shower.

Over the last few days, he had watched some of the fucking going on and began again to feel a hint of yearning there. He noted who partnered up the most with whom. Dark-haired Jaxon preferred the fairness of Calder. Torrance and Seth, the twins, always stuck together, but liked a third or fourth when they got horny for more. Still, it was hot watching the two of them, mirror images, make out together. And they did. All the time.

Aiden and Finn often paired up. Li Po often joined Cam, but Zanti stayed to himself, which concerned Ren and in turn made him feel weird because he still did not like that feral-charged guy who never spoke, and who had treated him so brutally as if by choice. It was hard for him to understand why the others tolerated him, for beautiful as Zanti was, he behaved like an errant child, often making faces at the others, scowling, stomping about. Li Po said Zanti did not use sign language because he didn't want to talk at all, not even that way. He wasn't deaf, so he didn't need others to sign to him. He was a weird guy. He could make noise. Squeal. Groan. Li Po had said early on that Zanti's refusal to speak was a deeper issue and no one except maybe Cam knew the truth as to why.

But that didn't make Ren feel softer toward him at all even after Li Po had said that Ren was the first to make him come.

The other three men, Tomo and Michael and Aaron, were also more loners. But they sometimes joined in group sex, and Ren had seen them with the twins several times. And of course, he'd seen Li Po and Aaron together one time. But these past days, Aaron seemed to be more interested in making love to his grand piano.

The first invitation Ren got to join in a group sex marathon came during the third day of the storm.

Rain lashed the window panes. Wind pulsed about the mansion. The air had an ionic charge to it. Everyone's auras spit and twisted in purples and blues. Everyone's except Zanti's which, when Ren did spot him, still twisted blackly about him.

Ren was wound up and restless from pretending not to watch the twins blow each other on one of the couches across the pool.

Li Po and Calder approached him. Jaxon stayed back a little.

It was Li Po who made the first move. He shrugged a little, not shy but unsure because even though he and Ren hung out playing games, they had never even touched.

"Want to play for a bit?"

Ren sat by the open window, feeling the cold breeze across his shoulders, his body covered in goose bumps. His cock cringed against his balls for warmth, but Ren didn't care. He liked the cold. But now he was ready for some warmth. Something steamier. Maybe a little kindness if not downright comfort. As long as Zanti and Aaron weren't involved, he found himself interested. Although Zanti made him wistful still, and confused.

He suspected Master watched their antics through his hidden cameras. They could never know when they were being watched, but if Ren hoped to gain more of Master's attention, playing would help.

"All right." Ren sat forward. His hair was damp in the back from the rain coming through the window.

Li Po's face froze in a moment of shock, his features sinking into him a little, his mouth slightly open. Then he lit up with a wide smile, blinking fast, cheeks flushed. "I was hoping!" He held out his hand.

Ren reached up. Li Po's palm was warm and Ren felt their connection instantly in his blood. It warmed him. Little fires prickled at the base of his spine. Li Po's fingers wrapped around Ren's hand and he gave a tug. Ren came to his feet, casually noting Li Po's cock jerk once, then begin to lengthen. Little pink trails of light began to flash against Li Po's skin.

Good. Ren hadn't lost his talent yet. He would know exactly how to bring this man to the pinnacle of ecstasy and drop him joyfully into it. And because he liked Li Po, he might possibly join him there with a minimum of effort.

Before Ren could even blink, Li Po leaned forward and hugged him. "Sweet," the man whispered in his ear.

Ren realized that he'd never asked Li Po the obvious questions even though they'd spoken the most. How long had he been here? He knew Li Po spoke a lot of languages, but did he have other hidden talents?

There was a long couch by the waterfall, half of it with a back, half without, and that was where Li Po led Ren, with Calder and Jaxon following. The part of the couch without the back was wider, and big enough for four men to sit together in a circle, and even lie down. The cushions were thick and soft, and had white coverings which the cleaning crew changed every day.

As they all sat, it turned out they positioned themselves with Ren more in the center, the others flanking him, staring at him.

Ren said, "I'm sure you've all heard of my talent by now and want to see for yourselves what I can do."

Li Po shook his head. "You're our guest." He touched Ren gently on the shoulder. "Please? Will you lie back?"

Ren had not expected this. Even at the Palace, everyone had wanted his hands on them, his ministrations, his caresses, kisses, massages and more. They didn't know why they wanted it so much more than with others, except that he was gifted in the art of bringing on the best orgasms. His test subjects had all gossiped and raved.

Here, though, the men knew. Even if Zanti couldn't or wouldn't talk, Aaron talked. Finn and Aiden had seen how Ren had made Zanti even crazier than the guy really was.

Ren hesitated. "Don't you want to test my abilities?"

"We do," Li Po replied, smiling over him, pushing gently. "But later. First, as I said, you're the guest. And guests deserve a certain initiation. That is, if they want it. Do you?"

Ren looked into Li Po's amazingly expressive eyes and said, "I do." And let himself be positioned until he was lying on his back, legs slightly spread.

Hands began to roam over his shoulders, chest and legs. Tender and warm. He let these men take him flying.

Li Po was at his shoulder, bending low, and his scent was like the beach, all frothy and spiced with salt wind. He ran his fingers through Ren's braids—braids he'd kept after his night in the mask. Li Po paused to trace the curve of one ear, his fingertips sliding over it and to his jaw. Li Po touched Ren's eyelashes, leaned down as Ren closed them and kissed his lids with so-soft lips. Li Po's breath was hot, like a sudden blaze of summer.

When Li Po reached Ren's own lips, the kiss so kind and tender that Ren broke open a little. His eyelids fluttered. *Yes, thank you.* He was glad Li Po was his first real kiss in the harem. So friendly. He wanted that man in his arms but he waited. He was their victim for the moment, their prize. Or perhaps they were all his prize, for none of them appeared right now to have anything on their minds but seeing to Ren's own rising lust.

Ren's mouth parted. Li Po's gentle tongue pressed the insides of his lips, nothing more. No demands. Just stroking and petting, as if he was a fine acquisition, maybe even beloved. Like a pet.

Calder ran his palms up and down Ren's chest, massaging the pecs and nipples, working the ribs. He was reverent and calm as he did this, focused.

Jaxon caressed Ren's spread thighs, fingertips delving along the delicate skin of the inner part of his leg where Ren was very sensitive. How did they know? It was driving him crazy.

His cock had risen of its own accord. The air wafted across the tip, a cool draft, letting him know it was already wet.

They treated him like art, making a slow and thorough process of their creation, taking their time, making every part of him whole, special, loved. Jaxon caressed him down to his toes. Calder made circles that encompassed the tender areas under his arms. Li Po had graduated to kissing his throat, making his whole body more sensitive than ever.

Another might glance at them and only see sex and four men and unified arousal. But it was all built on a precious extension of energy that took its time to sink through Ren's skin and suffuse him in white light. For white was what he saw when he felt pleasure, as if his own aura was absent of all the colors he saw on others. As if he were missing the thing his own touches sought. Yet he wasn't unsatisfied. His orgasms always blossomed through his whole body. His own ecstasy often startled him, and that amazing drug was what had propelled him to want to be owned this way, claimed, a slave for life. But to a master who might love him—well, his hopes had been too high.

These men were powerful substitutes. How could he be disappointed?

He was not.

And oh how they knew what they were doing.

The rain battered the outside walls of the atrium. Millions of tiny drum-puff sounds all around him. The touches all over his body drummed a similar pulse inside him, his veins humming with heat, his vision blurred, his eardrums filling up with a sound from within his head that might be like a cat's purr, only wasn't. It was brain and mind locking onto a distant planet called Bliss, and the storms there were made of euphoria, wet and warm and sucking at his every cell.

This was the dance and the origin of awe: life, birth, death, over and over.

Ren didn't think he would have wanted to become a slave to pleasure if he had not recognized this about the sexual act, about lovemaking and orgasms. It was spiritual to him, like a religion. He couldn't stop it. How it took him over. How he wanted it more the more he had.

Sell himself to pleasure slavery? He would have paid to become a slave!

Li Po came back to his lips and the kiss liquefied his insides, the tongue soft and probing, entering him like the sweetest liqueur. Calder began to lick at his nipples now. Jaxon kissed up and down the insides of his thighs. Their hands followed their tongues. They massaged, caressed, stroked.

No one touched him yet on his cock or balls. They did not turn him over, but they did lift his limbs, and position him into a more vulnerable stance so that the backs of his arms and legs were exposed and touched, and the place where his thighs met his buttocks was revealed. They spread him so his crack opened and he could feel the cool air on his hole.

The rain sounds mixed with the waterfall's constant plunge. Water and wind. Those were Ren's totems. And of course hands and lips and tongues.

Li Po pulled back and his hair was like a dark rain around both their faces as he looked down at Ren. "I would like to taste further of you," he whispered.

Ren nodded. Permission granted.

Li Po moved down to a nipple. He and Calder sucked nipples simultaneously before Li Po dropped lower, tongue diving into the divot of Ren's hip, then savoring the back of his thigh where it met the curve of buttock. He took hold of Ren's leg and put it over his shoulder, then traced his tongue along the underside of Ren's balls, which instantly drew up and rocked inside their sac, eager for more. Just when Ren's leg was starting to feel uncomfortable, raised up and pushed aside, Li Po crawled under and through, letting the leg rest back on the cushion, and he was between Ren's legs.

He licked up his balls, laving the sack, then swirled his tongue around the root of Ren's cock, which twitched with impatience, though Ren himself was not. He loved delayed orgasms. He loved the process.

As if sensing this, Li Po took his time, licking around his cock before driving his tongue up along the underside with quick, wet licks. Ren's stomach was already soaked from pre-cum. He loved having his cock sucked almost more than getting fucked. He already imagined the silken warmth, the suction, the movement of the mouth up and down his shaft.

He wanted it but not fast. Slow. Delicious. Weaving pleasure upon pleasure.

Every inch of Ren's cock was thoroughly investigated before Li Po took the tip between his plump lips.

By now, Jaxon had taken over the area of his balls, licking them over and over, kissing the skin between.

When Li Po finally pushed his mouth over the tip, tonguing Ren, offering the first bit of suction, Ren's body fizzed with the vibration of arousal so strong he never wanted it to end. Calder paid careful attention his nipples, which now felt huge and tight. His chest heaved.

Li Po lowered his mouth further down the shaft. The lips circled him in a tight band. The suction increased. The wet warmth encased him. Saved him. Rebirthed him.

That was what it was like. An experience more than play for Ren. Always. More than just fucking. He could give it. How he saw the color coalesce and suffuse the skin of others guided him, inspired him. But he could take it just as well. He had not forgotten this, only mourned the change of his environment. That was all. And then to have his first performance become less about pleasure; he had failed to come then. Master had to have noticed. Ren hadn't yet come since coming to the harem.

He wasn't ashamed. Only annoyed. And made to feel more like an outsider than he already was.

This was how Master should have seen him for the first time. Li Po, Calder and Jaxon brought him to life.

Li Po's mouth moved slowly upon him and Ren's buttocks squirmed and tried to lift from the couch. Gentle hands held him. Soft mouths kissed and sucked on him. All over his body. Moving, wetting, sucking at the skin. But Li Po's mouth on his cock never let up, never relented, and his cock thrummed happily in its new, hot nesting place, twitching and throbbing, causing Ren to soar higher and higher on his own storm brewing within, ready to explode with the force of a hurricane.

Damp fingers found the skin behind his balls, then brushed teasingly over his hole. Of course he would let them fuck him for the asking, now that they'd broken through his dam, his grief and irritated resentment.

Li Po pulled up, milking with his lips, and licked all about the tip of Ren's cock, lighting even more fires. Ren bucked. Li Po held his hips with his hands, fingers curving around like a hug. He went down on Ren again, all the way so he could feel the throat muscles pulling, tightening on him.

Ren's head went back. His eyes rolled up. The crest was there quite suddenly, the stimulation on his nipples and balls extending the sensation until he saw the peak and knew it would be a long and glorious fall. No wings. No net. Nothing.

His body jerked. He hurtled ever higher and then everything froze. He was pumping now, straight into Li Po's mouth, the top of his head opening into white on white on white. His cock pulsed hard. He felt the spurts one after another. So many. The way the wetness grew about him. It was too much for Li Po to swallow all at once. He felt the overflow on the base of his cock, and rolling down to his ass. To the couch.

He had his breath held. He let some of it out, then stopped, continuing to come. A cry broke free from his throat. He heard it like a bell dipping itself into the wind. Heard the storm try to swallow the house. Heard the rain and the waterfall as one.

Honestly, in that moment no one on Earth, he believed, had ever experienced a better orgasm. It was all about him. He was the center, the focus, pure force, the universe itself.

The men licked and caressed and kissed him as he came down. It took him a long time. He would have been shaking if they weren't there to still him. He would have fallen if he weren't already lying down.

Kisses wrenched him out of his body, then back into it. On his ribs, his arms, his neck. Li Po was at his lips again, and he tasted himself upon them, salty and cool. Like foam.

Ren raised his arms up and embraced Li Po, hands on the backs of his shoulders, rubbing the smooth skin.

"Such a delight you are," Li Po said, rising a few inches above his face. Smile turning to a low laugh. "Gourmet all the way."

Ren loved Li Po right then. His heart opening and closing. The others were nice, too, but more like beautiful blurs. Li Po had taken charge, and Ren liked men who did that. Who knew what they wanted and what to do. But Li Po was not his master.

Still, Li Po was clear in his vision, not blurred, but bright and forward and someone he knew he wanted to hold on to in this harem. Someone special.

Yet still, his mind went to Zanti. Did Zanti have someone special? And why did he even care? The silent boy had taken him until he'd bled. It had been almost an insult. Almost. Except for one fact. Everyone said Zanti never came. Never. But he had come inside Ren. What in all the world could that mean?

He didn't want to think about that. Lovely Li Po was in front of him now, and had just given him the time of his life with two other beautiful men.

When Ren finally had the strength to feel like himself again, to sit up, to see the clouds of color that mixed their auras together, he said, feeling a genuine smile cross his face for the first time in days, "Who's next?"

All three of them were aroused, no question. And Ren, when excited, needed very little recuperation time. It didn't matter, though. For the first time since entering the harem, he was ready to give.

No one answered him right away. He saw movement out the corner of his eye. Zanti at the edge of the pool in silhouette, then turning his back and walking away. His stomach lurched. Had Zanti been watching them? Why? He blinked the image away.

"All of you?" Ren asked with a grin, distracting himself from that thought. Before they could shrug, or shy away, or move forward—however their personalities drove them—Ren bent to lick a line of green light that blinked at him, tonguing up Calder's thigh. Calder gasped, his long stiff cock twitching.

Ren loved to use his gift to help men discover erogenous zones they might not even be aware of. Young or old, smart or not-so-smart, men were impatient. They wanted to fuck. They wanted the final bliss. But Ren knew—and these men had to know as well— bliss could be as exquisite in the process as it was in the outcome. You could spend an hour thinking you were coming the whole time only to be drowned by the final orgasm. Sex was fun, but it was also an art. And Ren painted with his whole body.

Even though Ren's first play with Master had been somewhat unpleasant, it had taught him that Master knew this as well, that most men simply wanted the outcome, the orgasm, but there was so much more. Did he have impatient *boys* in his harem? Ren thought not.

The others realized Ren had chosen Calder as the next and moved around so Calder was in the middle of their circle.

Calder's pretty, midday-blue eyes widened and took on a bright sheen. His fair hair, sweat-damp at his forehead, sideburns and ears, framed him with darker locks, all starting to curl at the ends. He was so damn cute it melted Ren from the inside out just to look at him. Muscle, bone and cock were the only hard things about him. Everything else was soft, soft and malleable, his ass the sweetest heart-shape, his chest all gentle curves, and all topped with the face of an angel.

"Lie back, sweetheart," Li Po said to Calder, then looked at Ren.

Ren smiled. He didn't mind if Li Po gave orders. In fact, he liked it.

That boy, all creamy-skinned and willing, with a bubblegum pink cock, did as Li Po asked. He was like an offering to the gods, of milk and gold, with soft innocence but certainly not a virgin.

Ren began to point out areas of Calder's body that needed attention, when the aura of Calder pinged electric like circuits connecting on an energy level beyond ordinary awareness.

The juncture between neck and shoulder. The back of the jaw. Left side just above the hip. Bellybutton. Juncture of thigh. Back of the knee. Little toe. Of course his cock radiated pure light, but that was ignored for now.

The rain had slowed. The waterfall was louder now, and Aaron's piano rumbled along slower, the chords more thoughtful as if he were composing now, thinking it through.

Ren was aware of everything around him as well as Calder coming to life on the cushions, of the warmth in the room from the heaters combined with the rain scented, cooler air coming from the window he'd opened. Of the dew of the waterfall misting over them. The shadows of the other men moved about the room; the music undulated over it all.

The other's followed Ren's commands, touching Calder where Ren indicated. His skin glowed. He brimmed with pleasure in voice, tightly shut eyes, and salt-sweet musk of arousal.

Calder opened his blue eyes and begged Jaxon to fuck him. Ren nodded and Jaxon, more than ready, slowly entered his body. Ren loved to watch actual lovemaking, and this was it. Calder and Jaxon clearly had feelings for each other. Their tenderness with each other was like a confession of their desire. Need defined. Both their bodies radiated pink and pale blue. At the juncture where they joined, red fire encased them and shot tendrils of sizzling energy into the air.

It was natural for Ren to see such things and sometimes he forgot that others were blind to it.

They came together in each other's arms while Li Po and Ren rubbed their backs, kissed their necks.

Li Po was next.

By that time, Ren noticed they'd drawn an audience, but Zanti was not among them now. This happened at the Palace, too. All the time when Ren focused his attention on one or more, others stopped to watch. Their masters allowed it. Master Holden had understood, and tried not to look too proud.

It wasn't that the other slaves at the Palace—or here in the harem—hadn't witnessed great sex before. Of course they had. All the time. Ren understood it was something more. They saw it in him, and in his partners—something greater than just sexual joining. Something that went to another level of bliss, soul-deep. It could have been love, but Ren could manifest this energy for anyone, those he cared about and those who were strangers to him. Onlookers could see the scope of the performance beyond mere fucking, though few could describe in words why.

The way Aaron interacted with his piano might have been one way to compare it. Fluent. Not just hearing and playing the compositions, but being a part of it.

Ren's partners were his compositions. His paintings. His poems. His plays.

Li Po stretched out before him, Jaxon and Calder, hard as steel, light brown skin stretched and yearning, sparking blue, then gold, then orange.

Ren loved the feel of him. Satiny, tight. He kissed him, cupped his head, felt his own heart open. Li Po had been the kindest to him of all. It affected how he saw him, how he touched him, how he brought him to life.

It wasn't long before Li Po bent his legs back, his cock bobbing, and pleaded to be penetrated. He was polite. He did not use crass terms. He did not say, *Fuck me.* He said, "Please. I need you inside." His gaze sought Ren's.

Calder and Jaxon smoothed their palms over his arms, legs and chest. Ren licked the straining cock, then lower. Wetting him where his aura had turned to a fuchsia-petaled flower flashing at his hole.

When Jaxon had taken Calder, he'd revealed a drawer beneath the couch filled with toys and vials of scented oils. Ren used something that smelled of flowers, spreading it over himself and onto Li Po. He went slowly, taking care, but the entry was easy. Li Po so open and willing.

Ren had been ready to go again for a while now, his stamina just fine, burgeoning, actually. Li Po was so warm and welcoming, his eyes blurred. He did not always love to top, but he loved Li Po in this moment, so open and needy, and his body flamed for him.

Hands caressed Ren's buttocks and the backs of his legs as he thrust slowly in and out. Another hand cupped Li Po's cock and balls, then lower, fingers framing where Ren entered Li Po. His strokes into Li Po and the strokes of those fingers—Jaxon's—heightened everything, and the world swayed and brightened, full of so many colors he could not name. It was as if color shot from his eyes, and suddenly Li Po was thrusting up, hands reaching for Ren. "Deeper. Oh. Oh." Jaxon stroked him and he came as Ren angled himself into him, knowing he'd hit his prostate.

Li Po's essence fountained from him, painting his flat chest white.

All the colors of the atrium and the men and Li Po's blooming aura gathered about him until he flew up into all color—pure white. Ren came as the whiteness went into him like snow and hot ash simultaneously.

Suns, moons, stars surrounded him. His senses returned and he realized he'd collapsed on Li Po, who held him and stroked his back, breath puffing against his neck.

This was the world. The gift of it. Wholeness. Completeness. The self divine.

Calder and Jaxon lay beside them. All four men were in a daze for awhile.

Their audience moved about them, curious, but no one spoke.

Ren dozed in Li Po's arms. When he finally opened his eyes again, Li Po's were closed. His breathing even and slow.

Later, one by one, they each got up and went to the showers.

After bathing, Ren went into his alcove to take a nap. He woke with Li Po pressed against his back. "Sorry," Li Po said. "I needed to touch you, feel you. I'm still not quite down from that ride."

Ren turned and kissed him. "It's okay." But for some reason, he'd felt Zanti in his bed. Just for a moment. But there was no reason for it. None. Li Po's scent and touch were distinct. Ren had only been dreaming, then, and dreams were not something one could control.

"What I mean is," Li Po said softly, "we all have to respect each other's space, or this would be a very difficult place to live. We don't go where we're not invited. You didn't invite me here. But can I stay for a while?"

"I said it's okay. I meant it." Ren kissed him again. Li Po's mirror-like hair brushed Ren's forehead, warm and smooth. His lips were rose-petal soft.

Ren could hear the rain continuing to attempt its plunder of the world. He pulled Li Po close.

Chapter Seventeen

Consent

After lunch, Cam, tablet in hand, came up to Ren.

"We need to talk."

It had been four days since anyone had been called upstairs by Master. Since Ren had worn the mask. Li Po had spent much of the past night in his alcove. They mostly cuddled as if both needed that more than anything. But early in the morning, he'd left. And Ren stretched out, glad for the extra room. He liked Li Po, but he still liked his space.

Still, Ren was happy about having Li Po to focus on. Li Po was like a healing force. Solid. Good. Sane.

Now Ren's body tensed and he glanced beyond Cam to see if Zanti was about. Zanti had not eaten meals at the table for days. He lurked in the shadows, a darkly blooming flower, his aura nearly black, his unusual, feral beauty aglow but distant.

Ren did not care what Zanti did. He told himself this over and over. He just wanted him to stay away from him. But all that was a lie. Ren was intrigued if nothing more. Zanti was an enigma and he would be fooling himself if he thought he wasn't curious about the guy's story.

Not seeing Zanti anywhere about, Ren shrugged. "Sure."

Cam said, "Let's go sit."

Cam led them to a couch in the media area. As Ren sat, he said, before Cam could speak, "I've been thinking of making a request to Master. Has anyone ever asked for a yard?"

Pulling his leg up and folding it under his chin, Cam replied, "You mean outdoors?"

"Yes."

The other man laughed.

"Don't laugh. What if I wanted to garden? You know, like Aaron's hobby with his piano."

"Yeah, we all get what we ask for. Within reason. It can take time. I'll make a note. But we have plants and a waterfall and special lights here that make it seem like the outdoors. We get our vitamin D from those lights. But once in a while Master has allowed the twins and Tomo to go running on the grounds. Accompanied, of course."

"Really?"

Cam nodded. "Me, well, I'm not one for running. And if I want fresh air, I open a window."

"What about field trips?"

Cam shook his head.

Ren noted that none of the men suffered. But their world of captivity was incomplete. If they noticed, they soon learned to look the other way. Ren knew all about trying not to think about the things you couldn't change.

"Something else I wanted to talk to you about." Cam looked away, head tilting. He gazed at the waterfall for a moment before again facing Ren.

Ren leaned back. Took a breath.

"Zanti," Cam said softly.

Ren didn't want to talk about Zanti. Not to Cam. Not to anyone. He almost got up right then. He pressed his mouth tight, teeth cutting into his lower lip. Instead, he attempted to keep control of the conversation. The fact that Zanti shadowed Cam a lot made him ask, "So, are you two a thing? Like lovers?" Though he could not imagine what Cam saw in that guy aside from his hellishly, ethereal beauty.

Cam opened his mouth, then closed it. There was a pink essence of light playing about his blond curls. "No. Zanti doesn't take lovers."

Ren sat forward. "Sorry I asked. I was going to take a swim. Do you mind?"

Cam's hand shot out, steadying Ren. He wasn't rough or even firm. Just insistent. "Please. Let me talk for just a minute. I know you're curious."

Ren leaned back, feeling his brow furrow.

Cam took his hand away. "I want to tell you about—about him. At least what I know."

Throat going a little dry, Ren thought about getting up and getting a soda.

"Zanti isn't like the rest of us."

"I sort of noticed."

"I mean, right, he doesn't talk. He's odd, of course. He obeys Master, but not for the reasons you think."

"What reasons? We're all slaves. We don't have a choice and we know it going in."

"It's not like that. I'm like the greeter. You know, how I received you, checked off the stuff to orient you into the harem. My tablet has files on all of you guys. Histories. Bios. The webpage the Palace made for you. All your videos. Your essay. Master put me in charge of that. He greets each slave he buys after Niko prepares them. But I'm the hands-on guy. So I know stuff. Zanti can't talk, but I have his profile. His history. At least part of it." Cam tapped his tablet. "All here."

Ren looked at the man's forefinger tapping the glass of his screen. "So?"

"Zanti is the only one of us not here by consent."

"He's not a trained slave?"

Cam shook his head. "Not in the way you know it. Or I. I'm not Palace trained, but I had private training. Consensual training. Then I had an owner before I came here who furthered my training in all ways. For two years. He died."

"I—I am sorry, Cam." He wanted to ask if they were close. But he didn't have to. He could see it in Cam's now-clouded eyes, and in the way his aura drew in and grayed.

"It's fine now. I'm happy here. I really am. Master found me and bought me and brought me here. A lot of our stories are like that."

And Zanti's? Ren did not care, but then again, he did. That damned boy was on his mind. Often. His head began to ache, which was rare for him, and a sign of stress. And what was Cam really trying to tell him? That Master was some sort of altruistic collector?

"Zanti was taken when he was underage," Cam began.

Ren closed his eyes and put his fingers to the bridge of his nose. "By Master?" Why was he asking? He didn't want to know anything about Zanti.

"No. Master has given me permission to tell you this much. Ever heard of Mister X?"

Everyone had, Ren thought. He'd been caught several years ago. The most notorious kidnapper and serial killer of the Northern provinces. Ren had been about fifteen when the guy had been caught. Mister X kept his victims, all men, in cages in his basement in deplorable conditions. Some had been there for years. Others he raped and killed and dumped. He had been known for cutting off their hands and heads so if their bodies were ever found, they would be difficult to identify.

"Why are we talking about serial killers now?" Ren asked.

"I'm trying to tell you!" Cam let out an exasperated breath. "Zanti was one of the boys in the basement."

If that was true, then how had Zanti come to live here?

"He was there for three years. Can you imagine? He was fifteen when he was abducted," Cam continued. "Tortured. Raped." Cam lowered his head. He whispered the rest. "Over and over. Still a boy. Just a boy."

Ren felt himself go cold. It wasn't because he didn't care that an innocent boy had been treated this way. It was the opposite. He didn't want to see. He didn't want this to be true. Zanti's truth. Somehow, it tainted the harem.

Cam said, "Do you remember any of the details of that case from the media?"

Ren really did not. He shook his head.

"The cops had no leads. Everything they had to finally solve the case came from an anonymous tip."

"Yeah, I sort of remember that." Ren sighed.

"The thing is, and I'm not really supposed to talk about that... but after what happened with Zanti the other night..." Cam paused. "You'll keep this to yourself, right?"

"Keep what to myself?"

"Master has connections everywhere. I don't know much about him except how his tastes run here with the harem, or who he even is. But Zanti... Zanti came from Mister X. Master bought him for a large sum."

Ren's blood turned icy. "Master had contact with a serial killer? With that guy?"

Cam nodded. "Master rescued Zanti. They others were too far gone. Remember the news? The film footage? They were catatonic. There were five in the basement. Three died pretty quick.

The other two are in institutions. But Master got Zanti out of there first before the cops broke into the house. He made a deal with the killer. Then the cops came, acting on that anonymous tip."

"You think Master was the anonymous tip?"

Cam nodded.

"But Zanti… he's, he shouldn't even be here, then?"

Cam nodded. "He wasn't for a long time. He had a year of rehab, all on Master's dime. Master oversaw all of his treatment. Master communicated with him daily by email and text. Zanti never talked but he would respond to Master through letters. The only communication I've ever heard of. He doesn't write anything for me. Doesn't even try to sign. But with Master, he did. It's in his file. The letters between them. I am the only one who's seen them. But after what happened to you… that's never happened before. Zanti isn't really violent. And he never has had an orgasm that I have ever known of. This, you coming here, it's changed things. Zanti is weird, but he doesn't hurt people. Aaron told me it was like a rape for you and I saw your face when you came downstairs after that night. I'm sorry but I don't know what happened. Master let it happen for some reason. But you came back hurt. And Zanti hasn't been the same. And you need to know that. Master told me you needed to know the background, at least."

Ren's shoulders hunched. He wasn't sure what to feel. And he certainly didn't like the idea that maybe he had disrupted the harem. Had Master done all this on purpose? "All that happened was a stupid play. A story. Zanti was the star. He liked it. Until I touched him."

"Until you touched him?"

"Yes. He didn't like me to touch him."

"He doesn't like to be touched. But he will for Master's sake and he's used to the others. He will obey anything Master tells him to do. But him not liking *your* touch… well, that's not what the others are saying. He liked your touch too much."

"I don't care what they're saying. He hates me and I don't know why. Master didn't tell him to hurt me. He did that for revenge or something." He didn't want to say anymore. He didn't want to talk to Cam.

"I know Master didn't tell him to hurt you. It was you he reacted to. And he doesn't hate you. He's dealing with the fact that you made him feel."

"Maybe he doesn't want to feel." Ren's skin heated. He tried to keep his voice down.

"You touched him and that can't be undone. What he wants and what he feels are a conflict for someone like him."

"The others touched him."

"Yes, but you *touched* him. I repeat, he doesn't like to be touched. Not even by me. He follows me around, hangs around me a lot, I guess he likes me in his way. We are a *thing* as you described it, but not in a sexual way. He sleeps with me once in a while if he can't sleep alone that night. He trusts me. But we're still not all that close. But he does not like to be touched beyond that, in a sexual way, except in a play for Master it's okay because he's a character. Not himself. But you touched *him*. That's what happened. From what I hear, anyway."

Ren re-played the moment in his mind, even though it was the last thing he wanted to think of. How Zanti's aura had burst to pinks and lavenders. Pleasure centers on overload.

"Zanti liked it," Ren whispered, but not with pride. Zanti had liked it, but had not given consent. He'd made a mistake, then. He'd read Zanti wrong, all the colors, the auras of Zanti spoke a different language, one Ren did not himself speak.

Cam gulped. "That's the problem. He liked it but maybe he doesn't like that he liked it. So you got the brunt of his frustration. And I just wanted you to understand."

It was a lot for Ren to take in. All he could think to say was what he'd already said. "He shouldn't be here."

"Master invited him. He accepted. But like I said, Master rescued him. Master is everything to him. All of this…" Cam gestured about the atrium. "He didn't ever in his entire life consent like we did to being a pleasure slave. He doesn't have a brand like the rest of us. There's the reason."

Ren's eyebrows rose. "You told me it was because he was so strange you thought he would freak out at the pain."

"I lied. It's about consent. It's about Zanti and his rescue and everything else. Do you understand now?"

"No. I don't understand. I still don't know why Master would have him here in the harem. It seems wrong."

"Zanti is safe here. He can relax here. He's like the wiriest, slipperiest guy, but on rare nights he curls against me and relaxes. Finally. He can sleep. He doesn't dream. He's safe. He's as happy as he'll ever get. He would not survive out in the real world. This is what he knows. This is familiar to him. As long as it's safe. He'll play roles, but as Zanti himself, he does not play with the rest of us."

"But why did Master—" Ren was going to ask how Master could have let the play get as far as it did, with Zanti's actions turning toward sexual assault.

"Master doesn't control Zanti," Cam said as if reading his mind. "I'm sorry about what happened to you. And on your first visit upstairs. But I have looked at your profile and I know you were bought and brought here for reasons more than just Master's whim. What I mean is, I saw you with the other guys. Li Po. Jaxon and Calder. You're different. You're very special with that talent of yours. You said Zanti liked it when you touched him. That's not normal for him. And there is the reason, perhaps, that you are here."

"For Zanti?"

Cam nodded.

No. It couldn't be. Ren thought about the play, about the evil count who'd bought Zanti and kept him to try to break through to him. No one could touch Zanti. Until Ren in his mask came forward. The play had been more than just a play. A carefully planned metaphor? A test?

"Aaron told me Zanti came," Cam said. "Uh, orgasmed. Zanti doesn't do that. He can get hard, but he doesn't ejaculate. He doesn't finish. Not even for Master's plays. He performs. He's pretty and he does what he's told. He can make the others come." Cam smiled wistfully. "But he doesn't do that himself. Come, I mean."

It would have been nice if Ren had known this beforehand. Keeping him in the dark did him no favors. And now, with this new information, what was he supposed to do about it?

When Ren did not immediately reply, Cam sat forward. "So now you know."

Ren could only nod. The information was too much all at once. He had made Zanti respond. Come. How was that even a good thing? It had obviously made Zanti hate him all the more.

Finally, he spoke. "I don't know what you want me to do about this information. Zanti should stay away from me, of course, if he doesn't want to feel. And he should not be part of any plays. Master should know this. But Zanti should also be made to understand that none of this is my fault. He did try to hurt me— No, he *did* hurt me."

"I know. I know." Cam held his hand up. "So we all have to live together here in somewhat harmony. I do my best to orient newcomers, putting in requests, supplying Master with reports."

"Reports?"

"Yes. I submit one very day."

"About us?"

"All of us, yes. It's my job."

The change of subject helped Ren focus. More questions pummeled his thoughts. "But you have actually never met Master?"

"No. I spoke the truth about that before. I haven't. Not me. Not any of us. Except I think Zanti has. I can't know for sure. If I ask him direct questions like that—anything to do with Master— even though he trusts me, he won't even nod or shake his head. I can get him to acknowledge liking a movie, or if he's hungry, but that's about the extent of it."

How had the conversation gotten back to Zanti? Unable to let go of his resentment, Ren focused his interest on Master.

"You put in requests to Master." Ren did not form his statement as a question. "Put this one in. *Ren would like to meet Master.*"

Cam let out a long, low laugh. The skin around his eyes wrinkled, clueing Ren into the fact that Cam was older than he let on. Maybe as old as thirty. But he wore make up to soften his features, and his hair was so bright and thick and curly it gave him a boyish demeanor.

"Everyone asks that at some point," Cam replied. "Everyone except Zanti, of course."

"And their requests are refused."

"Well, duh."

"Put mine in anyway. I don't want to be left out," Ren said.

Cam tapped his table half-heartedly.

Ren said, "Do you know why Master sees no one?"

"Only gossip and theories, so no."

Ren sensed movement behind him, and turned. Zanti was sidling up to Cam, a rather vicious look to him, which was normal. But still. Vicious was the only word Ren could think to describe it. Or feral. He liked that word. Wild. Untamed. It did not excuse Zanti's behavior, but gave some reason to it.

But more words quickly came to him as he kept his gaze averted. Ethereal. Devilish beauty. Bewitching, striking, dazzling asshole. And surviving victim of a notorious serial killer.

Had Zanti been eavesdropping on their conversation?

His heart skipped, then quickened. He blinked hard.

"Zanti," said Cam in a welcoming voice. "Ren and I were just talking."

Zanti's chest rose as he took a deep breath and held it. His eyes flickered. His aura remained dark, almost solid black. Ren could not read him.

Zanti's gaze switched from Cam to Ren and back to Cam. His mouth was a tight line.

Ren said, "I'm sorry if I ever made you feel uncomfortable."

Zanti's eyes filled, but the tears were like angry sparks, not sadness, not forgiveness.

"Zanti," Cam said softly. "Nothing Ren does here is his fault. You know that. You hurt him. Ren has apologized. Can you? Maybe just shake his hand."

Ren watched the man. He looked as if he were about to explode with emotion.

Zanti lifted his hand, then batted at the air.

"Zanti." Cam cocked his hip. "Come on. We all have to get along. And Ren is new. We need to help him fit in."

Zanti crossed his arms over his chest and turned away.

Ren stood quickly. A hurt came over him, turning to annoyance. "I'll tell you what. I'll just stay away from him."

Zanti turned back to look at him, brows narrowed as if he were the hurt one.

"What?" Ren held his hands to his sides, palms up.

"Well," Cam said. "If you're rejecting him it just makes things more awkward."

"I'm not. He's rejecting me."

"Zanti? Is that true?" Cam asked.

Zanti let out a whoosh of breath and turned his head so his long bangs slapped across his face.

"I'm not rejecting you," Ren said again.

Zanti shook his arms, his beautiful body shuddering in response.

"Well, that's my answer," Ren said. "I'll stay away from him. And if Master calls us again, I'll protest it."

"You can't."

"I will." Ren turned. "I'm going for a swim. Don't forget. Tell Master to think about a garden for us. I want a garden. I don't care if it takes a year like Aaron's piano. And please put in the request that I also want to meet him."

Cam tapped his tablet screen again.

Zanti glared at him as he moved away. Ren pretended not to notice. But he couldn't help but hear a strange sort of hum that came from Zanti's direction.

What the fuck? Was the man growling at him?

Despite Ren's conviction to dismiss the guy, and not care, his spine tingled and stiffened at the sound. The body's instinctive response to a threat. But Zanti was not a threat, was he?

His thoughts fumed. He held no ill will toward anyone. Ever. Not at the Palace and not here. He'd had rough sex plenty of times and held no grudges because of it. But Zanti—even now that he knew more from his talk with Cam, for some reason it only made things more complicated.

Ren saw Li Po walking toward the pool, and called out to him. "Swim?"

Li Po gave him a thumbs up.

Together they met by the side of the pool and dived in.

The cool water muffled all sound. Ren's vision blurred. The only auras underwater were refractions of real light rays shattering as his legs and arms broke the liquid surface.

With Li Po beside him as comfort, Ren swam laps with powerful strokes until he was worn out, until he couldn't think anymore.

Chapter Eighteen

Fight

Daylight stabbed its silvery rays through the open window.

Two nights in a row, Master had called for men from his harem, three at a time. First the twins and Tomo. Second, Aaron along with Calder and Jaxon. But not Ren.

Maybe Master had heard Ren and Cam's conversation. Or maybe Cam had put it in his report that it was best of Master kept Ren and Zanti apart.

The ones called had returned with sexually satisfied grins on their faces. All fucked out.

Li Po said to him, when Ren mentioned feeling a twinge of rejection. "There are some of us not called for as much as a year. Then suddenly we're requested several nights in a row. It doesn't matter really, does it?"

Ren shrugged. It did to him. He wanted to live for Master. Be everything for Master. He was perfectly fine playing with the others. But he could not feel that somehow this feeling of being left out was about Zanti.

Li Po smiled and reminded him, "There are cameras hidden everywhere. Everything we do here is a show. Seen by him." He grinned. "When you have sex with me, he's probably watching."

Ren lifted his chin. "You're right." He smiled at Li Po's sweet face. "That's a great idea. Let's make him watch right now."

Li Po took his hand and pulled him to a wide, soft couch. They were good together. Really good. Who wouldn't want to watch?

Well, one person who watched was Zanti. Again. And he scowled at Ren when their gazes met. Then he flipped him off.

"What the fuck did I do?" Ren murmured. He was incensed. He scowled back, shaking his head hard.

"What?" Li Po asked. He hadn't seen.

"Nothing." But it disturbed him greatly. The mad boy had it out for him, and for nothing he had willingly done to him. If Zanti thought he rejected him, he needed to be told otherwise.

Ren decided to have another talk with Cam. Later.

After Ren and Li Po finished making love, they rested in each other's arms, then took a dip in the pool.

Ren held his breath and swam the full length of the pool underwater, feeling his chest expand, his muscles burn with an enticing tingle, encased and enchanted by the water's embrace. It comforted and calmed him. Everything was white and blue, bright and cool. Clean and chlorine fresh. In this moment, he did not long for a different life. This was good. He felt accepted, even somewhat loved by Li Po although they weren't really in love. Maybe things might escalate to that. If he couldn't have Master's hands-on love, he could have Li Po. Li Po did not have the penchant for taking charge that Ren might like, but sex was good with him. Great, even.

Propelled by a new energy at his thoughts, Ren did not stop at the pool's wall for a breath, but pushed himself off in the other direction to see how far he'd get holding his breath. Could he do two lengths?

The opposite end came closer and closer. He was letting out little bubbles from his nose, but he knew he'd make it. It was shallower here. His feet hit the bottom and he popped himself up like a dolphin, water showering from his body as he gasped for air.

He heard echoes of a voice. Master's. But he'd missed the command. But most of the men of the harem had gathered and as Ren stood dripping in the water, clutching the side of the pool, they turned their heads to stare at him, eyebrows raised or narrowed, mouths in tight thin lines or opened in some strange look of disbelief.

"What?" he said breathlessly. "I'm not…"

Before he could finish, or even register that something had happened that concerned him, that Master's voice had given a command which he had not heard, Zanti strode toward him so quickly he did not have time to react.

Cam, not seeing Zanti at first, wiggled his tablet in the air. "You and Zanti have been called. Shall I make a protest?"

"What?" He looked from Cam to Zanti, whose face fell. Then anger blackened his aura and white sparks flew from the edges.

Ren looked up at him as Zanti approached the side of the pool. Angry fairy. Wicked imp. Aura like pitch surrounding that beautiful body, those beguiling eyes.

"Get away! I've done nothing to you! I would think *you* would want to protest!"

Quick as a blink, Zanti's foot came up and smashed itself into Ren's chin, sending him reeling backward. Well what the fuck did the guy want, then? He heard Cam's startled voice. "Zanti! Stop!"

Without really thinking, the water buoyant enough to delay his fall, Ren snatched at that foot trying to avoid it, and pulled Zanti into the pool on top of him.

The splash sent a million water droplets into the air. The liquid of the pool's surface enfolded them both as they flailed, arms out, Zanti's legs kicking at Ren as he went under, butt first.

Ren came up, braids whipping the water that flashed about his head. Zanti's body was already launching himself at him, like a fish, and down they went, the water pushing at them as they sank. Water got up Ren's nose and stung. In a burst of bubbles, he gave an underwater cry and shoved, but Zanti's arms were already coming about his shoulders, his hands at Ren's throat.

Cam's very short list of rules came back to him. *No fighting in the harem.* Cam had said men had been permanently removed from the harem for fighting, for violence. But Zanti had an edge. He was a favorite. The rescued orphan. The tortured boy from a serial killer's cage.

Zanti was not here by his own will, but through some agreed-to plan of Master's that was different from why Ren and the others were here. They were all pleasure slaves. Except Zanti. Zanti pretended. Zanti obeyed Master's commands. But he was different. The rules were different for him.

It dawned on Ren, even as he fought for the surface, for breath amid Zanti's crazed attack, that Zanti was exempt from being banned from the harem, or taken away, or sold. But Ren was not. Was Zanti manipulating Ren in an effort to get Ren tossed for good?

The two men came up to the surface, gasping. Zanti had his hands around Ren's throat. Ren gripped his forearms, fingernails digging in. In the distance, men yelled but Ren could not determine if they were frightened voices, or excited and encouraging the fight.

A louder voice came through the din, strained but deep. Cam's voice. "Stop! Stop this at once! Zanti! Ren! Stop!"

The water frothed and lapped the sides of the pool in great waves, some swells arching over the tiles just enough to get the closest men wet.

Zanti was a slippery, feisty devil, surprisingly strong. Ren could feel his own throat closing. The hands at his neck clenched hard but they were both wet and luckily Zanti could not get enough purchase to go any further with his attempt to strangle Ren.

Ren bounced on the water's surface, kicking up to keep them from both going under again. He flailed, hitting Zanti in the chest and face. Zanti's grip gave way and his fingers slid down Ren's chest, scratching over his still tender brand, making Ren livid.

It was simply too unlucky for him—or ironic, perhaps—that he'd just been feeling good, calm, and content to be part of this harem-family. Now this. It was so unfair!

Ren bobbed back in the water and Zanti smashed his palms hard on the surface, legs pumping, moving toward him.

Cam continued to yell. Men's voices echoed words of disbelief. "He's crazy!" "This won't end well." "Look at him go!"

Ren backed up more in the water, but Zanti was an unexpectedly fast swimmer. They met again, hands clashing, bodies wrestling and went under again, both coming up sputtering. Ren shouted between breaths. "You crazy fuck!"

He never bullied, or called others bad names. Not even when he was a kid. But right now, on this day, in this harem, he couldn't help himself. *You crazy fuck.* He should not have said it. He felt bad. Zanti was a victim. This wasn't his fault. But then Zanti shouldn't be in the harem. It was Master's fault for putting him with the rest of them.

Cam was still calling. "Zanti! Zanti!"

Suddenly there was more motion. White on white. Bodies. Splashes.

Ren could not comprehend any of it until he realized he was being held by another man dressed in a white shirt and white shorts. A groom. And Zanti, hissing and spitting and panting, was being held by another groom.

The grooms wrangled them both from the pool, all four of them soaked and dripping on the tiles. Zanti still fought, but Ren held himself back, no longer giving any fight to the groom who held him.

Ren looked about him and saw all the other men standing in a semi-circle, watching. Cam was crying. "This is wrong. So wrong." His tablet lay at his feet, the glass shattered, puddles of water seeping around it, and Li Po was absently petting his hair.

Ren was still mystified. What had happened? Why had Zanti attacked him? He gazed about him. Everyone watched him. The groom still held his arms behind his back.

Calder stepped forward, cheeks flushed, eyes wide. "If you didn't hear it, Master called you upstairs."

"I know. Some of us have been called." Cam had re-stated the order when Ren had surfaced for all to hear.

"He called you and Zanti. Just you two. No one else," Calder finished.

Him and Zanti. Alone. Well, yeah. That was just nuts.

Unbidden, an image of Master Locke came to him. If Locke could see him now, dripping and enraged, would he be disappointed? Why it mattered to Ren in that moment what Locke might think, Ren didn't know. But just that thought, that image of Locke in his regal stance, with his powerful dark gaze made Ren calm down.

But before Ren could say anything, the groom still holding him spoke. "Come with me."

The groom gave a tug on Ren's arms, holding them tight by the wrists. The guy was slightly shorter than Ren, but strong. It didn't matter. Ren wasn't going to resist.

The groom shoved him toward the entrance behind the waterfall where the door to the room of masks stood open.

He heard shuffling behind him, and beneath the constant fall of water, bare feet hitting tile. A voice said, "Cooperate or you will be bound."

Ren glanced over his shoulder to see Zanti in the grip of the second groom, the fiend half-heartedly trying to pull away.

Ren wondered if the groom might really tie Zanti's hands and feet together and then carry him. He surely looked strong enough. But Zanti, still shrugging and tugging at the groom's grip, complied enough to walk on his own two feet.

Past the threshold and into the room of masks they went. Ren thought they might stop there and get a scolding from Master through all the hidden speakers. But they kept going until they reached the porch, then down the steps and along the path that led to Niko's house.

Ren's skin prickled at the thought his first and only visit to that house. His brand itched, the supreme pain of it still fresh in his memory. Niko had talked about punishments for misbehavior. Whippings, even.

Was this where they were headed?

But certainly not for Zanti. Nothing so extreme for the boy who survived Mister X.

They walked along the flowered path, the green of the grass between the buildings and along the hillside so brilliant it hurt the eyes. Birds called. The sunlight was warm and yellow. Ren blinked at the glare.

As they walked up to the tiny porch of Niko's house, Ren's groom opened the door with a key. Niko was nowhere to be seen.

The grooms led Ren and a somewhat subdued Zanti through the front living area and down the hall to the large shower room. There they met two more white-clad grooms waiting with soaps and towels, the huge shower already turned on and steaming.

With a few sharp commands, the grooms ordered them both into the shower. Ren stayed as far away from Zanti as he could.

The grooms washed them all over with handfuls of liquid soap that smelled of deep summer and overgrown gardens. The enema tube was stuck into Ren first, and he nervously made his way to the toilet.

Zanti made a soft cry as he was similarly dealt with.

Ren stood by his groom drying off while Zanti suffered and glared.

When they were clean and dried, the grooms escorted them into the next room where Ren had gotten the brand. His muscles tensed. He felt his breathing quicken.

Inside the room was a long, black couch Ren had not seen on his first visit. His groom shoved him onto it at one end. Zanti's groom pushed him to sit at the other end.

Another groom approached with a tray of two drinks. Ice water in wine glasses where the condensation was already beading. Ren took one.

When Zanti was offered his own glass, he shoved at the tray and turned his head, his wet dark hair falling into his eyes. His collar chimed with his fast breaths.

Ren was thirsty so he sipped at the cold water, feeling it go all the way down into his body.

The four grooms stood, arms crossed, watching them. Two were on Zanti's side of the couch, two on Ren's.

There was no sound in the room but their breathing, both men still huffing a little. Ren's heart hammered, nerves on edge. Even though the shower had cleansed his body, he'd begun to sweat again.

Minutes passed and the guards said nothing, did nothing. They just watched them, their auras muddy with indifference.

Zanti, back stiff, hands clenched into fists, looked ready to pounce. Ren had his own hands clasped on his lap.

They waited.

Finally, footsteps sounded in the hallway.

Black bowtie, white shirt crisp and new, black slacks perfectly creased and shoes polished to a dark shine, Niko entered the room. The table with all of its implements—the branding iron and other things Ren could not recognize or define—had been pushed against one wall. But it was still there. Would Niko go to it and choose something among the collection to punish them?

Elegant as a prince, Niko walked to stand in front of the center of the couch, hands behind his back, and stood looking from Ren to Zanti. The grooms now flanked him like guards.

Niko said, "You do not have the power to decline. There will be no protests of Master's orders through Cam or in any other manner." He glanced at each of them in turn again.

Ren looked away from Niko and at his naked knees. The glass of cold water in his hand felt heavier and heavier until he thought he'd drop it.

"Master has called upon you two. You will go upstairs together. You will cooperate. You will not lay a hand on each other until or unless Master orders it. Do you understand?"

Ren's hand shook a little and his glass of water sloshed over his thumb, the ice pinging. Did they not understand he had not started the fight?

He nodded once, looking up. Niko's brows were narrowed. He looked quite powerful and severe. For a moment, he wondered if Niko was playing a role, if he was really Master masquerading as the butler-guy. But no, Niko's inflections were off, the tone of this voice and accent all different. Niko had an aura of placid blues mixed with infusions of gold. That did not mean he wasn't capable of telling lies, only that he appeared momentarily complacent while doing his job to bring two slaves into line.

The end of one of Ren's braids, still damp, dripped onto his thigh. With his free hand he wiped the water away, while trying to see out the corner of his eye if Zanti might also agree to Niko's demand.

Zanti's posture never changed. His fists were jammed into his thighs. He faced away from Ren enough that Ren could see the knobs of his spine. For a moment, he remembered touching him, that hard body, that silken skin. Zanti had liked it because Ren could see the pathway of lights that even Zanti, who hated to be touched, exuded. He could see the areas where Zanti's body secretly longed for at least a soothing caress. But it didn't matter. Synesthesia aside, seeing or tasting lights and auras or not, this would not be easy. If Zanti wanted him, it might be different.

Niko moved to stand in front of Zanti. "Zanti, you will behave. You do not wish Master to place you elsewhere, do you?"

Zanti's only response was to take a slow breath and part his lips to let it slowly out.

Niko went on. "If you disobey," he turned to look at Ren, "either of you, the grooms will see to your immediate punishment." He walked to the long table with all the tools and devices and picked up two long tubes, not unlike that which had branded Ren.

A heat of prickling adrenalin threatened Ren's veins.

Niko handed the tubes to two of the grooms, who held them firmly at their sides as if they'd used them before and knew what to do.

"What are those?" Ren asked.

"They produce an electrical charge. If either of you is out of line, they are instructed to use them. You won't like it, believe me," Niko replied sternly.

Ren looked down again. He saw three raised welts on his chest from Zanti's scratches. They didn't hurt, nor had the skin been broken, but they were pink and a testament to the fact that they'd been fighting.

Surely Master would never torture Zanti with a device like that. Especially after rescuing him. But Zanti's cooperation was not a given.

"So," Niko said. "Do we have a problem?"

"No, sir," Ren replied. He put his glass to his lips and drank another sip of the cold water.

Zanti remained stiff and still. His chest rose and fell with deep breaths. Apparently, that was good enough for Niko.

"Very well, then. You are prepared. No make up. Let your hair dry naturally. Ren, your braids are a bit unkempt but Master has given no instruction that they be undone."

Niko motioned for both men to rise. The grooms stood at attention. Two for Ren. Two for Zanti. Less like grooms, more like bodyguards. Or enforcers.

Ren quickly stood, but Zanti was slow, almost lazy in his obedience. His dark eyes flashed about the room and his mouth curled as if he'd just eaten something bitter.

The grooms escorted them down the long hall where shadows swept their feet and the air was very still. Ren thought he heard Niko, left behind in the branding room, chuckle. Or maybe it was the air ventilation system kicking on. He couldn't be sure.

Chapter Nineteen

Upstairs

They went into the mansion by a different entrance, this time around the side of the house and toward a smaller back porch.

Ren knew this was intentional so they would not have to go through the harem atrium itself. Maybe Niko or Master thought Zanti would get worked up again? Whatever it was, Master wanted no more disruption, that much was obvious.

Two steps up led to a single black door that opened onto a black and white checkered floor and a wide hall. Small round lights dotted the ceiling. Several closed doors on the left made Ren speculate as to what was behind them.

They came to a staircase at the end of the hall. It was wide but curved upward. Its steps were carpeted in a thick, flowered pattern and cushioned Ren's bare feet. The only sound made was the quiet footfalls of the four grooms and two slaves, and the faint jingle of Ren and Zanti's slave collars.

At the top of the curving staircase they came to the second floor where Ren had been brought the last time. But they were at the other end of the long hall that Ren had only glimpsed twice. The two grooms leading the group opened the second door. They all walked into a large bedroom with a huge bed splashed in pale lavender and white spreads and pillows. It stood in the center of the entirely white room. White carpet, white curtains, white walls and white coffered ceiling. It was like walking into a world of froth and snow. The bed was like the pale, flowering centerpiece.

The scent was fresh like just cut fruit, apple and pear, as if the room had been newly set up and thoroughly cleaned, the carpet wet-vacuumed, the linens air-dried and everything sprayed down with that soft, fruity fragrance.

Ren's stomach grumbled and he realized they were missing dinner.

The bed had a headboard, white-cushioned, and dripping from its upper corners were sparkly, gold chains that ended with lambs-wool lined white leather cuffs. More gold chains and cuffs were draped across the bed's foot as well. For the ankles.

Ren shut his eyes a moment. He did not want to think about having sex with Zanti when he was so angry. But for Master he would do anything, of course. Besides, he had a long-term agenda. He wanted to eventually meet the guy. And he was determined to do it if he had to seduce his way through the entire harem, the grooms, and even Niko himself.

He opened his eyes and glanced to his left. Zanti stood flanked by two grooms, his head back, staring with a frozen, bored look at the ceiling. Distant and often pissed. That was Zanti.

The room was well-lit, but the curtains drawn, their filmy, layered materials like ghosts upon ghosts looking on, blocking the outside dusk.

For about thirty seconds they all waited. The stillness overtook the room, and the mind, even for that short amount of time. Was Master even around?

Finally a breathy sound moved about the room. The speakers had been turned on.

"Welcome, Zanti. Welcome, Ren."

Were they supposed to respond? Zanti could not. Or would not. Ren had no idea what to do. At least this time he wasn't wearing a mask. Or a cock cage.

"You may proceed." Master's voice rang out, slightly mechanical as always, low-toned and melodic.

Ren turned to see if the grooms could make sense of the order. One was already moving toward the bed, lifting one of the wrist-cuffs. The other flanking Zanti said to him, "You. Move to the bed and sit so your wrist can be cuffed."

Ren's grooms stood back, waiting.

Zanti whirled away from his groom like a haughty child and marched toward the bed, head held high. He did not sit as instructed. Instead, he lifted his wrist toward the other groom, palm up.

The groom reached up with the cuff and Zanti's hand shot up. He acted as if he was going to hit the groom, but he didn't. His hand waved in the air. He jiggled his pretty rump and stepped back.

The other groom said. "Cooperate."

Zanti had his lower lip caught between his white teeth, as if holding back a grin. He was playing with the grooms, teasing them, Ren realized.

The second groom behind Zanti said curtly, "Sit!"

Zanti turned toward him, made his body curve as if flaunting his beauty while at the same time goading the groom.

Ren wanted to protest right then. How could anything ever work with Zanti? But of course they were going to chain him so he would stay put. Ren didn't like the idea of it, but okay, it might be necessary. But why Zanti if he didn't want to be there? He could not imagine, now that he knew about Zanti's past, touching him as he was chained to the bed.

"Master?" Ren asked to the room at large. "Please. May I ask you why?"

The groom nearest Ren threatened him with the tube. "You will be silent and follow Master's orders. No questions!"

Ren stiffened, eyes on the bed.

Zanti tossed his pretty head, his hair settling around him like liquid. And that aura of his, so dark and grim. Coal-red scars sliced it open here and there. The edges were jagged as if it wasn't made of light but of thin slices of onyx stone, broken. His streamlined body, so slim and burnished the goldest shade of brown ever seen, undulated to tease and taunt. It was as if he wasn't human, and not just in appearance, but in spirit. In his heart. And after what Cam had told him Zanti had been through, how could he be human any longer? No, he'd been transformed. But to what?

A pang of empathy, or maybe it was pity, strummed lightly inside Ren's stomach. Mixed with his dislike of Zanti, it only irritated him.

Zanti played the grooms well. He lightly dodged each man as they tried to grasp him. He did not run or attack or show any alarm. He just played. This went on for some time.

Finally, a groom said, voice raised in frustration, "You will sit or you'll get the tube!" He held up the shocker device.

Zanti backed up, light on his feet, bouncing on his toes. A fairy child grown adult in a human world.

The groom, clearly frustrated, lunged.

Zanti's aura abruptly went white. His mouth opened. His eyes rolled up. Maybe he was going to faint, but the groom kept coming forward, and now the tube emitted an orange light that hissed.

Ren saw Zanti change, but the grooms did not. All they saw was the spoiled, brat boy acting like he owned the mansion and all of them as well.

Maybe Ren did not want to be up here with Zanti, but suddenly he didn't like to see the groom threaten a broken boy with pain even if he deserved it. He didn't think. He just reacted. They were only a few feet away.

Ren found himself leaping in front of the groom with the tube. "Stop!" That was how he found himself between Zanti and the groom.

The groom looked livid.

Ren was confused. A part of him, still smarting from the fight, wanted to see Zanti punished. But the other part had seen the black aura for too long, the damaged boy. That was the part that acted without thought, on auto-pilot.

Zanti reached out and touched Ren on the shoulder. Then he pushed Ren, not hard but not gently, and shook his head back and forth.

But Ren stood his ground, until the groom lowered the tube.

In that moment, as Ren turned to see if his other grooms were moving to get him back in line, he saw Zanti jump onto the bed with a smug smile, ass first, body bouncing, and hold out his arms like a sacrificial god.

The groom with the tube stuck the instrument in his belt, walked around Ren and fastened the cuffs about Zanti's wrists. He turned to the ankles. Zanti teased him some more, pulling his feet away, but his glittering, brat gaze, as if it was all a joke on them, never left his face.

Now Zanti sat on the bed, back against the pillowed headboard, wrists and ankles cuffed, looking again like the prince who owned the place. The chains did not strain. He was as comfortable-looking as a trained dog on a leash. Only Zanti wasn't trained. Or so Cam said.

The omniscient breath went around the room again. "Forty-five. Six. Eleven. Nineteen. Leave."

Ren watched the dismissed grooms line up and exit the room. Numbers. They were numbers. Ren could not help himself. He looked up at the ceiling as if that was where Master, the mystery man, might be. "They don't have names?"

A rush like a breeze. Maybe a slight crackle. Zanti was staring at Ren with cool detachment, but the smirk was gone.

Through the speakers, the voice. "Those are their names."

"Numbers," Ren said quietly. He wasn't trying to argue. Was he? He was mostly annoyed and, worse, trying not to fume at now being alone in the room, *upstairs,* with Zanti.

Ren stood very still, looking everywhere but at the bed. Yet he could not help but *see* Zanti. The man's aura was no longer the shocking white it flashed to when Zanti reacted to the threat of the tube. Nor was it back to black. It grayed about him in a jagged halo. Gray, to Ren's mind, meant a person was unsure, conflicted or confused.

Master did not speak. They waited. Ren shifted his weight from foot to foot, his braids slithering about his shoulders. The silver dangles of his collar were cool against his chest. Zanti sat still as a sculpture.

Minutes passed.

Able to take it no longer, Ren said to the room, "Are there orders?"

The answer came quick. Surround-sound. "Do as you wish." There was a sound like a snick and the silence of the room deepened. The speakers had been turned off.

What did that mean? They were here to put on a show. But they had not been specifically told how. Or what to do.

Do as you wish.

What if what he wished was to do nothing?

But that would not impress Master.

"This is ridiculous," Ren said to no one. He crossed his arms in front of him. He turned away from the bed. Chains clinked.

Ren refused to turn to see if Zanti was moving. His stomach rumbled again. This was the dinner hour. They had nothing. There was a bathroom off to the left, door open. It would have water and that would be it.

Was this a test to see who could outwait whom the longest?

Ren hung his head. Chewed his lip. It was hard to know how fast or slow time passed in the harem, let alone here in this white room.

Ren turned to the bed again with his brow furrowed, eyes half-closed. Zanti reclined amid lavender and white, a trapped nixie-thing, his demeanor showing no frustration at all now. His aura was still gray. He looked completely relaxed, perfect in line and form, skin unblemished, stomach lean and flat, hips narrow. His cock was flaccid and pink against slightly darker, perfectly round balls. Beauty made of hate. Beauty without a soul. No colors zipped about his skin. Nothing Ren could see yet, anyway. Zanti stared straight ahead as if looking at something no one but Zanti could see.

There were no scars on him at all. Cam had been right. Zanti's scars were internal. You could not see them. But you could feel them in his looks, his behavior, his lack of a voice.

"You're at my mercy now," Ren said coolly.

All Zanti did was blink.

"Why did you attack me? I've done nothing to you. You're the one who hurt me. Why do you hate me?"

Zanti's brows furrowed slightly. His aura did not change.

"If Master thinks this is some way for me to take revenge upon you, he's wrong. I won't." Why did he say that? To let Zanti know that he could but didn't want to? Maybe.

"I don't want to touch you want me to," Ren said.

Zanti blinked and stared. Sometimes the chains gave a little rattle. The speakers in the room remained silent.

"You hurt me," Ren said. His teeth were gritted now as he spoke. "Intentionally. I am a stranger here. Unsure. You knew that. You made me feel even more unwelcome. But okay. Maybe you had your reasons. I know more now than I did before. Cam told me quite a bit about your history."

Zanti's head tilted but he did not look at Ren. He did not smirk or scowl or hide a smile. But his eyes flashed. Not a glitter like usual, but something else.

Ren was conflicted. He didn't want to think about what all Zanti had gone through in his short life. But he did. He couldn't imagine the terror, the horror. Pain. Waiting for death which would be preferable to anything else. But Zanti had not been rewarded with death. His stay in Mister X's dungeon had been longest. He'd had to live. That was the torture.

"I'm sorry that happened to you," Ren said softly.

Zanti hissed and turned his head away.

160

"I won't do anything. I won't touch you. Master said to do as we wish. I don't wish to touch someone who doesn't want to be touched."

Zanti tilted his head all the way back and gave out a long, hard sigh, almost a moan.

Ren realized he was looking over Zanti's head now to a point in his aura where a sort of heart-shaped red mass formed. It had an inner glow and two white spots on it like distant stars. It was not bright red like lust or pleasure, but like a burn on skin that might never heal. A weird anomaly. It glared like Zanti often did, those two white stars within the redness like eyes. The shape hovered in his aura like a misplaced thing, a monster caught in a net.

He couldn't imagine what Zanti had been through. But why take it out on him?

Zanti did not like that Ren had made him come. Ren figured that out easily. If he didn't want to feel, why not leave him alone? And yet here Master had put him, with Zanti, and then gave the order: *Do as you wish.*

Still confused, Ren decided to sit. But not on the bed. Instead, he lowered himself to the floor, the carpet soft against his backside. He crossed his legs and leaned against the side of the bed.

For a while, he worried a hangnail on his thumb. He listened to Zanti not moving on the bed. He rubbed the balls of his feet on the plush rug.

"I suppose I'll just sit here for awhile. You can't get mad at me for that, can you?" Ren asked.

More time passed. Ren had his hands clasped in his lap and realized, as he looked down, they were trembling. Nerves, of course. The unknown always made him wary. He could do as he wished. Master's orders.

"I don't know what to do. So. I guess I'll just mumble to myself. Although I don't mind the quiet."

He waited. When he heard no movement from the bed, he continued. "I read auras around people and on their bodies. I can see where and how to touch others for maximum pleasure, which is an asset as a slave. Except with you, I guess. You're hard to read. Your aura is usually very black. Black is all colors at once, you know."

Still no response from the bed.

Ren took another deep breath. "Why did you kick me in the pool?" He thought about his question. "Do you hate me because I made you feel?"

He heard a hiss from above. He stayed still, not looking. He didn't want to see that red monster in the aura again.

"If I had known you were going to respond badly, I would have changed my course that night during the play. I would have touched inexpertly. I would have worked hard to cause no response in you. I can do that, you know. I can touch you opposite of what the colors of your aura show me. I can see where you don't want touch and deplete arousal. I just never thought of doing that before now."

The covers of the bed shifted.

Ren wanted to peek but remained still. He concentrated on breathing for a long time.

Finally, he said, "I don't want there to be bad energy between us. I don't. I want you do know that. If you want to fight me, fine. But I won't fight back. Okay?"

Nothing.

Quite tired now, Ren wondered if he could get up, pound on the door and alert a groom. Maybe they'd let them go back to the atrium and have a late dinner.

But he didn't do that. Certainly Master was watching or they wouldn't still be in this room.

Ren closed his eyes and a doze came over him.

He woke with a start. He glanced about him. How much time had passed? The room, still white on white, still warm, hadn't changed. He could tell only by the slight darkening of the curtains where they covered the rectangle of the window that it was full dark out.

Ren glanced over the side of the bed and saw Zanti on his side facing away from him, his arm at an angle where the cuff pulled the chain taut. He couldn't tell if he was sleeping or not.

A growl erupted. Ren's stomach. He was hungry and thirsty. He could do something about the thirst, at least. He got up and went into the bathroom. He used the facilities and then cupped his hands under the sink faucet and drank the cool water.

The bathroom was also white, with white towels and white tile and a short, white rug. He was careful to make everything stay right and clean, using one of the towels to wipe up the water drops he'd spilled on the countertop. He folded the towel neatly and put it back in place.

Zanti was staring at him as Ren came back into the room. His aura was gray. Not content but not angry. The red monster was gone.

Ren started to look away, but then thought Zanti also might be thirsty, or have to pee. He approached the bed. Zanti's eyes moved, tracking his every move.

Ren reached out to Zanti's wrist to undo the cuff. Zanti pulled back an inch, then stopped.

Ren shrugged. "It's fine. I just thought you might have to pee."

Zanti frowned, took a breath and held out his arm. Ren undid the cuff, then walked to the foot of the bed and undid the anklets. Lastly, he unfastened the second wrist cuff.

Ren said, "Go ahead and attack me if you want. I told you I won't fight you."

Zanti ignored him, scooted off the bed and walked casually into the bathroom. Ren heard the toilet flush, the sink turn on, the water flow and splash.

When Zanti came out, he leaned against the doorframe, scanning the area, gaze locking onto the door.

Quietly, Ren said, "Yeah. I'm hungry, too."

As if someone had been listening all along, the door opened and two grooms walked in. Forty-five? Six? Ren did not know who was who. The grooms motioned to them and Ren and Zanti followed them into the hall. They all moved down the corridor toward the main staircase, the one that led to the atrium. The grooms no longer packed the shocking tubes. There were no chains, no masks, nothing to deal with. Without a word, they escorted the two slaves to the entrance to the harem, opened the door and ushered them in.

The room was dimmed. It was nighttime. Some of the men were already in bed. Others were watching TV or dozing on the couches.

Cam jumped up from one of the couches and ran to Zanti. He had a new, unbroken tablet in his hand. Li Po, Calder and Jaxon approached Ren.

"What happened?" asked Li Po.

"Were you punished?" asked Calder.

Cam looked from Zanti to Ren. "Is he okay?"

Ren nodded, dismissing the fact that Cam did not ask if Ren himself was okay. "Nothing happened. Master only talked for a moment. Then we were locked in a room. That's it."

Air hissed from Cam's mouth in relief. "Are you hungry?"

Zanti turned to look at the kitchen area, his dark eyes widening.

Cam said, "Yeah, thought so. We saved you some dinner."

"We did," Li Po said to Ren. "Full plates."

They all went to the kitchen table and sat. Cam took plates from an oven. Zanti and Ren ate silently. This was the first time since the day Ren had arrived at the harem that Zanti ate at the table. Fried chicken and mashed potatoes, still hot. They also had bowls of fresh-chopped fruit.

As they finished, Ren saw Zanti look up at him. Before Ren could look away, Zanti met his eyes. His gaze was still, not jumpy as was usual for him, and his aura began to turn from the gray it had been most of the night to a pale blue.

A pang hit Ren deep inside, deeper than he'd ever felt. He didn't know if he wanted to cry or tear his hair out or yell or run. He only felt the wash of it, like deep loneliness from a distant place further than even the stars.

Suddenly, he tasted sparks and fire, but also sweet longing.

Pushing back his chair, Ren got up. "I'm tired," he said.

Zanti got up, pushing his chair back, too. Their eyes met.

Cam grabbed his tablet and stood as well. "So is everything good between you two? I can report that for the night?"

Ren said, "Fine. It's fine. No more fighting from me. I can say that much."

Zanti ducked his head and moved away.

Ren followed him across the large space, past the TV area, the couches, down toward more lounging areas by the pool, past the waterfall and into the bathroom. Zanti was there. They did not look at each other.

Ren took his time. He brushed his teeth. He saw Zanti step into a shower and heard the water come on. There was nothing to wash off, but maybe it soothed. Ren found showers comforting sometimes.

He looked into the mirror and saw the scratches, three red lines evenly spaced down the upper part of his chest. He touched them but they didn't hurt. He rubbed lotion on them to soften their indentations and soothe the raised skin.

As he stared into the mirror he saw a young man with bright eyes and a pretty face. Stunning, even, but not nearly as extreme in his beauty as Zanti, nor as delicate. He could never see his own aura. He had no idea what it might contain. Would his colors be brilliant or muted? Or maybe gray to black like Zanti? He came from grief, but he wasn't that broken.

On impulse, he raised his hands and began to undo his braids. There were dozens. Slowly they unraveled, leaving his brown hair rippled. Shining. Almost as wild as Zanti's. Why did he keep comparing himself to that man?

Ren left the silver rings that had decorated his braids in a pile in his private drawer beneath the bathroom counter. One was big enough to fit half-way down to the second knuckle of his fourth finger. He put it on, stared at it, then left it there.

The shower turned off. Zanti stepped out as steam rose around him.

Ren's heart skipped again. Like a magnificent myth, Zanti was. Something from another world. His eyes stung to see him.

Zanti looked his way, canted a hip and crossed his arms over his chest. If giving pleasure hurt that man, then Ren would refuse. But if Master ordered him? The conflict of that sent a rush of pain through his stomach. He would protest, then. Even if it meant being taken to Niko's house and punished.

For longer than felt comfortable, their eyes locked and half a dozen feelings assaulted Ren. How many times had he told himself the annoying man deserved nothing from him, that Ren did not care? But each and every time he'd had that thought, he'd been lying to himself. For he did care. Zanti had hurt Ren, but Ren was beginning to understand why, and he was coming to learn the dynamics of Zanti were a lot more complicated than words like "brat" and "spoiled" and "feral fiend."

Master had put them together tonight for a reason. And this was only the beginning.

Chapter Twenty

Second Night

Late in the afternoon, Master's voice rang out.

"Zanti. Ren."

Ren's heart stopped for a beat. Started up again. He realized he was waiting for an attack that never came.

He did not look to see where Zanti was in the atrium. He already knew. Ren had been half-heartedly keeping an eye on him all day.

Right now Cam and Zanti were glued to their tablets, sharing a loveseat by the pool.

Ren moved past them and into the bathroom where he showered quickly. Now all the curl from the braids would be gone from his hair. But he would dry it until it shone. In the shower he cleaned himself inside and out. He used sandalwood soap. He wanted to look perfect. It was all for Master. Not for himself. And surely not for Zanti.

But apprehension coiled within. He did not want to be with Zanti if it hurt the man. Would he be forced?

When he came out of the shower, Zanti and Cam were entering another stall together. Li Po met Ren. "I'll help with your hair. Do you want make up?"

Ren let Li Po do whatever he wanted. In the end, he had some painted shadow about his eyes and his brown hair fell like liquid about his shoulders and chest. Li Po had trimmed and smoothed his eyebrows as well.

"You're a star," Li Po said.

"I don't want to go," Ren whispered.

"I know." Li Po did not say more. Earlier in the day he'd asked Ren about the night before. Ren had not been able to tell him anything. It was all too complicated. Li Po had stopped pushing. He was a good friend.

There'd been no more fooling around for Ren all day. Master had not ordered it and Ren was not in the mood. But he had loved playing with Li Po and Calder and Jaxon and hoped to repeat it soon.

Ren was first at the door and had been waiting some minutes with Li Po at his side when Zanti and Cam walked up. As soon they showed up, within seconds the door opened. Two of the grooms from the previous day stood there dressed in their usual white shorts and shirts. One motioned with his hand as the other said, "Zanti and Ren only."

Cam and Li Po stepped back.

Both Zanti and Ren stood still.

"Well?" the groom said.

Zanti made a sort of hissing sound, shrugged one shoulder and sauntered forward, hips swaying.

Ren followed, his heart rate speeding. He should not be nervous, he told himself. He'd been Palace trained. But it took every ounce of discipline and energy he had to follow Zanti into the anteroom that led to the staircase.

Up the stairs they went. Again, no masks. They did not stop until they walked all the way down the long hall and were at the door to the white room.

All four entered the room, one guard in front of Zanti, one behind Ren.

There was a small hum as the speakers came on.

"Zanti. Ren. Welcome." Master's voice filled the room with its rich, mechanized tones. "You both look stunning tonight. Thank you for coming."

Ren replied, "My pleasure, Master."

Zanti, of course, said nothing.

"Ren, I would like you to lie down on the bed and allow yourself to be cuffed to it."

"Yes, Master."

Ren's heart now wanted to slam out of his chest. He focused on breathing. Slow. In. Out. And let the lavender spread encase his back and ass, and allowed the pillows to support his shoulders and head. He put his arms straight out to his sides to make it easy for the groom to put the cuffs on his wrists and ankles.

The groom was gentle. The cuffs were soft. Ren might have liked this set up if it had been with Li Po or Calder.

Zanti stood in the center of the room, face averted, his gaze toward the curtained window. In profile he stood straight and tall, of exquisite pedigree if one were only looking at physical form and composition. Like all slaves were looked at and assessed. At the Slave Palace, Ren surpassed many, but if Zanti had been there he would have surpassed all. At least in appearance, stance and the man most likely to be labeled *fairy prince*.

Like Li Po in his shades of tan-brown glamour, Zanti was Ren's type. Despite everything that had happened between them, including Zanti's attack of him, he could not prevent the slow roll of longing that swept through him. He was too nervous to see Zanti's aura yet, but he'd seen it enough. The black. The white. The strange new bluish tint that had happened last night when he'd uncuffed him. Under normal circumstances, blue meant love. But Zanti was not normal.

At any other time, in any circumstance, Ren could have given Master a great performance, something Master might request again and again. But with Zanti? Even if his gut trembled with strange desires, his lungs felt frozen. He knew Zanti didn't want him.

"Zanti." Master's voice came into the room in liquid tones. "You are in charge. Do as you wish. But first, I would like to command that you be someone other than Zanti. A man who is a master, perhaps. A man who keeps a harem of beautiful young men. A man whose favorite is Ren."

This suggested command could change things. Ren lifted his head to see how Zanti responded.

For a moment, Zanti did not move. That blue aura came over him, so rare to see. Then, without warning Zanti threw his arms up straight over his head, fingers curled into fists. If this were a ball game or music festival, one might think he was reacting to a home run or a hit song. Instead, he seemed to hit at nothing. His body bent forward at the waist and he stomped the floor. He then stomped toward the farthest corner of the room and sat with his knees bent to his chest, his back against the juncture of the two walls. He wrapped his arms about his legs and rested his cheek on his knees. His hair fell against his shins.

Huddled like that, the answer communicated itself clearly. *No.*

"Would you prefer that I give Ren another name?" Master asked.

Of course Zanti did not respond.

Master continued, as though used to this sort of behavior from Zanti. "It is your decision. All your doing. I am hungry to be pleased but the final move is yours."

What a strange way to state it, Ren thought. *I am hungry to be pleased.*

But it was that way when lust, eroticism and sex were involved. Like a heavy hunger coming up from an uncharted depth. If Master was hungry, their job was to feed him. Simple as that. Except for Zanti. With Zanti it was not simple. Now Zanti got to make the final call. Like Master himself.

As Ren heard the speakers go off, and the faint static abate, he leaned back on the pillows. Another long night approached. Maybe he could get in another nap.

For awhile, he stared at the closed door the grooms had exited through. He listened to the silence. He ran his heels along the lavender spread, thick and soft against the bottoms of his feet.

To the room, he said, "You should be happy. You get what you want. You have a choice. Just like I did last night. But I thought you might like Master's suggestion." It was actually a brilliant plan.

Zanti did not move, not even to look up. The presence of him in the corner, even huddled, was palpable. The guy filled the room just by being. It had been like that when Ren had first come to the harem. Cam had greeted him, but Zanti who shadowed Cam and stood behind him had been the very first thing to hook Ren's attention. He had brushed it off then as due to the strange behavior of the man. But it had been more. Zanti fed emptiness with his beauty, his very being. It was probably why he was taken in the first place. If he'd had that sort of magnetism as a teen, something that could not be helped, and he crossed any predator's line of vision, or played fast and dangerous in the rougher sections of wherever he came from, he'd not last.

In a way, Zanti's life was probably an imprecise mirror to the story Master had told the first night when Ren wore the mask and Zanti had hate-fucked him. For a boy who abhorred touch, he was perfectly capable of responding, of using his wiles in weird plots for revenge even if it was just a story, a fantasy of Master's playing out *upstairs.*

The situation left Ren, though helpless, contemplative. He wasn't afraid. If Zanti tried to hurt him the grooms would come in. Ren had no doubt. But the rough Zanti—that one was the character Master would allow to come out and play, if that was what Zanti wanted. That character was the Zanti who might be a Master himself in some far-off fantasy in a parallel existence.

Ren turned his head to look at that pervasive dark presence.

Zanti sat in the corner like a forlorn child, aura black. He looked up as if he sensed Ren's gaze. One corner of his mouth curved up. A half-smile. But it was not friendly.

Zanti sat forward, stretching his legs straight out in front of him. He arched his back, stretching his alluring body, then bent his knees and pushed himself against the wall, sliding up it slowly until he stood. His aura wavered black to blue.

Ren watched him walk a zigzag path to the side of the bed. His cock was not interested in anything Ren presented, but it was pert and cute as it hung in the shadow of his groin. A deep ache pushed through Ren's chest, a weird tremble though he was not at all apprehensive. He'd already determined he would deal with anything Zanti might do.

Zanti walked all the way around the bed, then back, eyes shifting, taking in all of Ren toe to head. When he came back to where he'd started he reached out fast, his fingers on Ren's wrist cuff. He jerked it once. Seemingly unsatisfied, he used both hands to tighten it.

With Zanti leaning over him, Ren breathed in the scent of amber, the burning sweet of it. The dark boy within, and the darker man without, both Zanti through and through, pushed their blackened gaze and ashen aura into Ren. Zanti was two men in one, Ren decided. Young. Old. Caged. Uncaged. Victim. Predator. The mix was nearly impenetrable.

Zanti trailed his fingers along the bedspread, following the line of Ren's body but not touching it, his fingernails making a dim scratching sound against the material. He adjusted both cuffs on Ren's ankles, then the cuff on his other wrist.

Ren might have been thrilled. Might have smiled. But not for this tiger stalking him.

Zanti bent down and vanished for a moment. When he came up, he had a drawer filled with sex toys in his hands. It had to have come from under the bed. He put the box on the bed beside Ren. Within, Ren could see everything from dildos to sounds. Ren expected him to choose from the contents the most sadistic of toys. A whip, maybe. A cock ring with spikes. A dildo big as a fist.

Zanti choose a thin, short-ish dildo and a vial of clear lube. He opened the cap on the lube and poured it over the toy. Setting the lube aside, he poked the thing between Ren's legs with no preamble and pushed it inside him. Fast.

Was this to mock him for the night he'd taken him so fast? It was clear Zanti did not care if it burned. If it hurt.

Ren bent his knees and lifted up so the dildo slid easily, without pain, where Zanti wanted it.

Now Zanti stared at Ren's groin. There was no action there. Nothing down below was interested. Ren could have controlled that better, made himself hard with a thought. Instead, he decided to wait and see what more Zanti might do.

Zanti brought forth from the box a tiny red belt. In a most clinical fashion, he nudged Ren's cock aside and fastened the little belt about Ren's balls, tightening it so they pressed up, firm, round and reddish pink where the skin stretched.

This caused Ren's cock to stir, though he pretended he did not notice and kept his face emotionless as he watched Zanti make of him what he wanted, handle him, mold him.

Do as you wish, Ren thought. *I am beginning to think it's why Master bought me.*

Strangely, the voice in his head trying to reason it all out, the notion of it all, clarified a few things. Master wanted to see this. Master wanted him to comply. That level of obedience woke within him an ardor that intensified when he reminded himself Master watched them. Watched it all.

This revelation made it a lot easier. It was why Ren had wanted to be a pleasure slave in the first place. For the moment of pure obedience. For the moment when he did not have to make decisions. Did not have to lead.

Master, if he was smart, comprehended all of this. And Master was intelligent, obviously, or such designs like his elaborate compound or the stories he made his slaves perform would not be so artfully accomplished.

Ren still did not trust Zanti, but many things combined to bring him to a point where arousal became easy. Obedience to Master. The soft bonds and the soft bed. The idea that Master had a larger plan in mind than just this scene. The tragic-tormentor who was beautiful beyond reason. And the fact that Ren had not had an orgasm in two days. His libido usually demanded much more.

More than anything, obeying another was what Ren craved. Even if he was at the mercy of Zanti.

Zanti took a cat o'nine tails in hand. It was black with a silver tipped handle. The main short leather straps undulated as he moved. The tails were not tipped, thankfully.

Ren liked the idea of being helpless. His cock began to fill. He did not want to be hurt, though. The conflict ruled his mind only for a few seconds until he reminded himself Master was watching all. Master was really in charge and he was obeying what Master wanted.

Zanti gazed at Ren's hardening cock and one eyebrow rose. That raised eyebrow—knowing Zanti was looking at him intimately—caused another ache deep inside. For something. What? Acknowledgment. Impossible connection through pity, perhaps, or hate, or maybe something more. Beauty corrupted. Touch wanted/unwanted.

If he gave himself over completely to Zanti, what would Zanti make of that? After that first night of the play, Ren fought down his own anger and resentment. He'd worn the mask, and he'd suffered. But Cam said everyone who wore the mask and cock cage had a hard time. At first Ren avoided Zanti, rejected him, defied him. He had felt justified. He'd been well taken care of afterward by grooms and one doctor. Master's orders. He'd received comfort and affection from Li Po, Calder and Jaxon. And empathy even from Cam as Cam tried to explain Zanti's odd nature and terror-filled history, to explain Zanti's erratic character.

Giving myself to Zanti. That's what Master wants? Ren mulled that thought over.

"All right," Ren said aloud. "Do as you wish." He deliberately repeated Master's words and it was easier to accept when he did that. The ache inside him folded itself outward, like a snake uncoiling to a line. Then it was many snakes.

Ren's cock bobbed up from his thigh as beautiful Zanti stood there with his weapon of choice, the cat o'nine tails, and the weapon not of his choosing: his beauty.

Ren felt the dildo shift slightly as his muscles rippled with his arousal. The ring around his balls dug in, making him feel more exposed than ever.

Zanti looked at his whip, then at Ren, and frowned. Pouted.

With a fast motion, he flung his arm out but none of the leather tails touched Ren. He flicked them on the air above Ren's body. They made a slight wind and tiny popping sounds.

Ren's skin prickled at the non-touch. *Strange.*

Like some sort of deranged shaman, Zanti moved the whip all up and down Ren's body without touching it. He flicked it over and over, the tails almost but not quite making contact with Ren's skin. He teased him that way for long minutes, circling the bed, threatening every inch of Ren's skin.

After awhile, Ren began to squirm for any touch, even an outright beating. He felt drops of pre-cum slide from the tip of his cock.

His arousal, at first a shudder, became a wind. He watched Zanti move around him and couldn't help but swallow over and over, waiting for something to happen. Wanting it to happen.

He remembered that perfect, hard cock pistoning into him, rough and hurting and found himself even wanting that again. Anything to defeat that weirdly disturbed ache that kept folding and unfolding deep inside.

Ren could not keep his eyes off the man. He watched Zanti's graceful motions, memorized the curves of his body at different angles, kept trying to see his eyes, get them to meet his own. They wouldn't.

Zanti's aura was still undulating between pure blue and gray.

Finally, Zanti's eyes met Ren's a few times, dark and deep and concentrated, only to glance away, deny, reject, dismiss. But Ren paid attention now. Each time their gazes connected, the eyes gave him a falling feeling. He would never land because there was no bottom, only more faraway darknesses to pass through. But Zanti was present in those gazes, too, and with Ren right now. He did not play a role. He was not someone else. He remained focused. Tied to Ren in every action. Nothing escaped his notice. It was more than Ren ever expected, and it was strangely and supremely tantalizing.

Zanti did not just obey Master. He had no brand. Master's orders were: *Do as you wish.* Perhaps he did not see that order the same way Ren did, that he wanted to please Master only. That he wanted to perform. Zanti didn't care about performing. Zanti did what Zanti wanted.

I give myself over to you. He wanted to say those words aloud. To Master. And to Zanti. He opened his mouth, began: "I give..."

Zanti's hand whipped down between his legs, the tails of the cat curving and curling about his penis, the edge of the handle scraping the wet tip. His cock had been straining and now the sensation of weirdness, of roughness—no, not rough, more smooth, tentative and slow—made Ren arch up.

That familiar smirk came to Zanti's lips. The leather tails dangled, tickling, over his distended balls. Ren drew in a sharp breath. His muscles clutched at the slick dildo inside him.

He felt open and tender. At the same time his arousal shot higher than ever. He squirmed and thrust upward without control. And yet nothing had happened. Zanti had only really touched him, skin to skin, when inserting the dildo, and strapping his balls. His mind wanted to remember those touches now. It clung to anything it could for it wanted over that crest of pleasure. It wanted the tightening and soaring and froth of release. It wanted hands on him, any stroke or caress, any pinch or pat or even slap. It wanted Zanti.

Zanti's hand moved the tails up Ren's body now. He leaned over him, watching Ren's chest rise and fall. Then he looked into his eyes.

Ren saw the tease there, and a conqueror's conceit. He saw the glimmer and gleam of control. This was the man who had survived Mister X. The pupils had expanded making his brown eyes almost entirely black. Zanti smelled of amber and metal and the burnt remains of a poison fire. Ren inhaled, drew him in... Zanti's inhumanness, Zanti's silence, Zanti's fairy-boy beauty and his abyss-god gaze.

Zanti leaned down. His pink lips parted. "Come," he whispered.

Ren thrust up, bucking against the tails and further up, cock meeting the fine, hard skin of the underside of Zanti's wrist. His tender cock head swept along that skin, searching for a palm, for fingers to hold him. That never happened but he still burst from inside out, shooting his pleasure.

The orgasm rolled through him.

Zanti had spoken!

And Ren had come with barely a touch.

The boy's smile churned into Ren. Twisting him. Confusing him. The gray aura around Zanti went white as pure snow with edges of blue surrounding it.

Zanti shook himself, as if coming out of a trance.

As Ren's orgasm subsided, Zanti ran the whip through the puddle of cum on his stomach and chest. Then he threw the cat o'nine tails hard until it hit the wall.

Ren watched him, white-haloed now, kick the bed. He looked down and saw Zanti's cock had hardened. It pulsed beautifully, the head tender and pink. Pink light surrounded it.

Zanti turned away, his satisfaction at what he had done to Ren transforming to something else. Confusion at his own response, maybe. Or anger.

Ren tried to sit up. The chains caught, holding him in a half-upright position. The dildo inside him threatened to come out as he moved, then pushed back in. His balls ached still, as if no release had happened, the ring around them digging in and hurting now that his skin was so sensitive from coming.

In any ordinary circumstance between two pleasure slaves performing for their master, Ren would have encouraged his partner, asked, even begged him to fuck him, especially if he saw the other was aroused. But this was Zanti and Zanti didn't want to be touched. Or did he now? No brand. Not a slave. But part of the harem.

Nothing was as it seemed.

The door opened. The two grooms came in. They went to the bed and undid Ren's cuffs. He sat up now, asking one, "I can take this off now?" He indicated the band around his balls, the dildo.

"Yes. Leave those things on the bed and they will be dealt with," said the groom nearest to him.

Ren took care of himself, then slid to the end of the bed and stood.

The grooms stood by the door waiting.

Zanti turned, his cock still half-hard, and tossed his hair as he strode into the hall. It seemed he could not get away fast enough.

Ren began to follow, planning on heading straight for the shower after they were returned to the harem. The energy in the room changed. The air crackled.

Master's voice. "Ren. Stay. Forty-five, wait for him in the hall, please."

Ren watched as the grooms followed Zanti out.

Ren stood in the center of the room facing the bed and waited.

"Zanti spoke to you." Master sounded almost as amazed as Ren had been.

"A whisper only. One word."

"I heard."

"I thought he couldn't talk."

"He can. He chooses not to. He has written me notes now and again. But he has spoken only twice that I know. To me. Never to another. Not even to Cam."

Should Ren feel special, then?

Master said, "I am curious. When you first touched and tasted Zanti during the play last week, what did his colors display? And did they have a flavor? If so, what did they taste of?"

Master had been curious from the first and Ren's body churned in pleasure at the attention.

Ren had not tasted Zanti since. He thought back. He had been nervous and encumbered. The mask kept his senses diminished.

Ren swirled his tongue around his mouth, the motion stimulating taste and taste-memory. "The auras on his body did have a faint flavor, I think. Campfires."

"He tasted of campfires?"

"Smoky, a bit. How campfires smell. And—and of ash, fine and smooth but disintegrating."

"Ash," Master repeated. "Yes. Thank you. You may go."

"Master! Please! I have a question."

"You may ask but I may not answer."

Hair falling forward, Ren bowed his head. "Everything Cam said to me about Zanti. His history. He is unbranded. But if all that is true about Mister X and Zanti's terrible past, is he really here of his own free will?"

"Zanti is unbranded because I do not own him. Zanti is the only one of you free to leave at any time. He does not. He stays. This is his choice. Tonight, with you chained and Zanti free he knows he could have walked out of the room at any time. My grooms would not have stopped him. But he did not leave. His wish is granted to remain as long as he likes."

"But he fights me, the grooms, your commands. Maybe he stays because he has nowhere else to go?"

A soft rumble, like a laugh. "Zanti can go anywhere, all funds paid, any life he wants. He knows this. Now, you may go. No more questions tonight. Maybe tomorrow I will answer more of your questions. If you are ready."

"Yes, Master." *Ready?* Ready for what?

So it was true. At least he knew now. Zanti did as he wished. And he had wished to make Ren come. He had spoken because he had wished to speak. Had wished Ren to come without hands, without human touch.

Ren had come, but not without fighting for the barest brush of wrist against his yearning cock. He'd gotten it. He'd gotten Zanti's command. He had obeyed. Zanti had not obeyed. Zanti had gotten his wish.

What did that mean?

Chapter Twenty-One

Third Night

The atrium lights had dimmed for the night. Most of the alcoves were dark.

When Ren had left the white room *upstairs* one groom was waiting. Zanti and the other groom were gone.

In the dining area, Li Po motioned him over, keeping his voice low, knowing other men now slept. How much time had actually passed in that room upstairs? Ren had missed more than another meal. He'd missed the entire evening.

And where was Zanti?

Li Po had a dinner plate waiting for him, heated. Ren thanked him, then ate silently. Steak. Broccoli. A baked potato with fresh melted butter Li Po had just placed on top. Ren shoveled in the food.

He was so hungry he didn't care that he was sex-grimy. Li Po did not comment on his appearance. But he did softly ask, "Are you all right?"

Ren nodded. He thanked Li Po again and headed for the showers.

When he came into the main room and turned to head to his alcove, he passed several where men slept, some alone, some together.

Cam's alcove, shrouded in shadow, showed two men, side by side. He could not help but pause, taking them in. Cam lay on his back, the sheet stretched up to his hips. Zanti lay on his side, head bowed against the side of Cam's chest. Cam's arm encircled Zanti's head. Cam was the only one of the harem Ren had seen who touched Zanti. The only one Zanti allowed. And that was, according to Cam, only on nights when Zanti could not sleep. When being alone made Zanti too restless.

As if sensing Ren's stare, Zanti made a low sound and curled closer to Cam, eyes shut tight.

Ren turned away, his heart pounding, that strange ache returning in his solar plexus.

*

Stepping off the treadmill, Ren grabbed a towel and rubbed the sweat off his arms and chest.

Cam was staring at him from a nearby couch, haloed in bright green. Ren glanced about the room and saw Zanti on a lounge chair by the pool, tablet in hand.

It was obvious Cam wanted to know what had been going on upstairs. He cared.

But Ren avoided him, not comfortable yet to talk. Not wanting to reveal yet that Zanti had spoken. Granted, it had been only one word, and whispered, but it had been a word. If Zanti wanted Cam to know, maybe he could speak and tell him himself. Or Master could inform Cam. Master had seen it all.

When Ren had returned to the harem the night before, it had been obvious to those still awake, like Li Po, that he'd had some action. He had his own emissions all over him. He'd headed straight for the shower after stuffing his face. And this morning he'd slept in. He had not wanted to face anyone.

He was normally social. At the Palace he'd been around all different slaves at different times for classes, training, dining and recreation. But those men and women had all been friendly, exciting. *Willing.*

These men in the harem were willing, too. Supposedly. All except Zanti. But Zanti was different. He was not a slave. He was a free man.

Ren threw his towel in the gym hamper and came down the steps, thinking a swim would be nice now that he'd worked his body up to a sweat. He did not look directly at Cam, but felt his eyes on him as he walked to the pool.

All the other men were busy, some watching TV, some fucking on the wider couches beyond the waterfall.

He dived into the pool, the coolness enfolding him. The last time he'd been swimming, he'd been attacked. It was still fresh, still hurt even after the past two nights Master had forced him and Zanti to be together.

He swam with force, the water frothing in waves alongside him.

This wasn't over. Not by a long-shot.

What would Master ask of them tonight?

When Ren popped up at the other end by the waterfall for air, he saw Zanti watching him. Slowly, Zanti looked down, pretending to be interested in something on his tablet, but Ren had not missed it. Zanti was watching him, and a heat deep in his groin flared to life.

*

"Zanti. Ren." Master's voice resounded throughout the harem.

It was no surprise to hear the order again, but some of the men chuckled or grumbled from around the room at the two new favorites. How could there not be competition in the ranks? Anyone worth their salt as a pleasure slave would want to be number one to their master.

Ren prepared alone. This time not even Li Po was there to do his hair or offer make up. Since Master had not required make up from him, or braids after that first time, Ren did nothing but the required cleansing inside and out since he had not done it that morning. He dried his hair straight. Unlike some of the others, he did not need to shave. The Palace's depilatory was permanent on slaves like Ren who had chosen to be hairless but for scalp, brows and lashes.

Ren stood by the door and waited, knowing all the eyes of the harem were upon him. He kept his head down. The scratches on his chest, he noted, had healed. There was barely a faint trail of pink now from Zanti's nails on him during their fight.

He sensed Zanti before he saw him. His smoky cologne. His weirdly sharp presence that made the air almost prickle. When he looked sideways at him, Zanti was staring upward, as if the tall ceiling had all his answers.

Master must have been watching, for only seconds later the door behind the tree of life tapestry opened and two grooms motioned them forward.

Ren let Zanti go first. Zanti did not hesitate. He almost bounced, his tight, slender ass bobbing as if conscious to the tease.

Ren wanted to roll his eyes. But a warmth began within, slowly penetrating throughout his body. His balls shifted, tingled. Zanti turned him on. There was no denying it. It wouldn't have been at all odd, except the warmth that kindled inside him for the beautiful, annoying man trembled and tickled in a way that involved his emotions. Longing, loneliness and empathy took him into a weird yearning. He wanted Zanti. He wanted to hold him. To kiss him.

He shook his head, trying to clear his mind of such thoughts. His normal response to males was sexual, yes, and pleasurable. But other than feelings for Master Locke, and his hint of envy at Locke's close relationship with his slave Wulf, Ren had no trouble when it came to mixing up pleasure with bonding. He easily separated the act of sex from love. He had dreamed of an actual relationship with his master. Hoped. He never thought of anything but mild friendship for his fellow slaves. Li Po had come the closest to making him feel a deeper friendship.

He did not acknowledge what he felt with Zanti as friendship, but this other part, the yearning part, the longing – both sexual and non-sexual—that scared him. He wasn't ready to accept even the thought of it.

Again, the grooms escorted them up the stairwell and down the long hall to the white room.

Zanti tossed his head like a vain prince. He seemed to know what was coming. Already, he approached the bed, arms out, and backed up onto it. He lay down on the cool, lavender silks, his legs spread as the grooms attached the wool-lined cuffs to his ankles and wrists.

Ren saw a pattern. First one of them was restrained, then the next night the other. The first night, Ren had done nothing until, after what seemed like hours, he'd let Zanti go free. He had not touched him.

Well, just because Zanti had done things to Ren the night before did not mean Ren was ready to do the same in return. Unless commanded by Master, of course.

Yet Zanti, with no brand of his own, freely allowed the grooms to restrain him on the bed. He did not tease or fight this time. Even if Zanti hated him, it was consent, wasn't it?

Would Master's orders be the same now? *Do as you wish.*

The room smelled of body powder, clean and sweet, and like pears again. Sweet as syrup. There was a tinge of greenness, too, like rain. The harem smelled that way all day because of the constantly flowing waterfall. And Zanti, with his fiery cologne, made the outdoorsy atmosphere complete both in the harem and here in the white room. The aromas flowed through Ren's body, quickening him. His body liked it. He liked how Zanti smelled. There was no denying it.

The grooms exited the room without a word. Forty-five and Six? He could never tell any of them apart.

The static in the air changed. Ren sensed the speakers coming on even as he heard nothing but continued silence.

"Welcome, Zanti. Welcome, Ren."

Ren's gaze darted to Zanti who lay with his head back on a pale lavender pillow, dark and shining, a vivacious look on his face as he stared straight upward.

"I have new instructions tonight," Master continued.

Zanti pushed his lips out in a childish double pout.

Ren closed his eyes, feeling his muscles tense. He forced control.

"Ren, I want you to go now to Zanti's side."

Maybe Master would be a part of this? Instruct them through the evening? Not leave? That would be better for Ren, less stressful. He wanted a master, not to *be* a master.

"I want you to look at him, really look, now. Do not only go through the motions. Open and focus. Put all your attention on Zanti."

Zanti did not scowl or pout or give any indication he protested this command.

At ease for the moment, Ren stood over the bed, his gaze traveling the entire length of Zanti's body. It was compact, gorgeous, the natural tan of his skin making him gleam. He was paler on some parts of his body: the inner thigh, the underside of his wrists and elbows, the curve of skin just below the underarm. His cock lay uninterested between his legs, dusky pink, his balls a little darker beneath the thinnest dusting of shadow on the soft, wrinkled skin.

Zanti would make any man's mouth water. Swallowing reflexively, Ren noted Zanti's aura was not yet blue, but still gray with black edges.

He had to keep reminding himself what Master had said about Zanti being able to leave at any time. That Zanti was here meant he consented.

"What do you see, Ren?" Master asked.

Ren knew what Master asked. Did he see Zanti's aura? Did he see the colors of pleasure making intricate maps across his flawless, firm skin?

He took a deep breath. "His aura is gray outlined in black with occasional dots of white stars within it, maybe two or three at a time. Like flashes."

"Thank you for that." Master's breath hissed throughout the room. "Can you see more detailed lights on his body, anything at all? As you would on the others before you touch them?"

Ren surveyed Zanti, tilting his head, letting his gaze intrude upon the man from all angles. The skin was slow to show him its secrets. Zanti's secrets. He looked in places one would not ordinarily look. Beneath the eyes. Along the jaw. The line between his slightly curved pecs. At the edges of his hips and knees. On the tips of his fingers and toes.

He thought he saw flutters of pale light, like little glowings in these places. And at the base of his cock. Not really on the cock itself, but in the fold of the top of the thigh and below the pelvis, where the cock formed from his body into a lovely shaft. The penis rested between the tops of the inner thighs, but the dip on either side of the base undulated with the palest of pink-gold light.

It was nothing like the bright lights of other men that tended to stripe their bodies and their erogenous zones. Not yet.

Ren concentrated.

"Tell me what you see," Master again commanded.

Ren pointed to the eyes, the chest, the fingertips, toes and knees. "Here and here," he said. He did not touch Zanti. "The palest of flickers. Maybe."

Zanti frowned a little, watching him with all the suspicion of a feral animal. A coolness lay in the back of his eyes. Blue emanated from the pupils themselves.

"Pick an area and begin. Touch him," Master ordered.

Ren knew the order was coming. He'd already decided to start with the least intimate zone he could detect. He reached out and ran his nails very lightly over the side of Zanti's left knee.

Zanti jerked his knee up and the chain holding his ankle went taut. His eyebrows narrowed. His lips opened a fraction.

Ren touched him there again, watching the pale amber light flicker across the bend in his leg.

Master was quiet now, allowing Ren to find his own way. He didn't like it, wanting commands to guide him, still uncomfortable with Zanti's weird refusals of him even though he knew Zanti was here by choice, even though Zanti had broken his barriers last night and actually spoken to him. It was still as if Zanti was somehow trapped in a cage like a pet, a cage he had sauntered into it willingly.

Ren could not help but hold himself rigid instead of flowing; he was hesitant. But a Palace slave did not hesitate. The punishment for holding back or refusing an order resulted in isolation, the worst thing you could do to a sex-addicted, willing pleasure slave.

Ren saw Zanti begin to relax as he took his hand away. Under Zanti's eyes, a flicker.

No hesitation, he told himself. *It's a job.*

He moved alongside to the head of the bed and cupped Zanti's face, not looking for his reaction, simply doing. Ren's thumbs caressed the hollows beneath his lower lashes.

Zanti's face began to glow even as he squirmed. Around his lips a lavender light formed. Zanti could deny it all he wanted, but the truth was in the lights. Zanti wanted to be kissed.

Do not hesitate!

Ren leaned down and placed his mouth to Zanti's, inhaling Zanti's hot, rapid breaths. Their collars jangled together, meeting like two bells chiming the hour. This hour. One among many, yet oddly different for this moment Ren's own heart began to beat like the wings of a trapped moth. In his chest, the sensation opened him up, the usual feeling of arousal, but also something more. A deep thrill washed over him beyond amazement. There was a sense of wonder like that of a treasure hunter finally sighting his goal.

The kiss overtook him.

When before, he had wanted to retreat, now he pressed forward, lips moving, opening, demanding. It was a sudden shock of desire from one second to the next. Zanti's mouth fell open and he tilted his head back. Ren's hands still held him, cupping jaw and cheeks, the skin and bone of him molding to his palms, silken, smooth, giving off the slight scent of vanilla and an edge of dust.

The kiss became an entity unto itself with its own growing energy and fused form. It had its own atmosphere, and invaded their mouths and throats. Ren's body became lighter, like ghost-flesh, on a journey into Zanti's gray cloud which wasn't truly gray after all, but silver suffused with powder-soft iridescence. Zanti looked filled with rainbow dust. What could have been a conflict in his aura, Ren now saw was purity itself.

Ren gasped and Zanti hissed as they pulled apart for breath after the kiss's eternal-seeming lifespan.

Ren was harder than he ever remembered being, already on the cusp of orgasm. He stepped back and looked down at Zanti's body to see the glow all over it now; he instantly forgot the man's past cruelty toward him. He knew every step, now, everything he must—needed—to do. Unthinking, he climbed on top of the supine man to lie on him with his full weight, an embrace of the whole body.

Zanti's arms yanked at their chains. The bed shuddered with the strength of it. Ren reached up to undo one of the wrist bands thinking that was what Zanti wanted.

Zanti yanked his hand away, head turning. It was clear this was a communication. *No!* Almost like the other night when he'd hissed *Come!*

All right, then. Zanti wanted to be held down. He *liked* the struggle. Many did. So many at the Palace, Ren had learned. Masters, as well.

Zanti had also liked it when Ren was bound. *Come!* That word the only one shared between them, reluctant, forced, then not-forced pleasure.

Ren began to slide up and down Zanti's body, his cock pushing into silken skin, Zanti's cock answering with a wet drag across his belly. It was something urgent, desperate as loss. But also need, desire.

Heat pulsed from all sides. Had Master raised the room's temperature?

Zanti's body arched up, undulating, causing more friction on Ren's cock which slid along hot, smooth skin, the tip wet, everything melted, it seemed, licking flame.

The sensual beauty of Zanti, and the silver of him, his essence, rushed over Ren. Everything he'd learned in his short life in the harem, all he'd learned of Zanti brought a wave over him, an abyss-deep ache for past losses, the memory of childhood's profound and giddy happiness. It rolled over him—longing, loss, desire— pushing him up and up to the crest of ecstasy. He lost control and came, still holding Zanti's head, their lips pressed tight, everything turning to lavender rainbows in his head.

Zanti's release flooded upward and Ren felt it mix with his own, spreading from belly to chest. Zanti made a sound, a groan of agony and a sigh of pleasure, one and the same, as he kept arching his body his arms tugging at the chains, making a ringing sound to join the jingle of their collars.

Ren lay on top of him not moving, not caring if Zanti might be uncomfortable, not caring if they stuck together forever in this semblance of what—sex? Was that what it had been?

Ren might have dozed. He didn't remember, but suddenly he jerked to awareness remembering where he was and who was beneath him.

Moaning, he rolled to the side. This was Zanti. *Zanti!* After all Zanti had done to spurn Ren.

Ren slid off the bed and stood.

Zanti watched him warily as Ren undid the wrist and ankle straps.

Then Ren turned away. What had happened? They had had sex, but not. They had become entangled in pleasure, in something not-sex but like a weird, dark dream of pleasure.

There was a wind in Ren's chest. He felt like he'd been hit by a train as he walked into the bathroom.

He took a damp cloth to his chest and wiped away all evidence, then froze in mid-stroke. He had the errant thought he wanted to keep that essence on him all night if he could. Save it. Bring it deeper into his skin. He did not know why a surge of tears accompanied the idea. Or why his mind began to swirl.

With deep breaths, he composed himself. It wasn't hard. Forcing himself to remember Zanti's hard, cool eyes and childish smirks brought him to his senses.

When he came out of the bathroom, Zanti was gone and Ren was alone. No groom waited for him.

Out of the walls came the elegantly accented, slightly mechanical voice as Master began to speak without preamble. Without allowing Ren any questions.

"I will tell you now so that you no longer need to speculate. I bought you for Zanti."

Ren took a deep breath. Master had not bought Ren for himself and that hurt.

"Don't take it personally, Ren. Of course you are lovely. I am already enjoying seeing you as a part of the harem. You are welcome and I find you engaging, attractive, and well-trained. You talent fascinates me. But I found you while looking for someone I thought might be a good match for Zanti."

"I find it hard to believe you're a matchmaker."

"Yes, I understand that. It's unusual, but Zanti is unusual."

Ren did not state the obvious and say the entire set up was unusual.

Master's voice reverberated with a laugh. "My plan is working, though. Do you not think so?"

Swinging his hands in front of him, Ren looked down, then up. "You forced us together because I make him feel pleasure."

"Yes. But there is more. Compatibility. Chemistry. Maybe it's new for you to put words to, but I see it. I made a good choice in you, Ren. You have not disappointed me. I knew it might be hard for you, but in your profile I saw your strength. Your will. It's still early. You've lived here only a little over a week. And yet you are perfect. I knew you would be the right fit here. For Zanti and for the harem."

Perfect. Praise from a master to a slave was something Ren craved.

"Do you feel you fit in? Are you coming to see what you can accomplish?"

"Yes, Master." It was true. He did see. He did feel it. The beginnings of belonging. And for Zanti, something stronger than pity now. Something that fluttered its wings in his heart. That brought a sting to his eyes.

"Master," said Ren, pushing away his shock at such sudden revelation and praise. "I still wish to see you."

"No. Never. That is our deal. But you may see me through Zanti. Do you understand?"

Tears welled in Ren's eyes, blurring his vision. "No. I don't."

"You must learn to understand, then. There are some things you can have and some you cannot."

"Yes, Master." He wanted to ask why. He kept silent. He'd already overstepped the line between master and slave by making a request Cam told him would never be granted. He was shaking now.

"Go back to the harem. Spend the night. Rest, sleep, swim, eat. Tomorrow night you will return here. You will learn more. And I will take pleasure in watching."

Behind him, a door clicked open. He turned to see his groom beckon him into the hall.

Reluctant, Ren followed.

Chapter Twenty-Two

Night of Gifts

Ren came out of the shower. He could no longer smell Zanti on his body, no longer feel the coolness of his drying release, or the fever of his lust. But he could still taste him, not the campfire taste but the breath of forests after rain, a freshness in the salt of Ren's own uncalled-for tears.

As he passed by the sleeping alcoves, he saw Zanti in his own bed, not sharing with Cam. He lay in shadow, a sheet over his hips, one leg off the bed, arms up and hugging a pillow to his chest.

Zanti had chosen to stay here. In a harem of all places. Did it give him a sense of comfort? Of family? These were the things Ren himself had craved. It was a dream he could, at the very least, understand. Something he and Zanti might have in common.

Ren hoped to feel that sort of comfort some day. He longed for that inclusive feeling, of being wanted, being loved. He was already wanted by many of the men, so there was success on that level. It would take time, of course, for the full sense of family to develop.

But for Zanti who avoided them all, it was that much harder. Zanti might never get his wish to feel included if he couldn't relate to the men on a somewhat *sane* level.

Ren slept restlessly that night, his dreams filled with images of Zanti's smirking, unconscious beauty.

*

The next evening, when Ren and Zanti entered the white room, Master's low tones made the pronouncement. "Do as you wish, but you will not leave until you have both come twice."

What a command! Especially for a man who, as everyone in the harem knew, couldn't come. Or didn't. Not until Ren's arrival. But Ren could do this. His heart began to beat faster.

Zanti shrugged, one cheek plumping in a half-smile, and jumped on the bed. He reached for his own cock and wrapped his fingers around it.

Master's voice, lilting with what sounded like humor, said, "Coming by your own hand defeats the purpose and will not count."

A loose fist fell against the bedcovers. The muscles of Zanti's face slackened. The smirk vanished. But Ren saw the lavender glow at the tip of his penis and knew Zanti was in the first stages of arousal.

Stepping up to the side of the bed, Ren reached for the wrist cuffs chained to the headboard.

Zanti watched him, then pulled his hand to his chest as Ren offered him the cuff.

"No?" Ren said aloud. "All right. Move over, then. I'll secure myself instead."

Ren sat on the edge of the bed, turning when he felt no give to the mattress. Zanti had not moved. He was staring up at him through half a hank of dark bangs. His body had a faint edge of pale luminescence all over it, like the barest of lavender light shining through a black, closed curtain. His eyes were abyss-deep, inscrutable, the lashes glossy in the reflected whiteness of the room.

"Move over," Ren repeated. He scooted back until the side of his hip brushed Zanti's upper thigh. Warm skin on skin. Smooth. Firm. Zanti smelled of vanilla and spring this evening. Not a hint of fire which was almost disappointing until he remembered that Zanti's fire was from pain, not pleasure. Therefore, Zanti must be feeling pleasure tonight.

The places on Zanti's body Ren liked touching: elbow, knee, three inches down from the underarm, the hollows under those beautiful eyes, began to show a faint iridescence.

Did Zanti not want cuffs for either of them tonight? What did Master want? It was of great concern to Ren, and caused him more dreaded hesitation.

Ren's chest expanded with his deep breaths. His cock was already hard. Zanti was beautiful, there was no doubt. Ren couldn't help himself; he was drawn to that body even when he had tried not to be. But it was more. A space deep within unfolded to a width and breadth of longing. Like a hunger, it wanted sustenance. To be filled. The pangs he felt were almost pain.

He reached over Zanti's abdomen and caught the other man's hand, the one that had just touched his cock as if Zanti had wanted to make himself come to get this night over with sooner. Ren grasped the fingers, which were uncooperative and would not weave with his own. They were dry and hot, as if Zanti had a fever in his palms.

Ren looked him up and down. The things he wanted to do to him might not be welcomed. But he still wanted.

Zanti's lips parted slightly as if he read Ren's thoughts. Ren felt his own mouth tremble into the start of a smile when, without warning, Zanti gripped his hand and yanked, throwing Ren off-balance and bringing him on top of Zanti, their chests smacking together. Zanti reached up with the hand he had earlier curled against himself and placed it on the back of Ren's neck, gripping his hair, and he pulled his face down hard until their lips met.

Mouth already open, Zanti forced his kiss deep, tongue invading, taking over Ren's mouth. Ren put his free hand up on the pillow until the fingers wove through strands of Zanti's satiny hair. He could no longer see the colors on Zanti's body, but he didn't have to. The heat was all over him—all over them, and if it wasn't steaming up the room, then it had to be a dream.

Zanti pulled his hand from Ren's and braced it against his lower back, turning them as their kiss fought to deepen. They wrestled on their sides, hands going everywhere, and then Zanti forced Ren onto his back. Ren almost fell off the bed. He nearly laughed as Zanti pulled him back to the center of the bed, their cocks meeting, rubbing.

A force of desire swept through Ren making him gasp. It was so strong it stabbed at his groin, causing his back to arch for more friction, more sensation everywhere.

They were sweating with exertion. Long minutes passed. Deep groans. Even Zanti, who rarely made a sound, let out small, undefined, low cries.

Once started, they could not stop. Ren didn't know why, but Zanti in his arms, even in this fierce way where they were almost fighting each other, where their kisses were pushy and severe and would surely leave their lips swollen and trembling after, made the empty space inside him excite with the ecstasy of being filled up.

He wrapped his arms around Zanti who was now on top, fingertips straying over the rounded tops of his ass. He spread his legs so now Zanti's hard cock stabbed Ren's balls. He lifted himself.

Without any preparation, Zanti was inside him. It should have hurt. Maybe it did. Maybe the pain fed into the pleasure so seamlessly he didn't notice. Or maybe they just fit. Either way, Zanti was fucking him again, but unlike the first time, that first night they had done the play for Master, this time Zanti was like a graceful dancer in the act, smoothly thrusting in and out, his pre-cum and their sweat making things easy. Zanti did not stab into him. He did not go fast, but undulated like a swimmer underwater, everything flowing without beginning or end.

Ren had never felt anything like it, not even with the most talented of slaves back at the Palace. He bucked his hips and matched Zanti's rhythm, holding on tight, and Zanti lifted his head then and looked down at him, eyes like dark stars glimmering.

Ren breathed in and out, panting, and said, "More."

Zanti slowed, stroked his hand down the side of Ren's face as if Ren were his lover, then brushed their lips together with the barest of touches and thrust with ease in, out, in, sliding over Ren's prostate, causing his eyes to roll up.

He felt the increasing heat, the liquid spill deep inside at the same time his own cock swelled and his mind rolled up and up to white beyonds and slipped over into them, his orgasm like lightning throughout his body. A yell. An echoed yell. He made another strangled sound, opened his eyes and became aware of slickness between them and, incredibly, Zanti petting his hair.

Zanti did not push away from him like all the other times. Instead, he lay over Ren as if he owned him. Head against Ren's chest, arms loosely grasping Ren's shoulders, he rested. Or claimed. Or whatever it was he was doing with his cock still inside him, his heart pounding against Ren's own heaving chest.

Finally, Zanti sat up between Ren's legs and his cock slipped out. He gazed down at Ren with dark eyes through tangles of brilliant brown. His lips were slightly parted, flushed. His chest rose and fell with more rapid than usual breath.

The gaze swept further than Ren's upper body. It blew through him like rich weather filled with a promise of rain and perhaps some wicked wind. Ren's cock stayed half hard.

Ren's lungs filled with that wild weather promise. He wanted Zanti again. With his whole body. And deeper. He wanted to embrace the boy. Hold on so they could both fly together and maybe, just maybe, never fall.

Zanti lifted his chin. His chest expanded. He raised his arms, nudging his hair back from his cheek with his shoulder, tossing his head. Not like an actor or even a slave. But as someone proud. Touched but still untouchable. He knew he was beautiful. He wanted to show this. He looked as if he took power from the very air itself. He stood up on his knees and twisted. The curve of his hip was darkly perfect, smooth to the firm thigh that held it. His stomach muscles rippled, the skin taut, rigid. His cock glistened with sweat and his own release, dark pink with the recent fucking.

Ren held his breath. Zanti was a god.

Not tied down this time, Ren put his hands over his own head. That half-smile quirked at Zanti's mouth.

"So help me, I want you again," Ren breathed. He told himself it would be a good show for Master. It would highlight his willingness to obey. His stamina and his ability to get along with others, even if one particular other had not welcomed him in a friendly manner at first.

"Ahhh," said Zanti. Just a whisper.

Sounds from Zanti were so rare that Ren felt the shock of it like a tingle throughout his body.

Zanti opened his mouth and let out a silent laugh.

Ren reached up and grabbed his preening arms and pulled him down until they were face to face again. "I am Palace trained. What Master wants, Master gets." But really, this was what Ren wanted. More than anything.

Zanti shrugged one shoulder and brushed his lips to Ren's, still openly laughing, puffs of air pushing into Ren's mouth. Ren arched up and his cock hardened.

The second time took longer and was far sweeter even with Zanti's intermittent penchant for roughness. Ren wanted it, wanted that force that could not be held down, that bratty, standoffish creature that writhed so very enticingly in his arms as he fucked. He wanted to hold the broken boy and the healed boy, one in each hand, and fold them together as a single force.

In the afterglow, both still dazed, they lay side by side. Ren's hand lay on Zanti's upper arm, then slid down to his chest to feel the surging heartbeat. He had him in that half embrace, quiet and still on the white bed, for about thirty seconds. Thirty blissful seconds.

Then Zanti pushed his hand away, got up and went to the bathroom.

When he came out, the hall door opened. A groom took Zanti away. But not before Zanti looked back at him surrounded by an aura of pale blueness, his dark eyes open with longing.

The door closed. Ren was left alone sitting up. He closed his eyes wanting to remember the stormy scent of Zanti, the smooth feel of their bodies pressed together. The new blue aura.

A slight hiss preceded Master's voice filling the room.

"You are worth every penny," Master said.

Ren's eyes shot open. He tipped his head back.

"Palace trained, yes, but so much more."

"Thank you, Master." He had done well. He had performed and obeyed. And he had loved every moment. But now he wondered about himself. For within he held a secret he had only just realized. He had done this for Zanti, not for Master. And he had taken for his own pleasure, which was not against slave rules, but the entire role was defined by giving first. Giving and taking might become entwined, but the best slaves never forgot their place.

He must have shown his inner concerns through a frown and a tightening of his muscles, for Master said, "What is it? Are you unhappy?"

Ren shook his head.

"Are you still resentful and angry with Zanti?"

"No, Master. I have come to… to crave him, in fact. I don't know that he feels the same, however. I hope."

"You don't know? But my dear boy, that is why you were purchased. Can you not tell from his aura?"

"It changed. Yes."

"To what color?"

"Blue. But Zanti's different. I'm not sure what to make of it."

"What does that color tell you in others?"

Ren swallowed hard. "Love."

A chuckle. "Money is no object for me. I buy as I like. This compound. The statues you saw on your drive in to the compound, my staff, this house and all the things I like to collect. Including the harem."

Ren nodded.

"I am also a generous master. I spread my wealth. As Cam has told you, you may put in requests for things you might like to have and I will consider those requests. Some requests are very small. Jewelry. Hair ornaments. Fragrances. Special foods. Others are larger, such as Aaron's grand piano. It took me weeks to find just the right one for him. Weeks longer to have it delivered."

"I know. And I was purchased for Zanti."

"You are rare and beautiful, to be sure. And Zanti did not request you specifically. But throughout my relationship with him, there is one thing he has always wanted even though he did not have the words to say. A lover. And that is what I wanted to give him. But it would not be me. That is not what I do. You are here for more than to give Zanti pleasure, or to make him potent again. He had a companion in Cam, but never more. Cam was not equipped for more with such a broken man. But you... you're special."

Stunned, Ren sat very still.

"You were purchased as a gift. A gift Zanti may not have outright requested, but that I knew he needed. You have exceeded my every wish and expectation in that regard."

"Thank you, Master." Tears started as if from nowhere. Then a new understanding dawned and he knew why he was crying. He was Zanti's. Zanti was his master. And this was more than just a gift for Zanti. It was a gift to Ren as well. The very thing he'd always dreamed of, always wanted.

"Now that you understand more about why you are here, I am still your Master in the end. Should Zanti grow tired of you, you will not lose your place here. I run the harem. You all abide by my commands. But my command for you is simply this: I wish for you to give to Zanti all you thought you were saving for me."

"You want me to love him."

"Yes."

"And for him to love in return."

"I have always wanted that for Zanti. So, yes."

It was both a relief and a strange pressure he felt under his skin. "It's already happening, Master. I want him. I crave him. The rest will follow. And his aura was blue. If I can trust that color for him to mean what it means for others, he is feeling what you wished for him to feel." To be wanted. To be loved. No one ever said it would be easy. "I can continue to do this."

"Excellent. Now, the groom will assist you back to the harem. That is all. You may go."

*

It was the middle of the night. Everyone was asleep. When Ren exited the shower and went to his cubicle, hair still dripping, he slowed by Zanti's cubicle and saw him curled on his side in shadow. But something told him Zanti was not asleep. He almost entered the cubicle, a force pulling toward the young man, but he lost his nerve.

He moved on to his own bed and settled into clean sheets, exhausted.

His mind spun. Images of Zanti posing over him kept haunting him. He was aroused again just thinking of him. Wanting him. And now to learn that Zanti, who had no brand mark on his chest, who was not a real slave, was his true Master? He tossed about on his mattress for a while, letting himself become used to the concept.

All his life he'd wanted this. To be the slave of a master who wanted and needed him. And here he was falling in love with a boy he had disliked at first, only to find he was the boy's purchased gift, as if given to him by a benevolent father who only wanted what was best for his son.

Master had rescued Zanti. Now Master gave Zanti a slave to keep, to have, to own. A slave of his own.

Ren wanted to belong to Master. And Master had assured him Ren was owned by him first and foremost. But this new concept was not unwelcome. To be Zanti's special gift. A thrill raced through him. He liked the idea that Zanti could come to him at any time, claim him and he'd have to go with him, follow through without question.

He finally fell asleep with a smile on his face.

Chapter Twenty-Three

Three Long Nights

For three long nights, Master did not call upon anyone to go upstairs. There were no plays. And no requests for Ren and Zanti to enter the white bedroom.

Ren spent his days with Li Po and a few others. Sometimes Li Po and the others had sex together, but Ren could not focus and so he did not join them. He kept thinking of Zanti, looking about the room for him, finding him reading or napping or not finding him at all. Zanti made no moves toward him. Did not even seem to notice him. It hurt.

He missed Zanti. He wanted Zanti.

Ren sat beside him on the couch and Zanti ignored him.

He ached deep inside that Zanti wished to treat him this way.

On the third day, he sat beside Zanti one night after dinner and read while Zanti read. Then, when Zanti got up Ren said softly, "I miss you."

Zanti paused but did not turn. They both went to bed again alone.

Ren read in his bed until he could not see, then closed his eyes and slept.

Something woke him. He could not tell if he'd been asleep minutes or hours. He started to sit up but felt the body beside him, curled in, forehead pressed to Ren's upper arm. Ren turned his head and his breath fell across Zanti's fine, dark hair on the top of his head.

He could see the edge of Zanti's shoulder and part way down his naked back and side. Colors swirled in the darkness: plum, azure, red. The wounded colors. Cam had said Zanti sought companionship only when he could not sleep. When he was restless, afraid to be alone. The colors of Zanti confirmed that was happening now.

Ren had come to realize, over time, that healthy bodies were made of whites, golds, blues and greens with flickers of the other colors. Zanti was black, then gray, and then that rare white purity with a lavender iridescence of arousal, then that last final night, Zanti's aura pulsed with the pale blues of love.

But tonight the colors meant Zanti was hurting or lonely, just like Ren, and did not show the lavender or the blue.

That was fine with Ren. He did not need to make love right now, or even all the time. Just the fact that Zanti had come to him to sleep brought new feelings washing over him, the best of them all: that he was wanted.

Ren had a master now who wanted him. It had been his goal from the beginning.

Everything fell into place inside him, like pieces of a puzzle finding their true match, fitting just right.

Back in the day his high school teacher had told him: *You choose how you want to walk through this world. How you want to experience it.*

As hard as it was for Ren, he had believed those words. And they had brought him here. To a place and a man he hadn't chosen to love at first but now loved nonetheless. If he had it to do over again, he wouldn't change a thing.

He moved an inch closer to Zanti and, barely breathing, kissed the top of his head. A soft blue light began to flicker, there.

Ren's heart rate picked up. Zanti would never have to tell him his feelings. Ren already knew.

Zanti's hand moved up and fingers stretched over Ren's hip, then curled. His bent knee bucked Ren in the thigh.

Ren shifted closer. "I am for you always," Ren said, the whisper falling over them like a cloak, like a beginning of a new story, one that embraced lost boys and re-started their broken hearts.

Epilogue

Trust and Love

When Ren woke, Zanti was still with him, curled tight against Ren's side with the covers loose about his smooth waist.

Groggy at first, Ren had to remind himself of his new reality. He was Master's gift to Zanti. Zanti fought not to accept the gift, but now things were different.

Zanti had come to Ren's bed willingly for the first time. Just to sleep, but it was a start.

Ren did not want to move away from that wiry, taut warmth but he had to use the bathroom.

Deftly, he slid out from under the sheets, the air cool against his warm skin. As he exited his alcove, Cam came up to him, his face scrunched up, eyes narrowed. "Is he okay?"

Ren nodded. "Yes."

Cam stared over his shoulder at Zanti still asleep in Ren's bed. "Promise?"

"I promise."

"Because this is odd behavior. Zanti doesn't do that. He doesn't climb into bed with anyone but me and only very rarely now."

"It's fine."

By now, others had come up to listen in on the conversation.

Cam bounced on his toes, nervous. "Because I worry about him. I care about him. We all do even if he's different."

"I would never hurt him," Ren said.

"I know. But you didn't like him. And he's been rejecting you. Do you now? Do you care?"

None of these men knew the whole story. Even Ren was still trying to fit it all together, like a puzzle of auras sorting themselves out to paint his life.

As he thought about his answer to Cam's question, for of course he did care, but it was more than that, a strange feeling came

199

over Ren, like anticipation and nausea and longing and hope all in one. He'd only ever felt this way when pursuing his dream, when trying to please others because pleasure slavery meant everything to him. Now this was not about trying to please anyone. It was about something more. Enfolding Zanti in his arms. Holding onto him. Wanting him to belong to Ren as much as Ren belonged to Zanti.

That seemed to be happening, but it was still too early to say. To put it all into words.

He opened his mouth. He tried to speak.

Cam's eyes widened.

Ren did not have to turn around to see that Zanti had come into the atrium. He felt the body heat behind him. A soft palm brushed over his wrist and a hand folded over his own.

That broken boy. That bewitching man.

Ren's throat closed for a moment. All he could see were the recessed lights on the ceiling. Slowly, all the men's auras slowly came into focus. They were a pretty blue-green this morning, peppered with the grayish-mauve of curiosity.

Ren pushed the air from his lungs. Tried to find a voice. What came out was steady, still gruff with sleep. "I care about him. Yes. I care."

Zanti's hand on his squeezed. That one squeeze spoke trust and acceptance. Everything was first steps, but they were finally on the road.

"Zanti?" Cam started to reach out, then backed away. He tapped his tablet. "Anything you need, you still come to me, okay?"

"We both will. Always," Ren said.

Besides, that was Cam's job.

*

At breakfast, lunch and dinner, Zanti sat next to Ren.

During the day, they were never far apart.

Ren watched Zanti's aura shimmer from gray to blue. On anyone else it would mean they were unsure to love. Zanti was not that different. Ren could read the signs in his demeanor and actions. He was not holding back his feelings as much. His feelings for Ren. He wanted love and he wanted to trust more. But he was still unsure.

But in cases of lovers, wasn't everyone unsure?

200

Ren thought about Wulf and Locke. Their story—their love—what he'd heard of it, still had to be worked through, worked out until the blue tree of light rose from the tops of their heads.

Was this happening here? To Ren? To Zanti?

No blue tree. Yet. But Ren hoped with all his heart.

Ren waited all day to be called by Master. He could sense Zanti's anticipation as well.

But the voice never came. While Zanti read, Ren played a video game with Li Po. But his mind wasn't on it.

He found his thoughts wandering, his body hot, his heart locked in his throat too often when he tried to speak or laugh or even eat. He could not stop thinking about the way they'd lost themselves three nights before, how their kisses sought depth, how their bodies wrestled.

He looked down to find himself erect. It wasn't unusual in the harem. Lots of the men walked around sporting erections at various times.

Supportive as always, Li Po said, "You're mind isn't on the game. How 'bout some ice cream?"

Ren looked up as Li Po handed him a dish of frozen chocolate. "Thank you."

After they ate, Li Po said, "I'm off to bed now. Have a good night."

Still sitting, Ren looked at his own empty alcove, wanting to go lie down but afraid. Afraid that Zanti would not join him. Or maybe afraid that he would. For then what would he do? He wanted him so very very badly.

Finally, he forced himself up to prepare for bed. As he entered the bathroom, he noticed Zanti behind him. Together they brushed their teeth. They used the facilities.

Upon exiting, Ren said softly, "You are welcome in my bed any time."

Zanti stopped a few feet away, head down, body frozen.

Ren watched his aura go black, then red stripes criss-crossed it. He slumped, his mind disappointed to see those colors. He wanted to take back his words, which had seemed harmless, but how could he know? If only Master had called them, ordered them upstairs, things would be fine. They wouldn't be entirely on their own.

"All right, then." Ren turned and walked to his own bed. He pushed down the covers with a shush, and immediately heard bare footfalls and a wisp of breath. He looked up. Zanti stood at the entryway, his aura now glimmering clear blue as the water that lapped the shallows of the pool. His pert, sweet cock was semi-erect, unusual for him.

Fearful of opening his big mouth again, Ren simply held the covers up in invitation.

It worked. Zanti stepped into the alcove and sat on the edge of the mattress.

Together, they both got into the bed, the area heating up around them in seconds.

Without Master to set them up, without the cuffs and chains, all was new to them.

Finally, Ren whispered what he'd said the previous night. "I am here for you."

Zanti's hand touched the center of his chest, just a brush, palm down. Ren's heart danced and raced. His cock fully hardened. In the shadows he saw so many pink lights dancing across Zanti's skin, everywhere now, not just in the hidden folds of skin, not just at the base of his cock, or on his lips. But everywhere, rushing into his outer aura, pink mixing with blue to make that beautiful lavender iridescence that beckoned Ren, invited, consented.

Ren had never wanted anyone more than he wanted Zanti right now.

Zanti rolled toward him, his breath fanning Ren's shoulder, neck and jaw.

When their lips met, every cell of Ren's body opened in pleasure. His cock leaked against his stomach. He was doing his master's bidding. Both his masters. But it was more. He cared. He loved. He could admit that now.

Arms came around him.

It was as if he had found his home.

*

One Year Later

Ren placed the tulip bulb into the earth and smoothed dirt over it. Then he took a blue pitcher and poured fresh water all around it.

The leafy trees overhead provided dappled shade. A soft breeze made their branches tremble. The sugary fragrance of blooming flowers surrounded them.

When he was done with the watering, he looked up. Zanti sat on a clean blanket, dark eyes watching him, his bangs scattered across his face.

Here in the garden was the only area they were allowed to wear clothes. Lightweight shirts and shorts to protect from the sun. Knee guards. Slippers.

Ren got up and went to the blanket. Without a word, he lay down, tired from working. He placed his head in Zanti's lap, bent his knees, and crossed his arms over his chest.

"I never thought Master would give us this place. This garden." It was fenced with a locked gate, but it was theirs. Through a new door at the back of the atrium, they could go to it whenever they wanted. The other harem members were welcome as well.

Zanti ran a hand through Ren's hair, combing gently.

"I could not have asked for a better life," Ren murmured. "To be showered with gifts. To have everything I want."

He turned his head. Zanti was looking at him intently, a hint of a smile playing at the corners of his mouth.

"But the best part is you," Ren finished.

Zanti scowled. Ren had seen that scowl many times. In the beginning, it had meant something so different than what it communicated now. Before it had been about resentment, mistrust, maybe even a little hate.

But now the scowl came only when Ren got too sentimental. It was a fake-mocking of Ren's enthusiasm for their love, for now that Ren fit in so well here, he tended to say what he thought without embarrassment, never shy.

Zanti still did not speak except those rare times he might order Ren to "Come!" He would always be shy. Even now his cheeks tinted pink at Ren's words. The pink was a flush of capillaries beneath the skin, but there was also a pink light that flashed up to mix with his aura. And above his head a blue orb spun.

It always appeared whenever Zanti looked at Ren, or touched him, or made love to him.

Unable to see his own aura, Ren had to imagine he had one too, twin to Zanti's, for the spirit of love was strong in him. Zanti was the core of it. But he loved his mysterious Master intensely for bringing them together.

In his heart, finally, he'd become the pleasure slave of his dreams. Whole. Loving. And loved in return.

The End

Dear Reader:

Thank you for reading "The Slave Harem."

Please consider leaving a review. Word of mouth is like gold! If it weren't for the generous support of my readers, I could not be writing more books!

You might also enjoy subscribing to my newsletter. I put it out several times a year to announce new books and upcoming projects, and I always have sales and freebies to offer readers both from myself and other authors I enjoy reading. You can subscribe at the link below.

Or, if newsletters aren't your thing, it is very easy to sign up for my Facebook group Wendyland to keep up to date. I am there almost every day, and I post current updates all the time.

For new release notifications, it's also super easy to simply follow my author page on Amazon.

Happy Reading!

Love,

Wendy Rathbone

Contact links for Wendy Rathbone:

Join my Facebook group Wendyland. I post updates, cover reveals, snippets, sales and other fun stuff every day:
https://www.facebook.com/groups/718074255203918/

Facebook: https://www.facebook.com/wendy.rathbone.3

Newsletter sign up (if you sign up at this link you get a free copy of *"The Bodyguard's Valentine"*):
https://claims.prolificworks.com/free/k5uTgYuU

Amazon author page: https://www.amazon.com/Wendy-Rathbone/e/B00B0O9BMS/ref=dp_byline_cont_ebooks_1

About Wendy Rathbone

I love to write.

The reason I write romance these days is because the overwhelming power of falling in love is a game-changer. It makes sad people instantly happy. It makes bleak reality look sun-warmed and friendly again.

I have written in all genres: sci-fi, fantasy, horror, paranormal, contemporary, erotica, romance. But I keep coming back to romance as the main focus. Gay romance. Male/male romance. The idea of two men falling in love is irresistible to me. It's all I write now.

All my books are available on Amazon and most are in Kindle Unlimited. So if you have the urge, go take a look. See what's on the shelf.

Love to you all!

Wendy Rathbone

THE SLAVE PALACE
Wulf and Locke
WENDY RATHBONE

Conquered. Captured. Sold as a pleasure slave.

After being taken as a prisoner of war, Wulf fights his captors and is sold as a One-Night Thrall to be used and abused, then put to death. He is purchased by a high ranking master of the famous Slave Palace. Why Locke buys him, Wulf has no clue, but something about this master is intriguing. Instead of abuse, Wulf is plied with luxuries he has never known by a man who actually seems to respect him.

Jaded. Looking for a challenge.

Eminent Master Locke takes on a bet with his best friend that he can't train and tame a dangerous One-Night Thrall in ten days. But something about this slave stirs him like no other before. All bets aside, Locke has the urge to keep Wulf, as well as save his life. But Wulf is fierce, unwilling, and his consent papers have been forged. If Wulf doesn't soon submit to his role as a slave, he will be sent to death as a prisoner of war.

A sweet, slow-burn love story taking place on an alternate contemporary Earth where owning pleasure slaves is legal.

LORD VAMPYRE
Wendy Rathbone

When Lord Neverelle becomes a guest at Cliffside Keep, Vanni watches helplessly as Damion, the young man he's grown up with and secretly loves, falls for the alluring and seductive stranger. Lord Neverelle is danger incarnate, and soon takes control of the household.

Not satisfied with Damion alone, Never uses a vampire trick called "the tempt" to compel Vanni, who is swept into a love triangle that includes fiery passion and nightly threesomes.

Now Vanni must ask himself, is any of this consensual? And what about Damion—does he really want to be with Vanni, or is it all a sensual play controlled by vampire compulsion?

M/M and M/M/M romance.

The Imposter Prince
Book 1 in The Imposter Series
Wendy Rathbone

His love for an enemy prince threatens his very life.

Dare does not mind serving the spoiled and cruel Prince Darius. Growing up with him, Dare does everything for Darius including homework, bed play demands, and even doubling for him as the prince grows too paranoid to face even the smallest of crowds.

But everything changes in a single moment when Dare, while posing as Darius, is abducted by the enemy.

A captive in a new and hostile land, Dare meets another prince who seems just as indulged and rotten as Darius—until Dare gets to know him, until they fall in love. Against his will, Dare must continue to play the role of Prince Darius for real, or risk everything: his love, his land, and his very life.

His only chance for survival is to keep a secret from the one he loves, a secret that is also killing him.

A male/male, enemies to lovers novel of mad kings, troubled princes, abduction, fevers, cold dungeons, warm hearths, comfort, wine, and true love.

THE IMPOSTER KING

(Book 2 of The Imposter Series)
Wendy Rathbone

Their love made them close.
Their secret kept them closer.

Dare and Prince Malory are happily married and in love, but the secret of Dare's true identity as a mere servant threatens their romantic bliss.

Messages to the king of Brookfall go unanswered, and rumors of war unsettle both kingdoms. Until one day heralds arrive with bags of gold to ransom Dare and demand his return to Brookfall.

King Millard, Prince Malory's father, orders Dare to make the journey to see his father. But Dare is not the true heir, and if they meet, the secret he and Mal have been guarding will be revealed. Also, impersonating a royal means a death penalty offense. Worse, it could mean all-out war between their countries.

Panic. Despair. Lovers torn asunder. Personal sacrifice. More dark secrets revealed. An ending that will leave you breathless.

Ganymede: Abducted by the Gods
Book 1 in "The Fantastic Immortals" Series (A standalone read)
Wendy Rathbone

My name is Ganymede, and I have been betrayed.

Every boy my age dreams of leaving home to embark on a noble adventure, but never does any boy imagine it happening as it did to me. On the evening of my 18th naming day, when I expected no more than a chalice of wine and a few drunken flirtations to tempt my innocence, I was instead sold by my father to the god, Zeus - not because of anything particular I had ever done or said, but solely because I am considered beautiful among mortals, and my father found more value in a few gold coins than in the well-being of his youngest son.

To be honest, I never believed in the gods, but my lack of belief held no power in Olympus or on Earth. Now under Zeus's influence, I am kept drunk on ambrosia in the sun-lit halls of the immortals, alternately amazed and horrified at the power these beings hold over others, and how darkly they influence the progress of humanity itself. How very much I want to hate Zeus for kidnapping me, and yet he shows me mostly kindness, even on that fateful night when we shared a bed for the first time. Kindness, yes, but also a godly and unyielding refusal to take no for an answer... probably because he could read my ambrosia-fevered curiosity as much as my naive, inexperienced terror. He owns me, after all, just as he owns everything else, so perhaps it never occurred to him that a captive and a slave might not make the best of lovers.

Throughout my time at Olympus - who's to say how long I've been here, for time on Olympus is not the same as that on Earth - the only thing that gives me hope comes to me in dreams and visions. His name is Sable and he is a magnificent shape-shifter in the form of a giant raven. When he first spoke to me in my mind it was with a resonance unlike any I had ever known - his mind and mine sounding a single note together, a song without words, a promise of freedom, a glimpse of some distant but very real possibility of this thing we humans call Love. But now he is silent. Perhaps I dreamed his voice. Perhaps I have finally lost my mind.

ZEUS (Conquering His Heart)
Book 2 in "The Fantastic Immortals" Series (A standalone read)
WENDY RATHBONE

When I throw the lightning and summon the thunder, it isn't always out of anger, but often from a love so all-consuming it could only be the effect of Eros himself. Yes, he is beautiful. Of course he is. How could he be otherwise, with hair the color of sunlight and white-feathered wings that drape to the floor? And he is as ancient as the myth of time itself, an immortal with powers and glamour beyond my ability to imagine. He struggles to teach me wisdom, control, strategy, yet I sit here babbling like a child, for all I can think of is how I might try - at least let me try! - to prove myself to him in some way that will cause him to crave my company and my touch, just as I crave his.

I do not yet know how to be a god, for I am only 18 and still just a silly boy who has fallen in love with Love himself, while my father Cronus plots and schemes to lock me in his dungeon and make me his slave forever.

A male/male romance.

BUYING YOU
Wendy Rathbone

It's one thing to be a beautiful cover model on billboards, buses and magazine covers. It's quite another to be sold as one.

Prized for his looks, Dane knows it's shallow, but he is on his way to having it all. It feels good to be gorgeous, smart and have top designers from around the world requesting him.

When he returns to his hometown to participate in a small Date-For-Charity auction, it seems harmless enough—until a hooded man walks in and bids higher on him than anyone else. Dane is intrigued but nervous when he finds out the guy has vanished after the winning bid, leaving only a limo behind to whisk Dane off into the night.

Enemies to lovers, opposites attract, and hot steamy nights that challenge two guys' trust issues along with their biggest fears.

Eye Scry Publications
A Visionary Publishing Company
www.eyescrypublications.com

www.ingramcontent.com/pod-product-compliance
Lightning Source LLC
Chambersburg PA
CBHW020322260626
47156CB00004B/1328